JEWEL SOWERS

JEWEL SOWERS

JEWEL SOWERS

EDITH ALLON

Introduction by Karl Wurf

WILDSIDE PRESS

INTRODUCTION

KARL WURF

Jewel Sowers is the first of two early fantasy novels by Edith Allonby (1875–1905), a British schoolteacher and writer whose imaginative fiction prefigures later feminist and allegorical science fiction. First published anonymously in 1903 by Greening & Co., Jewel Sowers was followed by *Marigold* (1905), and both books are set on the invented planet of Lucifram—a strange, spiritual world described as "near Hell" and filled with shadow, symbolism, and satire.

Lucifram is a world of reversals and moral ambiguities, where characters grapple with truth, temptation, and self-awareness. In *Marigold*, Allonby explores these themes through a more allegorical and dreamlike lens than in her earlier work, using fairy-tale tropes to interrogate earthly values. The prose blends whimsy with critique, and the setting—otherworldly yet psychologically familiar—reflects the Edwardian fascination with theosophy, morality, and cosmic dualities.

Allonby's career was brief but marked by ambition. She worked as a teacher at St. Anne's School in Lancaster while writing fiction in her spare hours. In 1905, after publishers rejected her third novel, *The Fulfilment*, she ended her life by ingesting poison. A letter she left behind explained that the act was meant to force attention to her work. *The Fulfilment* was posthumously published that same year.

As the earlier of the two Lucifram novels, *Jewel Sowers* introduces many of the philosophical and fantastical elements that Allonby would deepen in *Marigold*. Its mixture of speculative world-building, social reflection, and spiritual symbolism makes it a unique and often overlooked contribution to early 20th-century imaginative literature.

CHAPTER I

AN INTRODUCTION TO LUCIFRAM

In the little planet Lucifram, that spun a brilliant and solitary course among the stars, exchanging annual salutations with them as the waxing and waning of the solar laws brought them out of the void and within hail, the people each and all walked upside down. The trees were upside down, the houses, the churches with their steeples, the palaces, the oceans, rivers, lakes, mountains, animals, and fishes, each and all, reversed our own conception of mundane propriety. Cultivate a patience with the seeming strangeness of this extraordinary planet, even to the reading of this simple book, and let that virtue lead you nearer to another sphere, more to your liking.

There were a few, indeed, upon this sphere who did their best to stand upon their feet. Sometimes they succeeded; but others were bowled down in the struggle and ended by standing once again upon their heads, or lying crushed, paying the debt they owed to Outraged Custom.

The circumference of this sphere was something like two thousand miles. It bulged out towards the north and south, with giant hollows to the east and west. And because *everything* that existed was contrary to our idea of things, all things looked normal.

When Nature and architecture combine to alter things, making them contrariwise, as people call it, what wonder if morality and all ethics blend with the custom?

To begin with governments and kingships. Unlike those upon a two-legged basis, a king was never chosen for his worth, but for his frailties. He was chosen to strew the path of his subjects with flowers which all might pick like little children out at play, and then would quarrel over.

Alas! To be a king in the planet Lucifram! That little planet topsy-turvy. Here, though a ruler might have the will of a Hercules to turn a somersalt and land upon his feet, some diviner instinct calling him to that, the pigmies around him pinned him with millions of tiny threads, an anchorage whereby to hold his head safe to the ground. Threads worked in gold! Held for the wonder of the multitude.

So for the kings. The Gods of all the stars looked down on them. They heard those faint sighs of weakness—those breathings after higher things—and pitied some, and smiled at others. And though in the topsy-turvy synagogues and churches the people prayed for them, no prayers reached heaven except those simple few the kings themselves breathed in solitude. Prayers that must travel very, very far, as all prayers must, and which needed the giant strength of great simplicity to bring them to the end of their weary journey.

So for the kings and princes. An arduous task is theirs—bound thus with chains—God only knows how hard! As each insidious little link might whisper, telling its own small share in the universal tale.

In our world we always speak of "Church and State"—a correct and steady way of speaking—but in Lucifram 'tis always "State and Church," and that is why the palaces and kings claimed our attention first.

The Church, composed of temples, synagogues, and priests, jumbled together in luxurious profusion, was dressed and bedecked so finely that the God the people worshipped fell almost out of sight. In their chief temple, in the greatest city, was a three-tailed golden Serpent, coiled around a golden pole above a table decked in red, and set with incense vessels. Dim and mysterious was that holy place, where priests, all flowing and bedecked in golden garments, came each day to bow before the Snake. Its three tails, the gold of them burnished like fire, spread out like fans on high, against a background of mosaic. Below, resting on the altar, was the great head, lying quite still; the genius of ages worked in its cruel fangs and awful eyes. Eyes never closing, jewel-glinting, green and fiery, all-surveying, all-watching. Those terrible eyes lit up the gloom, and compelled men to stand upon their heads as it itself was forced to do. For by the grim and dreadful fascination of those never-closing eyes, unconsciously the worshippers changed to position like to it, tails up, heads down, blinded by their religion.

In this temple the people sat in the big gloomy aisles, each on a little chair with a ledge in front for kneeling, and heard the priest from the pulpit, and the reader from his desk. Awed by the grandeur and the solemn dimness, they bowed and salaamed before the triune tails, hidden from the vulgar gaze by a red silk curtain blazoned in gold. And when the mighty organ rolled and rumbled, and the angel voices of the choir boys rang through the gold-washed rafters, their senses were stirred by some far hidden mystery, and their eyes would dim or kindle as they felt it; only the gleaming eyes within the veil remained unchanged.

Now it was customary for the priests who waited on the Serpent to fast a day each month and marry only once. A layman in Lucifram might wed twice. No priests could marry under forty. For laymen, the age was twenty-five for the first attempt, and forty for the second; that is, for the few who preferred company in their latter years to peace. But though the women, by Act of Parliament, enjoyed the privilege of marrying twice, just as the men did, there were certain things clearly beyond them, they being in Lucifram, as here, the weaker vessels. On those great days whereon the priest drew back the silken curtain and displayed the Serpent, all women were debarred from entering the temple.

And so enough for an explanation and a prologue. Take my hand, descend, and tread on Lucifram!

CHAPTER II

FRIEND AND EXECUTOR

In the capital of Lucifram there is a great park—a city park—planted with trees sown centuries since by the restless winds, when all was peaceful country. To the right stretches the city—work and pleasure, laughter and tears, and perpetual hurry-scurry. All round the park sounds and sights of human life, condensed within a curiously small circle, were in evidence. Silent streets, tall and shadowy, lit by occasional gas lamps, fringed on a brilliant thoroughfare, with omnibuses, cabs, and people hurrying everywhere. Most spacious squares, with fountains and statues, backed by huge buildings, erected both for grace and durability, lay on all sides. The mansions on this side of the park were in many cases of plain exterior. This gave the lie to the magnificence within. On the right side of the park, facing it and running along its entire length, was built the famous Greensward Avenue.

In the centre of the avenue, standing back under the shadow of the high walls of two palace gardens rising on either side, stood a large square house built of black marble. It was built in black, and the blinds were of deep red, the only colour to relieve it. Those were not visible till night came. Thirteen imposing-looking steps lead up to an imposing door, in black polished oak, rarely carved. Two narrow windows in the wall reached down on each side of it. The house consisted of three storeys and a basement, and to the back were pretty and extensive gardens protected by high walls.

The owner of this house was a certain Camille Barringcourt, who had but lately come there, within the last three years. With the exception of servants, he lived quite alone—a bachelor in the land of double marriages.

Now the house in which he lived was very appropriately called "Marble House." It had been built by a millionaire quite recently, despite its old appearance. The reason why it had such an appearance of age was because it had been erected from a spoiled cathedral in the remotest corner of Lucifram, where instead of worshipping the Serpent they worshipped the Toad. It had cost a vast amount of money to cart the marble and oak right over from east to west, but it was done right royally, and the house itself, from this point of view at least, was very interesting. No sooner was the great mansion completed, and royalty entertained on one single occasion, than the millionaire died. Men and women agreed on this, that his death was at least mysterious.

He was found dead in bed. So far as the doctors could tell he suffered from nothing, and had come by no foul play. He had died painlessly, in the big plain bed-chamber containing little else but the desecrated altar of the Toad, with a fac-simile of the Serpent rising above it—a shrine which all good people in Lucifram kept in their private rooms. And so he was buried, and the ladies mourned. He had been generous. And then his will was read.

All his vast wealth was given to charities; all went to charity except the house. That was left "To my friend, Camille Barringcourt, as a slight token of esteem, and in remembrance of the past." That was all. No one had ever heard or seen anything of this friend, and no one knew anything of the past. But lawyers, like detectives, have a way of hunting people up. In a little time it was spread abroad that Camille Barringcourt lived in Fairysky, or at least was staying there, a country which much resembled Italy on the Earth.

It may also be mentioned here that Camille Barringcourt and the lawyer were left executors of those vast charities.

The first thing about the new-comer's arrival that excited general interest was the advent of six horses. All were black as night, with long tails, fiery eyes, shining coats, and tossing, untamed heads.

Nearly all the little boys in that aristocratic neighbourhood were late for school that morning; or better, never went. Accustomed as they were to beautiful horses, they had never even in their experience seen anything to equal these. The six black horses travelled through the crowded thorough-fares singly led, each by a groom. Their trappings were of a deep red, and no unnecessary weight was placed upon them. The men who led the animals were men who understood their business, and had great patience with their coquettish, curvetting ways. Just as the journey was drawing to a close the traffic in the streets was for the minute stopped. Five of the six horses had passed the crossing, and the last was drawn up close to Lady Flamington's carriage. Whether it was her ladyship's hat (she was one of the best dressed and most beautiful women of the day), or whether her two thoroughbreds were ready to enter into the fun of the thing, and dance a lively impromptu pirouette with the new arrival, it would be hard to say. However, the black steed began a dance, anything but safe in the state of the crowded thorough-fare, and the bays in harness did their best to follow suit. It was a spirited attempt; then the groom for once lost his temper.

"Get up, you devil!" said he. The horse took him literally and reared up, despite his efforts to keep it down, dragging him with it, in its wild, un-tamable fury. The trampling forepaws struck on the cushions of my lady's brougham. What might have been the result it is impossible to say, for her escape on the other side was cut off by a huge lorry drawn up against her like a wall, but just at that moment a voice fell on the hubbub and the consterna-tion, and the "voice that breathed o'er Eden" on the day of her marriage had never been so welcome to Lady Flamington as that one now. At the same time a hand, the whitest, the most beautiful she had ever seen (so she told her friends after), grasped at the bridle.

"Waugh-o, Starlight—Starlight! Come, then."

The words, the tone, the caressing hand on one side, the firm hand on the bridle, were too much for the four-legged beauty. Won over by more words, more pressure on the hateful bit (even though silver), and more caressing patting on her glossy neck, she came gracefully down to earth once more.

It seemed to Lady Flamington that the stranger had sprung up from nowhere. As a matter of fact, he had sprung from the hansom behind, in which he was following, at almost walking pace, these six prancing treasures. Then just as the traffic was starting again he looked across at her.

"You are not hurt," said he. "I should have been bitterly sorry if that had happened."

For once her ladyship could find no words. She bowed, he raised his hat, the procession moved along. Then she knitted her brows thoughtfully.

"He should have been sorry in either case," she thought, and fell to studying his face in her memory.

Meanwhile the six black horses had turned into Greensward Avenue, where likewise at a quicker rate her ladyship's carriage was progressing.

All the way to the spacious private stables at the rear of the private grounds, Mr. Barringcourt, for it was he, led that most spoiled of all spoilt animals, Starlight. The little boys followed admiringly, till the big doors of the stable-yard closed cruelly upon them.

"That looks like a dook turned undertaker," said one.

Rumour had spread a report that Camille Barringcourt was a twice married gentleman, with a large family.

"How unlike poor Geoffrey Todbrook," said the ladies, and sighed.

But rumour for once was entirely wrong. One bachelor was dead; another succeeded him.

The new arrival settled quickly into his new home. Seeing it was already furnished, that was but natural. His servants were all foreigners, dark, tall, all very unlike the people on this side of Lucifram. Yet there was an inexpressible charm, dignity, and quiet repose about them that delighted and mystified everyone. Among them were some women, parlourmaids, sewing-maids, and housemaids apparently.

Each one of these servants, men and women, dressed in black, faced with deep red. It was a kind of uniform.

Now, a few words are needed as to the personal appearance of the Master himself. In figure he was tall, athletic, graceful, broad-shouldered. His hair was black and short, crisp at the ends, as Lady Flamington noticed when he removed his hat. People called his face "odd." It was dark and swarthy, with a strong forehead, and black eyes which were gloomy and deeply set. The nose was straight, bearing in its lines more sensitive refinement than any other feature of his face.

When he smiled he showed, though not obtrusively, a sparkle of white and even teeth. When Lady Flamington admired the beauty of his hands she was within the right. For strength and suppleness they would be hard to beat, and for whiteness also. This then, in short, was the figure of Camille Barringcourt, come to dispense the charity of his friend of the past; come to settle in Marble House, of Greensward Avenue.

Lady Flamington, some dozen houses off, persuaded her first and only husband to call there, soon after the arrival. He did so, hoping to see the fine black horses she had spoken of. Horseflesh was his hobby. He saw the gentleman, but nothing else in the way of interest, took a sudden fancy to him, and invited him over to dinner on Friday night. The invitation was as suddenly accepted. Sir James went home with some misgivings. He didn't know whether his wife liked swarthy men; she was fastidious. His wife had no objection to them. She was delighted to welcome any of his friends, except turf acquaintances and bookmakers.

On Friday night Mr. Barringcourt came. It was a little formal affair, one or two of the family circle and an intimate friend. The stranger sat beside his hostess for dinner, and they talked commonplaces. At last she turned to him with a pretty grace.

"You have not yet demanded my thanks," said she.

"For what?" he asked.

"You know for what."

"Your thanks would necessitate my apologies."

"I am surprised you never offered them."

"It was unnecessary."

"There I must confess to some curiosity. Do you remember you said to me, 'You are not hurt.'"

"Well?" said he, and smiled—a smile all the more charming as he bent his head to hers.

"Well!" she retorted. "I was hurt; your horse frightened me. To be frightened is to be hurt. Can you dispute it?"

"I never saw anyone stand pain better. Your face was a vision of—of—"

"Of what?" she asked.

"I do not understand your language very well, as yet. I shall improve in it; you must be patient. In a week or two I shall have found the word I need."

"And till then?"

"Learn to be gracious to a poor speaker."

"Ah! But I do not intend to let you off so easily. After telling me I was not hurt, you next proceeded to say, 'In that case you would have been deeply sorry'—you see my memory is good. Now, am I to understand that under the circumstances you felt no sorrow?"

"Most certainly."

"Now we shall quarrel, unless you can explain yourself."

"Is it necessary?"

"You shall discover how much so if you do not explain your meaning instantly."

"Then do not blame me if I sink still deeper into the mire. Under the circumstances, I was not sorry. I had been told on coming to this country I should find all the women forward—most of them ugly—the remainder plain. After three days' looking round me I had come to the same conclusion. Suddenly by the merest chance my eyes lighted on you. Can you wonder I should feel no sorrow?"

She frowned, then laughed, and looked at him.

"Where did you learn this grossest form of flattery?"

"I see your ladyship has no education to appreciate the truth."

"Talk to my husband about horses. I have no more to say to you."

"Is he a lover of horses?"

"Yes. He attends every Race Meet in the county."

Mr. Barringcourt smiled. "That speaks for itself," he said.

CHAPTER III

ROSALIE

Let us pay a call on Cinderella.

Alas! not a Cinderella with a prince and gorgeous clothing, but one without a tongue, or rather, tongue-tied.

Rosalie Paleaf, for that was her name, lived alone with an aunt and uncle. Both her parents were dead. She was pretty, of that fair delicate type called "picturesque." Her hair was of a palish yellow tint, glossy, but straight; her skin was fair and delicate. The eyes were grey, with dark curling lashes, and delicately marked brows. Her nose turned up just the least little bit, the most charming upward, delicate little curve in the wrong direction it would be possible to meet. The corners of her mouth, however, turned down with the saddest, most wistful droop imaginable. In fact, there was only one feature in her face that kept it from becoming most woefully pathetic, and that was the little, inquisitive, life-enjoying nose. To come back to her eyes for finishing touches. Their greyness was very pale. The pupils generally were large, with an equally black rim along the edge of the iris. Inside this rim the colour gradually paled to the pupil, which gave her eyes a curiously bright appearance. And then being tongue-tied! She had nothing she could talk with but her eyes, and so she used them.

Uncle and aunt were very kind to her. Who indeed could help being that? She was the gentlest, kindest creature, harmless and very helpless, with the sweetest face, the happiest manner, and sunniest smile upon occasions.

They were people of moderate circumstances in a very quiet way, and if Rosalie had not the hardest work of the house to do, it was because her aunt always insisted on doing it, with the help of an occasional charwoman. And so, when very young, she learnt to hem, and dust, and do the toasting. Later she got promoted to wiping tea-things, then dinner dishes, and ended as a fully-fledged young housekeeper, ready to bake and cook, darn, and make and mend, to sweep and dust, and do all work that is useful.

Beyond this her education had not progressed. She could read and write, 'tis certain, but very little more. Accomplishments were beyond the means of her relations, and had they not been it would never have struck them a child apparently quite dumb should need such things. So she stayed at home and was happy, except in the company of strangers, when her sad defect made itself felt under their pitying glances of surprise, however well they might try to conceal them.

But a child's happiness often constitutes a woman's misery. As the years passed by Rosalie began to feel her loneliness, her utter incapacity for the work of the world. She felt also something deeper, stronger, more unwordable. It was more real than anything else in her life, yet, because unseen, it was unsympathised with as having no existence. And so, although her happiness was gradually becoming overshadowed, she never fully recognised it till one October evening when she had turned twenty.

To look at Rosalie the spectator would never have taken her for that age. All her life had been spent in one long silent dream—the privilege of childhood.

It was the kind of autumn evening made for thought and sadness. The sky was very clear, with a suspicion of purple in it, and the gold of ages was in the west. As she stood by her bedroom window looking out at it, there came that terrible foreboding of sadness and sorrow that seems to do its best to crush young hearts, though perhaps it only moulds them.

And along with it came a longing for expansion, a weariness of the endless routine, the companionless silence and that nameless thirst after something, she knew not what. How could Rosalie, walking in the mist, having no speech or utterance, explain it even to herself? She wanted something, the purple of the sky suggested something—suggested, nothing more. And from that day forward the nameless longing grew, settling itself within her heart, finding no happier outside quarters. I do not know that she looked thinner or more frail, her physical strength was too great for that. No one beyond herself knew of the longing, and she attributed it all to discontent, and tried to stifle it.

At last one evening she understood. The inordinate longing for speech rushed over her.

But how to manage it? It is all very well to find out what you want to do—but how to do it? There was only one way—only one way, at any rate, that suggested itself to her, and that way was prayer.

Now, her religious education had not been exactly neglected, but Rosalie was one of those heedless creatures who hear a little and invent a great deal.

She had been told with great piety by her aunt of the great golden Serpent, its wonderful power, its relentless cruelty to those who crossed or vexed it, its generosity to those who did as they were told, and from those few rudimentary remarks she had built up a little golden temple of her own, quite an unseen spiritual affair, in which to worship the Supreme Being of Lucifram. She certainly gave to the gorgeous Serpent many qualifications she had never been told it possessed, but what of that? She was but a poor, helpless creature at best. But with a reverent, far-away love she had always worshipped the

Serpent, although as a sex she had been given to understand he reckoned her somewhat inferior.

But now, sitting up in bed, there came to her one of those terrible convictions, never to be misplaced, that are in themselves the sheerest madness or the sheerest sanity, that she must get her tongue untied. And the Serpent, being the strongest of all powers on Lucifram, was the likeliest to do it.

Next afternoon at five o'clock saw Rosalie kneeling in the famous temple, her head buried in her hands, praying in the silence as only sincerity and helplessness can pray.

"Oh, Serpent, give me my tongue! Let me talk," said she, a most natural request when coming from a woman.

Then she went home quite comforted, as only the simple can be.

"One does not pray for nothing," she thought "I feel the Serpent heard me."

And that night she was so happy, she did not notice her uncle's troubled look and silent way. She did not mean to be selfish, she was thinking purely of her prayer.

Some weeks went by, and every day she walked to the temple and prayed:

"Oh, Serpent, give me my tongue! Let me talk."

But no answer came to her prayer, and at last she got tired of kneeling down among the empty pews. The building was so big that she felt quite far away, so she picked up her courage and went up the big aisle, right up through the choir stalls to the steps rising towards the altar, hidden by the curtains. It was legitimate for any woman to go so far. She was perfectly within her right. So she went up the steps and knelt down quietly beside the golden railing.

And there she prayed to the unseen Serpent—prayed, and believed it heard her. Then she went home. How near she had been to that Unseen Power! How fervently she had prayed! The Serpent always answered prayer, always looked after the helpless.

On going home her ring at the door was answered by a neighbour with a white face and swollen eyes.

What was the matter?

An hour ago, soon after she went out, her uncle had been brought home after a stroke. Since then he had died, just after the arrival of the doctor.

Rosalie sank back against the lobby wall, her hands by her sides, her eyes filled with horror.

"Your aunt is upstairs in the back bedroom," said the neighbour, who had told the story as quietly as she could, as gently as its tragedy allowed.

Rosalie pulled herself together and went upstairs, trying the bedroom door at the back. It opened, and she was thankful. Her aunt sat in a chair, her head buried in the pillow of the one spare bed. Rosalie went to her and touched her shoulder. The elder woman moved slowly, and then sat up, smoothing her grey hair.

"I've been here long enough," she said dully. "I must go and see to things. Sit here, Rosalie. It isn't for you to be about."

Her dull grief repelled all sad advances. From the time that Rosalie found her lying there cramped against the bed she showed no further signs of weakness, no further signs of giving in, till the funeral was over.

Then when the blinds were drawn up once more, and the November light had flooded the room, she took her foster daughter in her arms and wept as only a broken-hearted woman growing old can weep.

"We went to school together," she said at last, twisting her wet soiled handkerchief around her fingers. After that she scarcely mentioned her husband again.

But now time showed a great difference in the little household, in addition to its greatest loss. Money troubles and worry, of late months thickening ominously, had helped to bring about the sudden end. There were no more happy meals at tea-time, no bread to toast, nothing but the barest, rude necessities of life. For they were poor, so poor that they scarcely knew how to look the future in the face. Both were very helpless.

The elder woman in a few short months had grown old, shrunken, and thin. She tried at times to smile bravely, to take interest in life and neighbours, but life and interest had gone for her in the old playfellow and life love. And more and more each day since her uncle's death Rosalie felt the want of speech. She could give none of that bright assistance that was needed. No better than a living shadow she was bound to go about the house. Yet still she went to the temple to pray in humility and faithfulness.

And then, as the spring came round, she heard vague, disquieting rumours of the little house being shut up. Her aunt was going to live with a married brother, whose wife had little in common with her, and she herself, Rosalie, was to be sent to a Home for the Deaf and Dumb and Blind, a large charitable institution, greatly enlarged and improved upon by the munificence of a dead millionaire, one Geoffrey Todbrook by name. Insufferable thought! To separate her from the only human being she had learnt to love, shutting them each within a dungeon of strangers! "O God! O Serpent!" What of the prayer of months, to give one atom in the multitude the powers of speech? Prayer of presumption! Its punishment the taking away of everything that makes some lives worth living, the precious gift of freedom.

And yet Rosalie set her lips hard, there was no drooping, and went once more, with faith supremely high, but heart all wrong and tortured, to kneel and pray to God within the temple.

CHAPTER IV

THE GOLDEN SERPENT

The afternoon was cold and gloomy, and by the time Rosalie reached the temple the little light that ever came there had quite died away. There were no Americans in Lucifram, no English tourists either, consequently the sacred building from morn to eve was silent as the grave except for matins and for evensong. But evensong was held at seven, and now it was but four.

Rosalie's heart was in that terrible state of aching which approaches physical pain. Speechless, she knew herself quite helpless.

For lack of speech she must be separated from one who had suddenly grown more helpless than herself, one whom she could not bear to part with, one who had grown accustomed to her great defect, and had never labelled on the door those words: "Home for the Blind—the Deaf—the Dumb—Incurables."

"Once I get inside there I am dumb for ever," she cried to herself, as she stumbled up the darkening aisle. "Oh, I cannot go—I cannot! I want to live like other people. To be free—free—free!"

And so she knelt down beside the altar railings, and buried her face in her hands against its golden bars.

"Oh, Serpent, let me speak! Give me a tongue like other people have. I cannot go to that asylum—I cannot really. I cannot live without my aunt. We are all in all to each other. What good am I if I remain a speechless log? I might as well be dead."

No answer. Darkness and silence. That was all. The impenetrable hardness of it sank to Rosalie's heart. Suddenly she got up and looked round cautiously, with pale face and dark-rimmed eyes. There was no noise. Nothing moved in the empty building save herself. Silent and trembling, she took a step forward inside the railing, then another, and her hand touched the crimson curtain. Again she looked around, assured herself again that she was quite alone, silently drew back the heavy fold and stepped within. The lights upon the altar, burning by day and night, changed the dull gloom to brightness. Her wandering, awe-struck gaze fell full upon the Serpent, its head and jewelled eyes all shining underneath the slowly swinging lights.

Here, then, was the hidden God that all things worshipped. This was the God who punished some, rewarded others, and wore the creeds of ages on its three-pronged tail. Her eyes were dazzled by the brilliancy, but the Serpent's wisdom gleaming from those curious eyes attracted her.

"Give me what I want! Give me what I want!" she whispered, and stretched out her white arms till her hands had clasped behind the Serpent's head. Then she leant forward and pressed her lips against the cruel, hardened, lifeless fangs, and whispered yet again:

"Give me what I want—just so that I may serve you!"

As silently she unclasped her fingers, rising to her feet. She passed down the three steps leading from the altar, and became aware, with beating heart and sudden tumultuous fear, that she had been watched.

For, stepping from the side way, came a stranger, stopping her progress outward to the other side of the veil.

"What is it that you want?" he said.

In his eyes there shone the priceless worth of wisdom's jewels, giving them in their brilliant expression something of the same impenetrable light the Serpent's had.

Rosalie became confused, and mixed the two together. How could she help it, seeing both had come together? But no words were there for utterance. She raised her hand to her mouth, her eyes to his face—eyes that had grown in sadness and in beauty throughout a lifetime—and then she shook her head.

"Dumb?" said he.

She nodded.

"Is that what you came to pray about?"

Again she nodded. She looked up at him, and her eyes sank. After all, it was the secret of a life, for none knew of these daily visits to the temple, and now a stranger had discovered it—the secret which had been guarded so jealously all these years.

"And you come in here to pray often?"

She shook her head vehemently, and pointed outside.

"I see. You stay outside?"

Again she nodded.

Then he held the curtain aside, and she passed out, he following her.

The church without was black.

Rosalie gave a muttered cry of dismay—the building was so large, its pews, and steps, and labyrinths all so intricate. But her companion produced a light that glowed like a thin taper, but burnt with a clearer and a stronger light, and plainly lit the church around them.

"Never trust to the church to give you light," said he whimsically, "unless, as now, you penetrate to the Holy of Holies!"

Rosalie smiled; she felt it was but polite, unaccustomed as she was to strangers.

Together they walked down the long aisle, and once she stole a glance up at him sideways, with great curiosity, to see what he was like. But the stranger was looking at her, and she bent her head downward again. She evidently did not possess the gift of sweet unconsciousness of self.

"I presume you wished to come away?" he said at the end of their journey, before he opened the heavy doors.

She nodded.

Then he laid his hand upon her shoulder.

"The Serpent must be very cruel and hardened if he withstand such a prayer as that you offered."

There was more amusement than pity in his voice and expression. Rosalie felt, but did not understand it. Never had anyone in her narrow life been able to put so much expression into a mere hand-touch. In gratitude she could have taken and kissed it many times.

They passed out on to the high steps leading from the temple. The rain was coming down in torrents. The street lamps glistened through it, and the passers-by were infrequent.

"How are you going home?" he said. The outside world seemed to have separated them.

She pointed to her feet.

"Walking? Well, hurry and don't get wet. It would be a pity to spoil the prayer by leaving no time for its fulfilment. Good-night!"

Then he moved away a step or two, and she stopped to put up her umbrella. Suddenly, however, he turned round, and came with quick strides toward her.

"See, here is my card. When you have made headway with the Serpent, and received an answer to your prayer, come and see me!"

And he scribbled on the back of the card "Admit Bearer," and then handed it to her, once more leaving her standing on the steps.

Then Rosalie, having succeeded in getting up the umbrella, and gathering up her skirts, turned in the direction of home. It was a walk of about twenty minutes, and all the way she thought of the stranger, of his interesting face, deep eyes and mellow voice, his hand laid so kindly on her shoulder. She remembered, also, that sudden perceptible change when outside the church, a mixture of harshness and coldness and pride, more shown in his manner than his words.

"I wonder what he was doing inside the curtain?" she thought. "Perhaps he had gone there to pray like me. I hope I did not disturb him." Then she sighed. "He looked a rich man, and he could say whatever he wanted to. There could be nothing he was wanting half so much as I."

On reaching home she was met by her aunt. As soon as they were seated at the frugal tea, the lady explained that a Mr. Ellershaw, an acquaintance of her dead husband, had called that afternoon to see her. On hearing how matters stood, and the separation that was imminent, he had told her of a post of caretaker he knew to be vacant, where the work was to look after a large building in the city let out in flats to different business men. There would be a certain amount of work to do in connection with this—and he did not know whether either of them would care for such a post; but it was there if they wished. It would ensure them living together, four rooms in the topmost storey. Rosalie looked across her tea-cup and nodded her head eagerly.

"You like such a prospect?" her aunt asked quietly.

She nodded again.

"It will be very hard work, and I am not as strong as I used to be."

Rosalie held out her hands and looked at them triumphantly. Then she pointed to herself, and smiled.

"You think you could undertake some of it?"

So together they wrote a letter accepting the post, and a week later left their old home, with all its memories and associations, to settle in a fifth storey dwelling amongst the skylights.

Rosalie felt her prayer in part was answered. They were not to be separated after all. Hard as the work might be, it meant freedom and the company she loved. She was content, went to the temple, knelt humbly and returned thanks. Then she went on praying for a voice with a faith born of simplicity and her own idea of God.

One day a priest found her praying there. He inquired the cause. Like the stranger, he was not long in finding it. He put his hand upon her head, and blessed her in the name of the Serpent's three tails. Then he went back to the priests' lodgings, and kept his story for supper. He was a jolly man, of the earth earthy, and his idea of the Serpent was that his golden coils were lucrative. The priest was not bad-hearted; he was simply mediocre. But he had a sense of humour—and who, indeed, but the soured and stupid have not?—and the idea of a girl kneeling by the altar railings (he had never seen her, as on that one unique occasion, step beyond) praying persistently to be allowed to talk when plainly she was physically beyond it tickled his sense of funniness. He laughed and shook till the tears ran down his face.

"And she believes it—*that's* the biggest joke," he cried. "Believes that if she prays long enough the Serpent will weary or turn merciful, and fulfil her prayer."

"According to our history of the past, with its wonders and miracles, that is not so impossible as it seems," said one, more thoughtfully.

"She'd best jump back a hundred year or two, and cap one miracle by another, then," remarked a third.

"What did you say to her, James Peter?" asked a fourth.

"Oh, I blessed her, and prayed to the Serpent to look serious, and the request was granted. 'Twas a miracle on a small scale, I can assure you. I could have roared right out."

"What is she like to look at?" put in a fifth.

"Pretty—sad-looking—just the sort of woman to get an idea. That is the sort we can't afford to quarrel with. They tip so handsomely on Sundays."

"Little or tall?"

"Oh, tall! Medium, at any rate. Couldn't smile if she tried. Sacred liver of the Serpent! What a sermon for one of you fellows with a love of sentiment to preach on Sunday."

"Wait till the woman is made whole, and sitting in the congregation. Then our fortunes are secured," said another drily.

And in this respect the priests of the Serpent were very different from our own. Amongst themselves they never acted the hypocrite—the heathen idolaters!

So next day, when Rosalie went to pray, one or two passed in and out silently to behold the phenomenon. After a time they grew accustomed, and took no further notice of her. After all, a woman might as well spend her time in an attitude of humble devotion. Experience generally proved those to make the best sort of wives.

Rosalie and her aunt had been established a little over six months in the new home, and the work was so hard and unaccustomed that it was beginning to tell on both of them.

The older woman was little better than a breakdown before she came, and gradually without much complaint, but growing silence, she sank into the bed of weakness more. It was a sickness from which she never rose.

She had been too old to face these sudden changes, was not made of the stuff that endures, or not enduring, fights. So then this cloud had only risen in mockery to sink the heavier. Where was Rosalie's prayer of love and thanksgiving?

The last week of her aunt's illness was very strange and unreal to Rosalie—strange and unreal when, after the second funeral within a year, she sat alone in the little empty four-roomed storey.

Her hands, roughened, though not coarsened, by hard work, were clasped between her knees. Her head had sunk forward on her breast, her open eyes saw nothing.

Vaguely she hoped that she might be the next to go, thought of her prayer for speech, and dashed the bitter tears from her dull eyes. What of her prayer? Perhaps to the Serpent it sounded nothing more than clamorous presumption and self-will.

Again she had been offered the shelter of the Home for Deaf and Dumb by those who recognised her sad position. Was she ungrateful? Many poor waifs there were, she knew, in that great city, with none to help them to the scantiest food and shelter.

"I can't believe you're either kind or just, and I won't pray to you any more!" she cried inwardly, jumping up fiercely at last. "I wasn't made to be without a tongue. I wasn't! I wasn't! You haven't the power to give me one; that's what it really is."

But no bricks and mortar fell to punish such an outburst.

"What have I done that I should be left here alone?" she continued. "I want to go along with aunt and uncle. You know I do. I can't live here alone."

But there was no answer. Gradually a calmer spirit came over her, together with a wish to find out that sphinx-like secret that wrapped itself in icy silence.

"What's the good of making me want to talk if you won't let me?" she asked.

Out of the vast silence a voice seemed to shape itself at last.

"Give up! Sacrifice!" it said.

It was such a very beautiful voice, and yet so very cold, that Rosalie shrank from it. Sacrifice was such a heathenish thing! Besides, what was there to sacrifice in the way of a tongue—she hadn't got one, not a serviceable one, at any rate.

"The Serpent's will comes first with all believers," cried the same voice out of the silence.

"I wish we could agree," said Rosalie, with no disrespect, and then fell a-thinking.

Yes. After all, it came to the old, old thing. A clashing of wills—one human, one divine—if such it could be called. And therein lay the only sacrifice that God or the Serpent ever needed. It meant the sacrifice of will.

Slowly and clearly the truth unfolded itself. If her faith were pure and unselfish, she must be willing to give up longing and praying for that which was beyond her, and still love and serve the Serpent even without reward.

And to what path did her duty point? The thankful acceptance of a shelter that was offered, a gentle surrender without bitterness into God's hands. An ending of a prayer He thought fit not to answer.

It meant a great deal to Rosalie. The priest had laughed at her simpleness in expecting the performance of a miracle. Perhaps would all else had they heard it; but to her it was a very real thing, the outcome of real belief, that left a shattered feeling of disappointment when the ending came.

"I thought the Serpent always answered prayer when it was real," she said, and felt suddenly like one moving uncertainly in unknown lands amongst a host of strangers.

The time was drawing round to autumn again, and now that her aunt had been removed, arrangements were being made for her going. Within the week, she had been told, she would go the Home. Those who had interested themselves on her behalf did not like to think of the lonely girl. The doctor who had attended the aunt and uncle had very kindly made it his business to remove all delays, such as often took place for those who were admitted.

Another woman, older and stronger, and more accustomed to the work, was engaged. She had been there for some time before her aunt's death. Rosalie, in this new and quiet mood, recognised the kindness that had been shown to her on all sides. But though she was truly thankful, she could raise no enthusiasm. The next day, when afternoon came, she dressed herself as carefully as her worn clothes would allow, and went once more towards the temple.

But with what different feelings! For two years past she had gone always with the same earnest prayer, with no doubt of its acceptance, and now she was going to give up the prayer and everything that made her life worth living.

It was just such another wet, dull day as that a year ago when, with excess of feeling, she had drawn aside the sacred curtain and stept within the Holy Place.

Today, as usual, she went and knelt beside the railings. All was growing dark. The same silence, the same utter emptiness, pervaded the temple now, as then. Now, as then, the great longing seized her to pass within the veil. So silently she rose, drew back the curtain stealthily, and stept within. The Serpent's steadfast gaze demanded her first glance. Then she looked round, but perceived no stranger. Assured, she ascended the steps and knelt beside the gorgeous table. With tenderness and love, the outcome of simplicity and pure devotion, she clasped her hands once more about the Serpent's head, kneeling before it.

"I'm sorry," she whispered, her lips close to the terrible mouth. "I made a god of my own tongue instead of you. But now I understand. And, oh! Serpent, teach me the right way to live, and keep me from growing bitter."

Then, as before, she imprinted a light kiss, tender and loving, on the unkissable mouth, and silently bowed her head some minutes on the table.

Then on a sudden Rosalie rose, her eyes wide open, and stared at the golden god. They stared in wonderment, but growing understanding. The light of dawning wisdom was in her eyes.

One minute, two minutes, three, passed away. She turned round suddenly, emerged into the church, dark now as once before about a year ago. A light was in her hand; she cared not how she came by it, but partly knew.

A priest from one of the choir stalls was watching her, with a feeble candle in his hand.

He called out "Treason! Blasphemy!" to see a woman thus emerge from behind the sacred curtain. It was James Peter.

Rushing forward, he slipped over a footstool, and fell down heavily. His light was extinguished. Down the vast aisle, with the lightness of a spirit, Rosalie ran. Her eyes were laughing, a flush was on her once pale cheek.

James Peter, rising, followed her. He puffed and groaned at every priestly step.

But when the door was open she turned and nodded to him in the distance. The door closed. He was in darkness. He had followed solely upon her light.

Not till the lights were brought for Evensong did he extricate himself from the toils of the massive building. Then he told his tale.

"I tell you she turned round at the door and called to me 'Bon soir, monsieur! Adieu!'" he cried for the third time to his companions.

"Good Lord! What does it mean?" said one.

"Was she not dumb?" asked a second.

"As dumb as the Serpent!" replied James Peter. "She went into the Holy Place, and is cured."

"A woman in the Holy Place!"

"Yes! I called 'Blasphemy!' but the damned footstool tripped me! Had it not been for that I had caught her and brought her up before the great High Priest."

"A footstool tripped you!"

"Don't speak so sneeringly, brother Thomas John. I said a footstool tripped me."

"And you lost the woman?"

"What could I do without a light?"

"Strike matches."

"I followed her eyes till the door closed, and forgot about them. Besides, not being a smoker, I never carry any."

"Did you say you found a woman in the Holiest Place?" asked others, crowding round.

"I did not find her there, I saw her coming out."

"Coming out! And never stopped her?"

"No!"

"But we must find her. What is her address?"

"I don't know. What's the punishment when we have found her?"

"In olden times it was to have her tongue torn out by the roots."

"But the Serpent had just given her one, I tell you."

"Nowadays, I expect, the punishment will be modified. Strict silence on penalty of death, maybe."

"But if the Serpent has given her a tongue, who then dare take it away?"

"How has the Serpent given her one?"

"I tell you, before she was dumb."

"Impossible! No woman was ever so afflicted—worse luck!"

"I tell you she was dumb, and is cured. She said to me at the door, 'Bon soir, monsieur. Adieu!' Very pretty words," and he mimicked the tone and gesture.

"This is sheer madness. There is no sense in the words!" cried another.

"Is it necessary for women to speak sense?" asked James Peter.

All the others laughed. He looked dangerous. And so they talked, and all gesticulated. But the mistake was on the part of James Peter—in part, at least.

He never heard the lady speak. It was his own imagination which coined strange words without meaning.

CHAPTER V

THE MASTER

Rosalie outside the temple never paused, apparently, to think. She did not take the direction of her old home, but flew on as if scarcely touching the ground towards that portion of the city where lay the mansions and the ancient park. The usually crowded streets were almost deserted, the rain kept wayfarers within doors. Nothing hindered her rapid movements onward.

Greensward Avenue was one long vista of shining pavements, dripping trees, and glistening street lamps. Here and there brighter lights shone from the entrances to houses. But on Rosalie sped till she came to the central house, which stood a little back behind high iron palings.

The door had two leaves, and opened inward from the centre. There was a vestibule beyond, and then another double door of thickest glass, polished and cut to shine like diamonds. Above the hall door a deep red lamp was burning, which cast its light well out into the street. The only furniture within the vestibule was a broad chair of oak, and a massive umbrella stand all carved with hideous faces, very ancient, no doubt, but not exactly beautiful.

Rosalie noticed these as she stood on the top step touching the bell, and because each face was very fascinating she would have continued looking at them had not the inner door opened upon the instant.

It was not a creaking door. It opened noiselessly and swiftly, and in the doorway stood a man.

He had none of the superabundant dignity generally associated with the servants in rich houses. His hair was not powdered, his dress was plain, and black.

Rosalie, so swift and impetuous until now, came to a standstill. She looked at him, and he at her. She had no voice with which to explain her errand, and suddenly remembered her only chance of admittance there was the card. For it was to Marble House she had come, the house of the man whom she had met in the temple just a year ago.

"What is it that you want?" he asked. These were the exact words with which she had been greeted by the master.

Then she remembered the card was hidden away in the bosom of her dress in a little silken bag she had made in an idle moment for it months ago. She must produce it, that was evident, and trust to Providence to do the rest. She turned round towards the many-headed umbrella stand, and began to extricate the card of introduction. The man stood there waiting, and when she turned round, flushed and flurried, holding the card, and glancing at him suspiciously to trace the smile upon his lips, she found nothing there, not even surprise. He evidently was old enough to be beyond it

Rosalie pointed to the back; he read it, then motioning her to sit in the chair facing the hydra-headed umbrella stand, went in once more behind the polished doors and closed them after him.

The door opened silently again before long.

"Come this way," said the low, serious voice.

The doors swung to behind them. They entered upon a large square hall. It was not brilliantly lighted, and the farther end was dim and scarcely discernible. But every thing was rich and massive, and highly polished. It reminded her in some indescribable way of the temple she had just left. Carved oak chairs, just as those seen in the sacred building, lined the walls, standing round in a perfect square, except where interrupted by some other article of furniture. These chairs seemed to be endless.

As Rosalie passed along she became accustomed to the dimness, and noticed from this farther end a spiral staircase ascending to the upper floor. It was built in polished oak, and went round and round in a way that reminded her of the Serpent's coils. It led to a gallery that overlooked the hall on all sides.

Three double glass doors of the same peculiar lustre as the entrance (which made the fourth) led out of this hall, one on each side, one being beyond the staircase.

Her companion passed through that door to the left, and she followed him. They came upon a corridor, and stopped before the last door on the left-hand side. Her guide knocked, then opened it. There was no name to give; Rosalie had no tongue to speak, no card to show. Then the door closed again, and she found herself in the presence of the man whom she had come to seek.

He was sitting by a table reading. A fire was burning in the hearth near by. A high shaded lamp stood on the ground beside him. The floor was thickly carpeted, the walls were lined with books from floor to ceiling, one other door led from the room.

The Master looked up as she entered, then got up, pushing the book away.

"So you have come," he said. He came forward and held out his hand.

Rosalie, trembling and uncertain, returned the hand-shake, nodding.

"What! you cannot speak yet?"

She shook her head, but as he was withdrawing his hand she clutched it eagerly, unconscious of anything but this one little sinking straw of hope.

This time he looked at her more closely. "What is it?" he asked.

She raised her other hand to her throat and mouth, then pointed to him, her eyes full on his face.

"I'm not the Serpent," he answered, and he shook his head and tried to disengage his hand.

But Rosalie's fingers tightened with a fierceness and determination altogether foreign to her. Her cheeks flushed, her eyes flashed angrily; she gave one little imperious stamp with her foot.

The Master looked at her and smiled—a smile that travelled from his eyes to the corners of his mouth.

"I see. You do not intend to go till I have performed an—an impossibility?"

Rosalie nodded in all seriousness.

"It is the gift of speech you're wanting?"

She nodded.

"It's very dangerous; leads people into all kinds of indiscretions."

She shook her head vehemently.

"You think you differ from the commonality?"

But Rosalie neither shook her head nor nodded. She only looked up at him with no other expression in her eyes except dumb entreaty.

"Come to the light," said he, "and try to look less ghostly. After all, if you can't be cured you can't. You're brave enough to stand that, aren't you?"

Again she nodded, still looking at him.

He pushed the shade of the lamp up. "Now open your mouth," he said.

Obediently Rosalie did as she was told.

"Why, you've got a tongue!" said he, bending his brows, and stooping down to her. "Can't you move it?"

But Rosalie could not. It was complete paralysis of the muscles evidently.

"Come with me, and I'll see what I can do."

He led her through the other door into another room. The walls of this place were lined with chests and cupboards with glass fronts, containing curious instruments. In the centre was a long table. The room was also fitted up with chairs such as dentists use, and a marble washing basin fitted with water pipes, hot and cold.

Yet when the light was turned on the general effect was cheerful. Rosalie found it so, at any rate, for renewed hope was springing in her heart. She sat down upon the chair he drew for her, and watched him whilst he went to the cupboard and brought out something shaped like a very long darning needle. It was thick at one end, very fine and pointed at the other. Then from another shelf containing flasks of glass polished and cut he took a liquid shining like silver, and poured some into a tiny crucible. With these he came back to her and placed them on the table. Then he looked at her, smiling.

"This will hurt you very much," he said; "but you asked for it, so you will have to go through with it."

Anyone but Rosalie would have noticed that the expression of his face was not particularly kind. But she noticed nothing. She leant back against the head-rest; he placed his hand upon her eyes. After that they were too heavy for her to open them. She opened her mouth instead.

It was a curious kind of pain, if pain it could be called. Never in the whole of her life had she ever felt anything so soothing. She could not tell how long the sensation lasted, but it ceased very suddenly. Then although her eyes were closed she felt (this was the curious part of it) a strong light shining into her mouth, right back to the roots of that so far silent tongue. It was a light that had the power to heal and strengthen, and for a long, long time it played upon every unused nerve and delicate muscle. At last all was over; the master laid his hand upon her eyes again and opened them.

"Now," said he, "the miracle has been performed. Are you satisfied?"

From long custom Rosalie nodded.

"You must speak," he answered, laughing, "if but to show your appreciation of the gift."

"Thank you," she said, quite perfectly, with just a little break in the word that took nothing from its sweetness.

"Did you find the pain very bad?"

"I nev-er felt it."

"Never felt it?" he repeated. "Give me your hand."

But her pulse was even, and he frowned.

"Where did you come from when you came to me?" he asked, bending his eyes down to hers with a keen, penetrating glance.

"I came from the temple."

"From the prayer?"

"Yes."

"Then you—" but here he stopped. "I see," he continued, but in reality he didn't.

"Did you expect I should be hurt?" she asked.

"I can hardly believe you were not."

"But I should have screamed. I made no sound."

"That was scarcely possible. For my own part, I always think it best to guard against screams, they are so unhelpful and unnecessary."

Now Rosalie looked at him, with eyes just as keen and penetrating as his had been.

"Why do you stare at me?" he asked, smiling.

"To see if you are disappointed."

Here he laughed.

"Be careful. Your tongue is getting rather out of bounds already."

"I think you would rather have enjoyed my being hurt."

"Well, what can you expect in a country where vivisection is disallowed? One must take what little pleasure one can get."

Here he led the way back into the outer room. When they were both through he turned the key and put it in his pocket.

"I rarely go in there," he said. "Few folks are fool enough to come to me. I have no ambition to become a doctor, and I shun the popularity that hangs upon the quack."

They were both standing by the table now, one on either side. Rosalie's eyes were fixed dreamily on a large glass ink-stand in the centre of the table. She was beginning to feel indescribably tired. There was nothing very wonderful in this, the operation had lasted longer than she was aware. But though tired, she was feeling remarkably light-hearted, longing to get outside and give herself two or three decided pinches to become convinced she was awake, and that this great good fortune of her prayer had at last come to her.

But over and above the tired feeling and the unreality came gratitude to her deliverer. The thought of this made her suddenly raise her eyes and look across at him.

Certainly his face was very proud, and the shadows lurking underneath his eyes and at the corners of his mouth gave it a dark, forbidding expression. It was not altogether pleasant.

"The feature I like best is his nose," thought Rosalie. "The one that frightens me most is his mouth; the one that most interests me is his eyes."

"You have been very kind to me," she said. "Is there any way in which I can pay you back?"

But he shook his head.

"I do not think you could give me anything tangible, but perhaps you yourself will be able to suggest something."

Rosalie flushed to the roots of her hair. "I haven't anything," she answered.

"Not even a soul?"

"What is that?"

"That part of you which under certain conditions becomes immortal."

"That part of me belongs to the Serpent."

"The Serpent passed you on body and soul to me."

"The Serpent did nothing of the sort," she answered vehemently, if slowly. "I—I—I—"

"You what?"

"I nothing."

His eyebrows came together in a frown.

"Yes," he answered quietly, "there is one way in which you can pay me back. Speak the truth in answering my questions."

"I'll try," said Rosalie meekly.

"Then put an ending to that 'I—I—I—.'"

"I came because I thought it was time. I got a little bit tired of the Serpent."

"Why?"

"Because it never took any notice of me."

"Are you sure?"

Rosalie's curious eyes looked up innocently and met his.

"Does that surprise you very much?"

"I confess that it does."

"Do you know, I'm very tired. If you don't mind, I'll come again tomorrow and talk it over."

But he shook his head, and smiled again.

"I don't think I'll let you go," he said. "Your answers are not very satisfactory. Besides, where is there you can go?"

"Oh, with a tongue one can go anywhere and do anything."

"You think so?"

"Yes."

And here from sheer weariness and exhaustion she slipped down in the arm-chair beside her.

It had been a very hard day, and the ending had told upon her strength. She had not fainted, however, she was only sleeping.

Mr. Barringcourt crossed the room and looked at her very narrowly, even dropping on one knee to examine her features more nearly.

It was a very pale, thin, and tired face he looked at, delicate and fragile, with dark lashes, and faint blue shadows underneath the closed eyes. The backs of her hands were rough, and he took each up and examined it as though he had been a fortune-teller—back and front.

Then he began walking slowly back and forwards through the room. His face, though handsome after a kind, was certainly not of the most prepossessing; and yet in repose his expression was one of weariness and contempt.

"What shall I do with her?" he muttered. "Keep her to prevent blabbing as usual. Keep her and bring her up to talk properly. When she is old enough, or rather fit enough, I'll let her out on a lease long enough to take her to the devil. Always the same! everlastingly the same! coming and going, with nothing to give and everything to ask. Dull to the very core, chattering like magpies, smiling and aping God knows what! Rich and poor, all of them alike. And for some reason best known to myself I stand it. What an excellent patient fisherman I should make!"

Then he sat down again very deliberately in his chair, and drew the book he had been reading towards him, at the same ringing a bell. The same man who had admitted Rosalie answered it.

"Take her away, and see she doesn't get out," said he, without looking up; and the other evidently understood so well that he never asked a question.

CHAPTER VI

NEW EXPERIENCES

When Rosalie awoke next morning, it was with a pardonable sense of bewilderment and estrangement.

Instead of the little bedroom, bare of carpet, and devoid of all furniture, except the poorest and the simplest, she found herself in one that was really palatial.

The bed had deep hangings of red silk, and she was not up to date enough to tear them down as breeding microbes and all things unhealthy. Then by degrees, her eyes travelling beyond the bed, she gradually became acquainted with the other things within the room, washstand, dressing-table, sofa, chairs; and here Rosalie gave a squeal of delight, and jumped out of bed, for there opposite was a wardrobe, as respectable as carved black oak could make it. But it was not the wardrobe that attracted her attention so much as the mirror set full length in its middle door—a mirror larger than she had ever seen before or dreamt about. Rosalie was not vain, but she had always entertained a great longing to see her feet at the same time as her head, and had thought it only a luxury and privilege accorded to the rich. When she had become accustomed to this novel vision she walked over towards the windows. Here, so far as beauty was concerned, a disappointment waited on her. All three of them looked upon a high blank wall opposite. It gave a sense of extreme dulness to the place.

Just then her explorations and discoveries were cut short by a knock at the door, and on it entered a woman carrying a tray holding a cup of tea. Rosalie, who understood nothing of this sort of thing, stared at it and the bearer.

"I'm quite better now, thank you," she said, shaking her head. "I was a little tired last night. I'd rather not have my breakfast in bed, if you don't mind."

"This is not your breakfast," said the other, in a voice so well modulated that many seemingly more exalted might have envied it.

"Oh, what is it?" said Rosalie, standing still with her hands behind her looking at it.

"A cup of tea to help you to dress."

She had the sweetest voice imaginable. Rosalie thought it the saddest she had ever heard.

"I shan't be ten minutes dressing," she replied decidedly.

"Quite an hour, I should say," replied the other.

"Oh!" gasped Rosalie. Then she clapped her hands together, caught up the flowing robe and skipped across the room to the bed.

"If I'm not dressed in ten minutes, my name's not Rosalie Paleaf."

Then with a sudden change to alarm in her manner, she turned round, growing alternately hot and cold.

"I say, where are my things? I can't see them anywhere."

"I took them away last night. There are your clothes for the day." And she directed her attention to a chair on which some very pretty and expensive *lingerie* was laid.

Rosalie looked at it, then drew herself up.

"I want my own clothes," she said. "These are too good for me; the others might be poor, but they were my own."

"I am afraid you cannot have them; you must dress in these."

The tears rose in Rosalie's eyes.

"I want my own clothes," she said again. "Auntie and I cut and made them together. They were the last pair of stockings that she ever knit."

There was no answer.

"Won't you bring them back?" said Rosalie at last, the tears still standing in her eyes.

"I am afraid it is against the rules of the house."

Then Rosalie got up with a sigh, and prepared to get inside the first garment.

"There is your bath first."

"I never bath in the morning; I always leave that till night."

"I think you had better do that which is customary."

Again Rosalie sighed, and followed her tormentress to an adjoining bathroom.

And so it took her well on into the hour before she was dressed, ready to leave the bedroom.

Mariana, who stayed to help her, insisted on arranging her hair, and after all arranged it much more becomingly than Rosalie herself had ever done.

But the black robe with its red silk facings, that fitted her companion so becomingly, suited her not at all. The fit was as perfect as it could be, but otherwise she looked quite out of place in it.

Breakfast was served on the same floor as that on which her bedroom was—three rooms away.

All this portion of the house evidently looked out on to nothing better than the wall mentioned before; but the beauty of the interior compensated for outside gloom. Rosalie was charmed with everything she saw, though somewhat awe-struck, and she took her breakfast shyly from the hands of what she described to herself as the handsomest man she had ever seen. She also made a mental note that he must be brother to the man she saw downstairs.

Rosalie had not gone all this time without grateful remembrance of that ordinary gift she had come to possess; but somehow there was some vague, indescribable thing in her surroundings that took away a full appreciation. She was longing to be outside, to talk with people more like herself, not all in black with red silk facings and knee breeches, and voices modulated to a soft perfection.

Rosalie's voice was sweet, but it was not the sweetness found in theirs. Hers was the outcome of expression, theirs of classical harmony. But how was she to get away? She dare not ask Mariana, for she was getting an uncomfortable idea that Mariana, from no ill motive, always thwarted and opposed her. So, watching her opportunity, she escaped and passed down the spiral staircase.

In the big hall below all was silent as death. Evidently no one was about.

She ran across to the big doors with a palpitating heart—outside them was freedom, she scarcely knew from what.

Alas! Another hand had touched the large glass handle before her own.

"Your card, madam. Your passport out."

"I have none. I shall not be away five minutes."

"I am afraid you cannot go."

"But I must go."

There was no answer. Exasperated, Rosalie stood and faced him.

"You let me in, and you can let me out."

"The orders are that you are not to pass."

"Whose orders?"

"The master's."

"Then take me to him."

"He is engaged at present."

"I'll go myself, then."

CHAPTER VII

A DEBT OF GRATITUDE

As Rosalie passed along the corridor her sudden decision was sealed by growing annoyance and a longing, almost amounting to fear, to get away.

With scarcely a pause she knocked upon the door, that door through which she entered last night. Without stopping she opened it. Mr. Barringcourt was there alone, at a table littered with papers, writing. He was indeed busy and engrossed, for on her entrance he did not raise his head, till accosted by her voice, and then he looked up sharply enough.

"You!" said he, bringing his eyebrows together in that dark frown which Rosalie had seen last night, and seeing had never forgotten.

"Yes. I want to go out."

"Impossible!" said he, with an impatient gesture of his hand, and returned to the paper.

"I want to go out," she repeated. "And you have no right to stop me."

"In my own house I have every right. Go away, you are interrupting me."

"So are you interrupting me."

He laughed, not altogether kindly, and looked up at her again.

"That is little short of impudent."

"I don't care. I want to go out, and if you won't give me leave, I shall take it."

"Take it then, by all means."

"That man at the door won't let me."

"Knock him down. It will be one way of surmounting the difficulty."

"He is such an elephant. I disliked him the very first time I saw him," she replied with energy, and as much simplicity as the truth occasioned.

"Well, go away and fight it out with him; watch the door, and bounce out when he's not looking."

"I won't do anything so undignified. I shall make friends with the kitchen people, and creep out that way."

"The kitchen door leads into the garden, and the walls are high, and the gate is locked. I keep the key myself, to ensure no one getting to the stables."

"Then give me leave to go out at the front."

"Now, why should you want to go out at the front? You have as beautiful a home as you could possibly wish for. What more can you want?"

"Fresh air and human beings."

"You have them here."

She shook her head. The tears rose in her throat, and were very hard to choke down again.

"It's the dismallest place I ever came to; and I'm no use. The people here always contradict me."

"You are the first person who has ever complained of them; and your opinion goes for nothing, your own conduct leaves so much to be desired."

"In what way?"

"In my time I have experienced much ingratitude, but never any quite to equal yours."

"I—ungrateful?"

"Most decidedly!"

"What are you wanting from me?"

"Quiet submission."

Rosalie's eyes opened wide, her lips parted; her expression was one of unfeigned surprise.

"What's that?"

"To do what you're told quietly. Now you *know*, there is no excuse for your not complying."

"But to submit means to stay here."

"Of course!"

"But I can't. Oh, I can't really! Anything but that."

"Nothing but that. You come to me with the most unusual request, and I am fool enough to put myself out of the way for you. Then you expect to go away, or rather slip away, without any more words about repayment. And when you are brought back, all this squalling."

"Nice people are quite content with 'Thank you.'"

"I'm not nice, and 'Thank you' never appeals to me."

"But if I stay here I can do nothing."

"Yes, you can mope."

"In return for a tongue?"

"Why not? It would be the height of self-sacrifice, and the perfection of thanksgiving."

Her serious eyes met his thoughtfully. "Do you really wish me to stay here?"

"I not only wish, but am determined on it."

"Then my self-sacrifice can never be spontaneous."

"You mean you are changing your mind. You are wishful to stop?"

"Not wishful, but if you want it, I'll—I'll try to settle down more cheerfully. After all, it's only just."

"That is so."

"Shall I often see you?"

"Never. I am not fond of inflictions."

He spoke so drily, and the words were so unkind, that Rosalie's wistful face grew paler. Yet still she argued to herself it would be selfish to wish to be free, to have a tongue and everything. And after all, the stranger was so clever that he must of necessity know best.

"Will you let me out just for an hour?" she asked at length, with a voice greatly subdued from the first clamorous outburst.

"Not for an hour."

"But I have an aunt, and she is dead. I shouldn't like strangers to take what once belonged to her."

"Where is your uncle?"

"He is dead too."

"Your people?"

"I have none."

"Where then, in the name of all the devils in Lucifram, do you intend to go to?"

"I thought when people knew I had miraculously come by a tongue they would—"

"Ah! I thought as much. You want to behave with all the absurdity of a hen that has laid an egg."

"Indeed!" said Rosalie, flushing.

"You want to get out just to cackle."

She was silent.

"You admit it?"

"I admit nothing but your want of manners."

"What a waspish, vinegarish tongue yours is."

"It's the fault of the doctor, then. If one cannot produce a sweet instrument one might as well admit oneself a failure."

"How was I to tell? Your face was so deceptive."

"Maybe so is my tongue. I was only speaking in fun. Let me out for one hour. Lend me twopence, and I will return, having spoken to no one, and in the right frame for being submissive."

For a short time he was silent. At last he said:

"Promise me faithfully you will return."

"I promise you most faithfully."

"Within the hour?"

"Yes."

"You understand perfectly that my reason for bringing you back is not for any personal gratification I should derive from it. It is simply so that you may not obtain any great or particular pleasure from having a prayer perfected."

"You speak plainly enough for the dullest mind."

"I'm glad. Now you may go. And remember, come back if you have any sense of gratitude."

So Rosalie passed out again into the farther hall.

"I have permission to pass," said she at the door, and then she stood outside.

It seemed to her when she reached the parapet that she had been out of the world for years. And oh! to be back in the world again! To see and hear the sights and sounds, so commonplace and ordinary, yet to her stilled ear so sweet again. Never had that terrible silent mansion struck her as so terrible till now she stood amongst the noise of work and life once more.

One hour of freedom. One hour with the light, jogging world, and then to pass once more beneath the shadow—a silent spirit in a silent world. The 'bus rattled on, taking its own slow time towards that quarter of the city where she had lived. She found the upper storey empty, and none had missed her. Yesterday the doctor had told her his intention of coming for her at four o'clock today. It was not yet quite twelve.

Each of the little rooms was now quite bare, except the tiny attic called her bedroom. In it were gathered the few trivial things she prized as belonging to days that were less dark than these. There was a necklace of coral, a collar of lace, a pair of gloves, kid, backed with astrachan, the last present her uncle ever gave her; a tiny brooch of gold, left by her aunt, and always worn by her, and but little else. One other thing she found, a book that in that planet compares nearly to our Bible. Sadly and lovingly she placed them all together, and kissed them many times, her eyes blinded with tears; and then a voice whispered:

"Why go back? Go to this doctor. Tell him everything, for he is kind. None would blame you for not returning to that prison mansion, even though under a promise. It was an unfair advantage."

But Rosalie shook her head.

"I must go back, because I promised. I asked everything in return for nothing. And God, in His own good time, will make the dark path plain."

The struggle gradually died, and Right conquered.

At last she was ready to go. Glancing round for the last time, she saw upon the mantelpiece a key, a solitary one upon an iron ring.

"It belonged to uncle's safe, the one that had so little in it," she thought. She took it up. Its dull appearance suggested so much dull tragedy to her. "I'll take it with me," she thought, and slipped it in the pocket of her dress.

Then she passed down the broad stone steps out once more into the street. Her brief holiday was over. The short hour was almost passed. She clenched her hands together, and drove back the blinding tears that struggled in her eyes. Gradually she drew nearer to the Avenue—how eagerly she had rushed there on the night before! The great black marble mansion came in view, its dusky grandeur having a certain sinister lowering to her understanding eye no different from a prison.

"I wonder when I'll walk along this street again?" she thought, and ascended the marble steps, hiding all trace of past emotion.

CHAPTER VIII

A BOOK OF INSPIRATION

"The master wished to speak to you when you returned," the attendant at the door said to her when he answered it.

Rosalie crossed the hall, feeling that vague sense of satisfaction that generally accompanies honesty, and which at times appears so poor a recompense.

This time on knocking she waited for the answer. When it came she opened the door and entered.

Mr. Barringcourt was in the act of filing papers, and generally tidying up the littered table.

"You are quite punctual," said he. "And what is more, astoundingly honest."

"You did not expect I should return, then?"

"No! Honestly speaking, I thought I had seen the last of you."

She shook her head.

"Gratitude brought me back at the expense of inclination."

"You should have yielded to temptation, and run away."

"Perhaps my action in returning was not quite so commendable as you think. I was much tempted to run away, and then—"

"What?"

"I could find no place to go to."

"You have no appreciative friends?"

"Not one."

"The doctor?"

Rosalie looked up quickly, and flushed. "Why do you speak of him?"

"I'm sure I don't know," he answered drily; "I believe I was meaning myself."

"Oh—yes—of course," stammered Rosalie. "I thought you meant Dr. Kaye."

"Then you had notions of appealing to him?"

Rosalie laughed. "You are not the pleasantest of companions."

"You might as well make a confidant of me. I am the only one you will find for some time."

"Well, yes, then," she answered, looking across at him with a timid glance. "I thought of running to the doctor, informing him you intended making a prisoner of me in a free city, and asking him to give me the benefit of his protection and advice."

"And you thought better of it?"

"You told me if I was grateful I should return. I was grateful, and though there seems something very topsy-turvy about the recompense you ask for, there is something in it that appeals to my sense of justice."

"That is why you came back?"

"There is no other reason."

Mr. Barringcourt all this time had been sitting in his chair by the table. Rosalie was standing at the farther side of it. Now he got up and walked over to the fireplace, where the fire was burning brightly.

"What is your name?" he asked.

"Rosalie Paleaf."

"Brought up by an aunt and uncle?"

"Yes."

"Always dumb, and therefore very much out of the world?"

"Yes."

"Where did you learn the little bit of knowledge you possess?"

"I listened to it. I was not deaf, you know."

"Could you read?"

"Yes, I can read. That is how I used to spend most of my time."

"Travels, novels, or biography?"

"A little bit of both—all three, I mean. 'The Life of Krimjo on the Desert Island,' which was my favourite, contained a little of all, I think."

"Ally Krimjo was only make-belief," said he ruthlessly.

"Indeed he wasn't! He had gone through everything he spoke about, the shipwreck and the loneliness, the savages and everything. Make-belief! Oh, Mr. Barringcourt, have you ever really read it through?"

"Yes, at the time it was written."

Here Rosalie laughed again triumphantly.

"That shows you don't know the book I'm talking about at all. The man who wrote it lived hundreds of years ago. Quite three hundred, I should say."

"At that rate I must be mistaken. Then if you are so fond of travel and biography, I have some volumes here all on that subject, written, too, about the time you speak of. You will have a great deal of time lie heavy on your hands; perhaps you would like some?"

Rosalie looked dubious, and her eyes travelled to the imposing-looking book-shelves.

"I never found anyone quite to come up to Ally Krimjo," she replied regretfully.

"You refuse my offer?"

"Not if you give me something interesting. But as a rule I don't like biographies, because the people always die. Now, Ally Krimjo—"

"You're quite right," said Mr. Barringcourt grimly. "Ally Krimjo hasn't died, so he deserves to live. Have you the Book of Divine Inspiration?"

"Oh, yes! I don't suppose there's anyone without that?"

"Here's one with pictures; look at it."

He took down from a shelf a heavy and ponderous volume of the Book of Divine Inspiration, as written and compiled in the planet Lucifram, and carried it without the least apparent effort to the table.

"Now come and look at the pictures. I'll show you a few, and then you can take it away with you and look at the rest."

He opened it at the first page—the frontispiece. It was a picture of the Golden Serpent, so lifelike that its appearance was most startling. The book, likewise, must have possessed the property of magnifying all contained in it, for suddenly the head and coils and tails seemed to enlarge to the same gigantic size as that within the temple.

"I don't like it. Don't show me any more of that book," Rosalie said.

"But why?" he asked, with apparent surprise.

"Oh! I don't know," she answered, almost whispering. "It's the Serpent. I don't like it."

"But you are the young lady who was kissing its head, and throwing your arms around it."

"Yes, I know. That was because I did not understand."

"And now?"

"Oh, now! I think it's cruel and deceitful."

"That's nothing short of blasphemy. The Serpent is a god!"

"Do you believe that?" she asked, suddenly looking up, and fixing his eyes with a look as keen as it was serious.

Two pairs of eyes, dark and light, each encountered one another—each trying to read the other's secret—and both for once inscrutable, dark and light alike.

"Yes. I've got a pretty good mental digestion; it can take most things," he said, the corners of his mouth curving into a smile. "Look! Miss—Miss— What's your name, by the way?"

"My name is Rosalie—Rosalie Paleaf."

"Well now, Miss Paleaf, let us turn to the second picture."

Reluctantly she turned round once more, to behold a forest jungle, as fine and beautiful a scene as one could wish. Its size and realism made her put out her hand to pull a twig of feathery foliage, when suddenly she was startled to see beneath it a pair of eyes, wild and yet intelligent, gleaming out at her. It was an animal shaped and sized much like a monkey. Behind it was another of the same kind, a partner in its joys and sorrows evidently.

Rosalie sprang back.

"Look at that hideous thing!" she cried in horror, pointing to it. Then recollecting herself, she said, with an effort at more self-control and appreciation: "Are—are they extinct now?"

"I don't know, I'm sure. What would *you* say?"

"I sincerely hope so, I'm sure. Put it away. There is something uncanny about that book. That creature startled me."

"It's an acquired taste. Here we come to another."

He had turned onward to a third picture, in which was shown a woman sitting on the roots of a tree, the expression of her face long and uncompromising, full of discontent. She wore no clothing, but her long and silky hair was sufficient covering. She was of no particular beauty, and her expression of discontent, mingled with curiosity, subtly introduced, and having little intelligence to enlighten it, gave the girl a feeling of repugnance. In one hand she held a fruit of brilliant scarlet; a mouthful was being eaten, and its taste did not seem altogether to her liking.

"What do you think of this?"

"I like it very little better. The man who painted it, judging from her face, understood human nature, and had very little mercy for it."

"There you are mistaken. It is a caricature," he answered softly, "painted one day by a man, and sent to his dearest friend—a woman."

"But she is eating a tomato."

"Of course! Let us continue."

The next picture showed this same woman standing beside a man who sat upon a rock cracking nuts with his teeth. As Rosalie looked the scenes began to move and become lifelike, pretty much in the same way as a cinematograph. At first the man did not perceive his companion, but turning suddenly, in the act of taking a broken shell from his mouth, he saw her holding the scarlet fruit, from which she had taken no more than two fair mouthfuls. On seeing this his jaw dropped, his eyes expanded.

Thin, far-away voices came from the picture, aiding the illusion.

"What for did you that?" said he, in a voice devoid of beauty and expression.

"To find out," she replied, in the same manner.

"But we die—we die—if we eat fruit of blood colour!" he cried, with superstitious horror in his voice.

"We no die, we live and grow fat. I eat, I live; but I miss something."

"What?"

"I know not. Eat, and tell me." Her look was cunning.

"I dare not."

"It is the best of all kinds—but for one thing."

"And what is dat?"

"Eat, and tell me. You be my faithful love."

Gingerly he took it in his hand, applied it reluctantly to his lips, sucking the juice alone.

"It wants—"

His low forehead wrinkled. He could not formulate his thoughts.

"What?"

"It wants—"

And then all round a million voices echoed:

"*It wants but salt!*"

"Salt!" he shouted, drowning the harmonic voices in his new discovery.

Hereupon the woman fell upon her knees, and almost worshipped him, kissing his hands and feet, weeping tears of pleasure on them.

"Scrape me some up," he uttered, taking advantage of her low position.

She did it with her finger-nails.

"Now stand back whilst I eat it."

"But I—I found it."

"Stand back, goose, and watch me eat."

"I found it first," she whimpered.

"Here's a seed—that's all you're worth," he answered. "Now I go to find more," said he, jumping up valiantly. "You bake bread and get me butter for when I return."

"I come too!" she cried. "You eat the whole while I worky work."

"Fool—toad—weasel—monkey! bake me the bread, or I your neck am breaking!"

And with that they disappeared from the page. Only the picture in its first stage remained visible.

"That's not pretty at all," said Rosalie.

"Few things are in real life," he answered.

"But that was caricature."

"Not in the way you think. It was caricature, I grant, but with a difference."

"Yes. I don't think the eating of salt with tomato could make a man really superior, do you?"

"No; but it was the fact that he discovered salt."

"But he didn't. He was as ignorant as she till the voices whispered it."

"Nevertheless, he caught the first sound."

"Yes, of course," said Rosalie thoughtfully.

Here Mr. Barringcourt laughed.

"You do not appreciate its true absurdity," he said; "but that, maybe, is scarcely necessary. Now, that picture, or series of pictures, was painted by a woman, and sent to the man who had sent her the first."

"But how about the voices?"

"Oh! she was no ordinary woman, by any means."

"Was she quarrelling with the man?"

"No. They were amusing each other in wet weather."

"They paint most beautiful scenery, but I don't like their men and women."

"You are not intended to. Now, shall we go on?"

"No; I'd rather not, really. It gives me headache, and I've had it ever since yesterday afternoon, except for that little bit after you had healed me."

"You are tired of the Book of Divine Inspiration?"

"I'm tired of the pictures; they are no better than caricatures and skits. I don't think that's a good book to keep in a house at all."

"You astound me! Were you not brought up to worship the Serpent?"

"Yes; but the Serpent disappointed me."

"I see. You only worship a God who is content to spoil you?"

She shook her head.

"I don't know," she said. "Perhaps I'll settle down again before long."

"I hope so. Has it ever struck you, Miss Paleaf, how completely you are in my power?"

"No," she answered, looking at him quickly.

"Well, you know, I found you in the temple, in the Holiest Place—the place forbidden to women. Do you know what the punishment for that transgression is?"

"No."

"To have your tongue torn out by the roots."

"Impossible!"

"Not in the least. In this one interview with me you have said enough against the Serpent to set all its scales and coils bristling, and its fangs working."

"I have said nothing."

"'Cruel and deceitful,' were not those your words?"

"Yes; but to tear my tongue out would not be to prove it otherwise. The Serpent's wisdom should assert itself and prove the opposite. You were also in the Holiest Place."

"Of course; but for a man the offence is not so capital."

"Tomatoes and salt," said Rosalie, and she laughed. He laughed also.

"Your impudence is only beaten by your ignorance."

"As often as I offend solely with my tongue, you must take the blame yourself. I think you must have oiled the wheels too freely."

"It is a good thing you have no relatives, Miss Paleaf; they would have missed you, disappearing so suddenly."

"Under the circumstances, I suppose it is."

"Were you happy with them?"

"Oh, yes! As happy as the day, when we were in prosperity. But this last year has been nothing but shadow and poverty, and I don't think I ever realised how many things I had to be thankful for till they were all gone."

"The gift of speech does not compensate for all things, then?"

"I don't know. I have had it so short a time."

"You are longing for freedom, and can find nothing to compensate for the bitterness of its loss. Is not that it?"

"I don't think it is only that. My aunt was only buried the day before yesterday. I should be very callous and ungrateful if I could forget her so readily."

"Yet you cannot deny the events of the past day have put a great gulf betwixt you and her."

"Yes; I could think she had died a year ago along with uncle. Poor thing! It would have been so much better if she had done so, I think."

"How long do you think your term of imprisonment will last?"

Rosalie shook her head.

"I don't know. The future has always been a blank to me. I never built those castles in the air that many love to build."

"How about your prayer to find a tongue?"

"I don't know. I longed to speak, but never looked into a future crowned by successful prayer."

"Well, your term of imprisonment here lasts three years."

"It is a long time."

"On the contrary, reckoned justly, a very short one."

"What do you mean by 'reckoned justly'?"

He took up a bundle of filed papers from the table.

"These are accounts of long standing," he answered gravely. "It is strange how quickly a high rate of interest accumulates. What you wipe off in three years or less by ready payments, some are leaving till a future date, till it accumulates and doubles, then maybe trebles, and some day swamps them."

Rosalie's eyes opened with unfeigned surprise.

"But whom is the money owed to?"

"To me."

"Have you all those debtors?"

"These are a few—a very few. People find out the softness of my heart, and then they come to me. Women with stingy husbands and extravagant tastes, men with limited brains and boundless ambition. Each and all, with many other pleas and reasons, call upon me and win me over to their way of thinking. I am always won. No simple-hearted fool within the country gives in more easily than I when I can gain security of person."

"But don't you tell them that you expect return?"

"No; I like them to think there's one generous person in the world."

"But that is scarcely fair. You ought to tell them what you want."

"The argument would be beyond them. Besides, it would come then too much like making bargains. I am no shopman. Those who seek me find me. Others stay away."

"But this is nothing short of madness. How can you make people pay without a signature or anything?"

"I never jest but when it suits my purpose. And for madness, I grant upon the surface it may appear as such. But each bill works backward—item by item, year by year. Mathematicians and philosophers looking through them would find a subject more than fascinating."

"But if when you show your bill the people refuse to pay, and say they never got the goods?"

"Why, then, one little snip and the fabric ravels out again, loop by loop, as it was knitted up. Back it goes to the fundamental working, as rigid as machinery, as true as time, and ends in nothingness."

Rosalie was silent for a time, and then she said: "Is that how it is you are such a rich man?"

But he shook his head.

"I am poorer than many people think," he answered. "And richer too—wealth is comparative. But now," he continued, with more energy, "I have come to the conclusion that your term of prison life shall not be quite so dull as you expected. You may come to me at any time, provided I have leisure. Moreover, you may borrow any book; amongst all these there will be surely some to suit you, even though it be but a uniquely pictured book of Ally Krimjo."

"But what are you expecting in return? You say you like people to esteem you generous, and are not in reality so at all. This generosity to me may end in nothing but a high percentage. It may bring me down to nothingness."

"You have the advantage of being young, you see. I might end your debtor if I tied you up in an unsympathetic prison, and let you out at last, to find I was too late, and your spirit killed by solitude."

He was looking at her with a puzzled and thoughtful expression, as if trying to weigh or settle something in his mind to his own satisfaction.

"I think you were easier to understand dumb than you are speaking," he said at last.

"Well, yes, because I would be less complex," said Rosalie wisely. "I was minus something before, now I'm not."

"Maybe. When will you come to visit me again?"

"Tomorrow morning, if I may. From twelve to one?"

"Yes. We'll arrange for that hour twice a week. It will be neither too long nor too often to bore either of us. The rest of the time you'll spend as best you can within the house and gardens."

CHAPTER IX

MARIANA

Rosalie went away again, upstairs to that corridor on which the rooms in which she lived were situated. Another meal was there in readiness, for the hour was now past one. She ate with little heart, the silent attendant by her side unwittingly depressing her. When the meal was over she went to a little sitting-room which Mariana had shown her, taking her small parcel of belongings with her, and shut the door.

Here a fire was burning, the only one in that particular wing, for they seemed to be chary of fires here. The room had little of brightness about it otherwise. Its walls were panelled oak without design or ornament. An oaken table on three legs, a few high-backed chairs, a rug before the fireplace, polished boards the floor; that was all. A narrow window looked out upon the blank wall opposite, giving the room a gloomy, darkened look. Yet there was something about this simply furnished room that Rosalie liked. It was less luxurious than any other in that house which she had visited.

She drew one of the high-backed chairs toward the fire, and sat down, her feet upon the fender. She had taken her small Book of Divine Inspiration from the parcel, and sat holding it idly in her hands, staring at the flames. After all, it was comforting to be able to hold something, something familiar and not strange, something that had been handled and read by loving hands and eyes, though now they were passed away for ever.

For Rosalie, despite her behaviour downstairs, was only playing a part. Laughing or answering, there had been ever in her heart the Serpent's tooth. It gnawed and stung with almost unendurable pain. O God! to be but rid of it for five sweet minutes.

So far as Rosalie was concerned, there were no late dinners in this house of mystery. She had ordinary tea at five o'clock, and then the lights for the evening were brought in, and the red curtains drawn. About seven Mariana knocked at the door, and entered.

"This is my evening for playing," said she quietly; "would you care to come and listen to me?"

"Thank you; I should like to come very much. What do you play?"

"Play? Oh! I always play on a violin; it's my favourite amusement. It's the way I always spend my night out."

"Night out," thought Rosalie; "what an expression coming from her lips!"

Aloud she said: "I'm very fond of music. Have you learnt long?"

"I don't remember learning, but I suppose I must have done."

She led the way along the corridor, down the slippery stairs, and turned in at the glass door leading from the central hall towards Mr. Barringcourt's study; but she did not go there. Instead, she paused at a door next to it on the same side. She passed in, and held the door for Rosalie to follow. The room within was dark, but it must have overlooked the Avenue, for lights from the outside shone weirdly in through the long windows, lighting up short lines of furniture, half a grand piano, a strip of table, an ottoman, and a piece of wall.

Mariana turned on one light. It was soft and shaded, but had not strength enough to illuminate the whole room. The farther corners were entirely in the shade.

"Will you not turn on more lights?" asked Rosalie.

"No; I like the twilight best. I can think and feel better when the light is low."

Then she uncased the violin which she had brought down with her, and tried the strings, testing them by the piano, which was now a little better brought to view.

Rosalie went over to a window—it was the natural instinct of a prisoner—and looked out of it with hungry eyes.

Passing, passing, never ceasing, went the traffic, and through the closed windows came the muffled sound of horses' feet, and wheels, and voices. Feverishly she scanned each face as closely as she could in the distance; but she read nothing on them but what one reads on a hundred faces every day. Her heart beat with an aching longing to touch the pavement again with free feet. Three years! It was a lifetime. One day in a house like this contained an agony of years.

"I am impatient," she said, and closed her lips patiently and tight.

She had forgotten Mariana's music—in the testing of the chords—till suddenly, after a short pause, she began to play.

Rosalie's attention was first divided between the music and the street. What was played seemed to fit in with her mood—a simple air of sadness. But this harmonic accompaniment had its dangers, for by degrees Rosalie felt her spirits, instead of keeping pace with it, begin to follow. Then the street claimed her attention less, the music absorbing it. And at last she turned round reluctantly and looked toward the player. Mariana, never an ordinary-looking woman, was by the one pale light quite extraordinary. The long graceful robe she wore made her look more than commonly tall. Her pretty arms, white and delicate yet, full of a certain indefinable strength, and the ivory whiteness of her face, had a curious charm and fascination in the dim lights. But beside her playing, the musician herself was insignificant.

From sadness her notes changed to melancholy, from melancholy on to misery, from misery to despair. Despondency, tragedy, hopeless complaint, and restless, weary wandering on those spiritual wastes where no light comes, or even narrow track to show that ever pilgrim passed before—this was her music.

Her face as she played betrayed no great emotion. The brightness in her eyes spoke more of mental activity and retrospection than of sentiment. Gradually the listener's eyes fell on the furniture around. Much of it, in conjunction with the rest of the house, was of polished oak, carved finely and curiously. Opposite there was a cabinet museum about the height of a man, and above it the carved head of some idolater's god, growing in clearness as she became accustomed to the light

But surely the music had affected it. Its ugly eyes, protruding and rid of all intelligence, altered slowly to expression almost human. For every quivering note struck from the violin found a resting-place within these staring orbs, filling them both with misery. Their dumb speech was terrible, but when Rosalie moved away, more ghastly still by reason of their persistence. She looked away. There on the floor beside her was a tiger-skin, a rug of worth and beauty, with a head and glassy eyes. Its eyes met hers. Their dumb misery told a tale beyond the power of speech. Shivering, she turned and moved away.

When would Mariana stop and take her from this wretched room? She had moved within range of the statues, those dim, misty forms of whiteness which rose like ghosts with out and upstretched arms to beckon her. Faces of cold, white, and deathly beauty, and eyes! Oh, terrible! all gazing into hers with that sad gaze and straining misery, reaching to the height and depth of agony.

It was enough. Had they but wailed, or cried, or uttered sound, the spell had broken. But here was silence—ghastly, terrible, because so secret and so unexpected.

At last the tension reached a limit. On all sides Rosalie encountered ghastly faces of long-suffering pain to which the music seemed to form a fitting background. Turning hurriedly to escape one face belonging to a child, set in a picture hung upon the wall, her glance fell by chance upon the mirror and revealed herself, strained horror in her eyes, with blanched cheeks and open lips. She scarcely recognised who stood there. It was enough. She crossed the room half running, and clutched Mariana's arm.

"How much longer?"

"The time is up. Alas! how quickly it has passed. Never again till next week, and then but two short hours. And yet you ask me, 'How much longer?'"

"Can you play like that, and never feel it?"

Mariana shook her head.

"It's the only time I ever feel, the only time I ever live."

"But it is pain and sorrow."

"Better than emptiness. Now I have lost the only thing I love. All week it lies quite mute, a thing of idleness, bursting with life. And when I take it up it utters so long a wail, so sad a sigh, that my heart returns to it, and we weep together till pain becomes an ecstasy and sadness joy."

"Oh, Mariana! what a life is yours!"

"No different from the rest. A life of grey tomorrows that come and go in endless twilight."

"Will you feel like this tomorrow?"

"No. Tomorrow brings a calm existence. Tonight I fill my heart with tears."

"What was it brought you here?"

"Oh! I loved not wisely, but too well, this little fiddle."

"And has it brought you to this pass?"

"Yes, if pass you call it."

"Then, Mariana, give it up!"

For her the dimness of the room had vanished, its fantasies and ghostly shadows thrown off with one great effort. She grasped the other's arms in both her hands, and stared at her, taller by her sudden force and fierceness. The other looked at her, and then recoiled.

"Give it up! The only joy of life—the only life beyond a dull existence! Why, I should die—the very thought would kill me."

"No! It would make you live!"

But Mariana only looked at her, and shook her head.

"Rosalie, can I play? Can you make anything out of it?"

"I never heard such music; but it is wrong—it's the wrong sort."

Then Mariana came close up to her, just as before she had drawn back, and, with a sudden weakness, drooped her head upon the other's shoulder, clasping her hands about her waist.

"Don't say that!" she cried, her voice little above a whisper. "I cannot bear it. I can do nothing more. There is no time. Once or twice I asked the Master would he listen, and he did. But he said there was no tune in what I played, no harmony of any sort—that all was a delusion, a fancy of my brain."

"But that was not the truth." And Rosalie held her very tight, that woman who in the morning had seemed so strong to her. "And he only said it because he knew you would be fool enough to take it all to heart."

"Hush! hush! It's treason to talk like that."

"Nothing's treason but failure. You follow my advice, and give up the fiddle. Then after a while you'll get it back again in such a way that even Mr. Barringcourt will not be able to say there's no tune in it."

Mariana looked at her, with surprise and misunderstanding on every feature.

"I can't give it up. I'm bound to play for two hours every Wednesday night, harmony or discord."

"Why bound?"

"It was the stipulation I made when first I came here. It's the kind of thing one can't break through."

"You don't want to?"

"No, I don't; but if I did I could not."

"You would rather live for two hours a week than seven times twenty-four?"

"I don't understand you."

"No, and never will."

It was Mr. Barringcourt's voice, and he spoke from the door, through which he had entered.

CHAPTER X

A CONVERSATION IN SHADOWS

When Mr. Barringcourt was in it, the great black house held its mysteries and shadows; without him they seemed aggravated fourfold. Not long after the Wednesday evening music, Rosalie stood in the centre of the hall suddenly smitten with the most chilly fear she had ever experienced in her life. No noise, no sound, not even the wind without, penetrated those walls of iron marble. Shadows and silence in endless vista met her eye. Shadows and silence like a sigh congealed, changed from nothingness into reality.

Dreading the loneliness, and her own want of nerve to go upstairs, she went to the door and accosted the keeper there.

"Does this house frighten you?" she asked.

"Not at all," he answered, most politely.

"That is strange, because I feel most frightened here. It is not haunted, is it?"

"What do you mean?"

"There are no—no ghosts?"

He smiled. "That depends upon your imagination, I should say."

"I want to go upstairs, and I dare not. You don't think me very foolish, do you?"

"Where is Mariana? Does she not look after you?"

"Yes. But she went away, nearly an hour ago."

"Shall I call her?"

"Oh, please do!"

He touched a bell, and a minute later Mariana appeared coming down the staircase. She looked as calm as ever. The short outburst of the evening had died away.

"I'm sorry to trouble you. But I really could not come upstairs alone. The house was so quiet that it frightened me."

"You will get accustomed to the silence by degrees," she answered, and led the way towards the staircase.

When they reached the little sitting-room where the fire burnt, Rosalie was pleased to find a white cloth laid there, with supper on it. It was a very plain repast, but cheerful, possibly because of the bright lamp and firelight.

"When do you have your supper?" she asked of Mariana.

"I have had mine."

"What is the time?"

"Almost ten o'clock."

"How late! That is the time I generally go to bed. What time do you go?"

"As soon as you are settled for the night I shall retire."

"Where do you sleep?"

"In the next room to yours. If you want anything in the night, you may ring or come to me."

"But then I should have to come out on to the corridor. I hate corridors."

"No. My bedroom opens into yours. Your door that opens into the passage is locked at night."

"By whom?"

"By me."

"Why do you lock it?"

"I don't know, I'm sure. You are safer with it locked, I expect."

"How long have you lived here, Mariana?"

"Three years this autumn."

"And how long has Mr. Barringcourt been here?"

"The same length of time. I came with him."

"And you are happy here?"

"I could not be happier—under the circumstances."

"Were you ever happier?"

"I think I was once. But it is a very long time ago. I don't remember how long, so that it cannot really matter."

"Where did you live before you lived here?"

She shook her head.

"I can't quite remember. I think it was a very cold and dark place, and one day Mr. Barringcourt came and asked me would I like to go away."

"And you accepted?"

"Yes. I wanted to get warm again."

"And are you warm?"

"Yes. Every Wednesday night. If it were not for that I should grow cold again."

A silence. Then:

"Who lived here before Mr. Barringcourt?"

"A man who died. His name was Geoffrey Todbrook."

"What?"

"Geoffrey Todbrook."

"Why, he's the man who started homes for incurables. There was one for the dumb and deaf and blind. I should have gone there."

"I have heard he was very charitable. He left this house to Mr. Barringcourt."

"Were they related?"

"No; I rather think myself the Master had let it to him on a lease. Then when the lease expired he died, and left a will to smooth all difficulties."

"Was Mr. Barringcourt living in the city before Mr. Todbrook's death?"

"Oh, no! I don't think he had ever been here before. He took me to the opera one Wednesday night, and he said it was only the second time he had been there."

"The opera? Did you like it?"

"Yes, I liked it; but it made my head ache. I was trying to remember something all the time."

"Do you often go out with him?"

"Oh, no; that would be to get oneself talked about. Besides, so long as we remain here, I am but a servant."

"Why does Mr. Barringcourt keep me here?"

"I expect you have some secret he wishes to discover, otherwise he would not trouble himself about you. When he took me to the opera it was to discover something."

"What?"

"I don't know."

"Then how can you tell?"

"Because, up to the time we went, and through the performance, he was very affable to me. Afterwards he took no more notice of me, and never has done."

"Don't you hate him?"

"Why should I? I had no secret. His conduct was permissible; and I had rather be left alone."

"And what secret can I have that he should be agreeable to me?"

"I cannot tell. Perhaps, like me, you have none. But if you have, rest assured you will not leave this house till it has been discovered."

"Have you ever had anyone staying here before in the same way that I am?"

"Not in my time. People with secrets worth knowing are few and far between."

"Then what can make the Master think such an insignificant person as I could hold a secret?"

"I cannot tell. I only said it might be so; there is no other reason why he should tolerate your company?"

Rosalie laughed, despite a very uneasy feeling in her mind.

"Do you ever have company here?"

"Yes. Last Christmas there was a ball, and we had two or three dinner parties and entertainments. Lady Flamington generally acts as hostess. She and Sir James are very friendly with Mr. Barringcourt."

"What is she like?"

"Very beautiful, I think, with very pleasing manners. She must be so to please the Master; he is so hard to please."

"Perhaps she has a secret?"

"Oh, no; I hardly think so. He makes a convenience of her."

"Good gracious!" and Rosalie laughed. "You don't give him an enviable character."

"I speak as truthfully as my perceptions allow me; but at times I may be wrong."

"And does she not resent being made a convenience of?"

"No; it is only self-respect that keeps her from falling in love with him."

"Is he then so agreeable to her?"

"He gives her everything that is not worth the having."

"What do you mean?"

"He gives her everything but love."

"But that, with a husband, no one would want."

Mariana's eyebrows rose. "There are double marriages on Lucifram, I'm given to understand."

"Yes; but no one thinks much of a woman who marries twice, unless she is a widow."

"Indeed," Mariana answered, and was silent.

"But is Mr. Barringcourt fond of no one?" Rosalie pursued.

"I never heard of anyone. He is cold and proud, and often takes no trouble to hide it."

"But then there are so many good and beautiful women in the world."

"They find partners, perhaps, that need them more."

After another silence Rosalie continued: "And Mr. Todbrook—what did he die of?"

"I think he went down the back staircase."

"In his own house?"

"Yes."

"What do you mean?"

"He died."

"In which room?"

"The one the Master sleeps in now. There is a portrait of him in the picture-gallery. Tomorrow you shall see it."

"What did he die of?"

"He had quick ears. He heard the spirit voices calling, and he went to them."

"Painlessly?"

"Like one sailing on a sea of glass. They say his end was merciful; and I know it was. He suffered nothing—he suffers nothing now."

"Is he in heaven?"

"I doubt there was too little pain for that; but yet I cannot tell. He may have suffered previously. Men's lives are strange. And the roughest rocks are coated by smooth waters. They keep their secrets all too well."

"I'm tired, Mariana. Shall we go to bed?"

"Yes. When you wish it."

So they rose and went together to the bedroom, which had a chilly air in it after the cosy room. When at last Rosalie was in bed, Mariana smoothed the coverlet and tucked the bed-clothes in.

"Leave me a light, won't you?"

"Yes; I'll put it on this table. But there is nothing to fear. An easy conscience may sleep well here, secure from harm." She moved away, but after a few steps returned. She stooped over the bed and kissed Rosalie's brow. "Good-night, little one. Sleep peacefully till daybreak." And then she went away.

Big tears rose in Rosalie's eyes, for the words had awakened in her a terrible longing for love and companionship, stronger and more powerful than ever Mariana, in her terribly set existence, could ever know how to give. For Rosalie felt that she was even now the stronger of the two, and wept for Mariana's solitude as well as her own.

CHAPTER XI

GARDEN AND HOUSE OF SHADOWS

The next morning the sensation of waking in such fine surroundings had lost all its charm. Rosalie awoke with a dull leaden pain at her heart, that gained rather than lost power as she recalled one by one the articles of furniture in this new home. The long mirror had lost its fascination; so had the silken bed-hangings. She did not jump out of bed, but rather lay there idly, with no wish to rise; oppressed with such a heaviness that to lie still seemed the only ease from all those aches and pains that twine around a heavy heart. As the grey light of early morning brightened and broadened, she curled in among the bed-clothes, and shut her eyes.

"If only they would let me lie here, and not disturb me! I would never disturb them, I'm sure. I feel so weary that the least exertion is the biggest effort."

Then she lay very still for a long time, till at last Mariana knocked at the door and opened it, bringing the customary cup of tea.

"I feel so tired, Mariana," Rosalie said, "and there's nothing to do. Don't you think I might spend the day in bed?"

"It is against the rules."

"Who makes all the rules here?"

"The Master."

"But he has gone away till tomorrow."

"That does not excuse us."

"But he would never know unless you told. I am tired, really, Mariana. I could just lie still, and never move an inch all day."

"You must get up."

"When I get up my heart aches."

"That does not enter into the consideration of the rule. You must get up, or you will be shaken out when the bed is made."

So very reluctantly Rosalie rose, with a day of nothingness and imprisonment before her. She was dressed in about the same time as yesterday, had breakfast served in the same room in the same way, and then walked out on to the corridor aimlessly and disconsolately.

Mariana had disappeared. Although Rosalie tried every door along the corridor she could not find her. Many of these were locked, and others she discovered to be bedrooms, furnished much as her own, with the exception of the little sitting-room and the room in which she had her meals.

At last, weary of this, she passed out to the high gallery overreaching the square central hall. She walked round it, and tried various doors leading off from it, but all were locked. Below, the dim hall lay in silence. Nothing of light or life was there, though it was not yet mid-day. She looked down over the high oaken balustrade, and sighed, and the echo brought her sigh back to her. She whispered "Rosalie"; the word ran round the arching dome, and then returned—a mocking, hollow voice within the silence. So the morning crept away, with no brightness to speed its dragging hours, no companionship, no occupation. Not a sound fell on her ear. So still was everything, the house might have been a City of the Dead.

At dinner-time she ate mechanically the food they placed before her. To refuse was simply to raise up insistence. Then she withdrew to the little sitting-room, to idle away what time would go, to find after endless waiting that scarcely an hour had passed. Then she got up and went back to the bed-room to bring her hat, and with the same difficulty as the day before, reached with safety the foot of the spiral staircase.

The doorkeeper was sitting not far away from it, reading a paper. She went towards him, and as she approached him he looked up, and then rose from his seat.

"Would you mind telling me which way I should go to find the garden?" she asked.

"Certainly. If you will come this way I will take you."

Rosalie smiled sadly.

"Suppose somebody got out or in whilst you are away?"

"No one would wish to go out, and the door only opens from within," he answered.

He walked across the hall, and she followed him to the glass door behind the staircase. This door likewise entered upon a corridor with doors leading from either side of it. The house seemed all doors, but at the farther end a spacious fernery opened out, the curtains (of deep red) which shut it off being now looped and drawn back, so that much beyond was visible. Through the magnificent fern-house he led her till they came to a door of glass leading down into the garden beyond.

The doorkeeper opened it, and let her pass through, himself following.

Outside, broad flights of steps descended by terraces to a lawn of smoothest grass. The terraces were paved in large squares of black and white marble, and from the central one a huge fountain was sending up showers of sparkling water to meet the brilliant sun. Beds of flowers, all of colours resembling scarlet geraniums, were laid out bordering the side walks. One magnificent bed of what looked like crimson gladioli ran up a steep bank bordering the left-hand wall. The high walls themselves were covered with creepers, all of brilliant red, just as autumn leaves are often found, and the only relief afforded was that of the dark foliage of the trees that clustered willow fashion in the rear portion of the garden. This was a kind of wooded avenue along which a carriage drive led from the big gates in the outer wall round to those stables where the Master's favourite horses were.

"This is the garden," said her companion, when he had brought her so far; "you will return any time before five. After that the doors are locked."

When Rosalie was left alone she walked across the lawn slowly, taking in all the beauty and striking nature of the scene. The gardens were large. The avenue and shrubbery beyond were shaded, and provided with many rustic and artistic seats. Rosalie walked along the carriage drive as far as she could, and then a sudden and unaccountable gloom seemed to fall upon her and all things. Just then a sudden bend in the road brought her full in view of the stables. It seemed to her for one instant as if against the gloom surrounding her they shone out in flashing whiteness. They were flat-roofed, though high, and the strong pillars supporting and ornamenting the building were an exact fac-simile of those used in the decoration of the temple.

And standing there looking at it, Rosalie smiled.

"I wonder whose idea that was?" she thought. "A devout architect and designer would never have thought of such a thing. But perhaps I'm mistaken; this may be a private place of worship. I'll go on and see."

So she advanced as far as the building; but whether it were stable or chapel she could not tell, for it possessed no doorway. She walked around it as far as she could on either side, till prevented by a wall of great height, but found nothing to serve as a clue as to the nature of its use. No sound came from within—none of the odour that generally characterises such places, either of sanctity or horses—and for the third time Rosalie walked round with growing curiosity. Marble, marble, all was marble, cold and hard and lifeless.

"I really think granite would be a welcome change," she said, and sighed and walked away.

But it was really pleasant and enjoyable to be in the open air. To be able to look up at a sky that belonged in common to prisoners and free men, there was some little consolation in that.

As she emerged once more from the wooded avenue, her eye fell full on the house. She was surprised and startled at its beauty, viewed thus from the back. Whereas looking at it from the street it showed as nothing but a large square mansion, almost ugly in its plainness, it was from here one of the most graceful and artistic buildings she had ever seen. It was turreted and towered, with polished oriel windows, shining with a lustre all their own against the dusky background of dark marble. The windows on the basement all opened on the ground.

"I believe this is the front, and the front is the back," thought she. "A kind of topsy-turvy, like the rest of things. What a magnificent door!"

This last expression escaped her involuntarily and aloud.

The door from which she had come was a small side one leading from the conservatory of palms and ferns, but in the centre of this huge construction of glass was a double door of thick carved glass, or some substance very like it, of fine workmanship and execution.

Rosalie went up the many steps towards it, passing the silver fountain that fell with almost a merry sound into the marble basin. Both leaves of the door were shut, and the carving represented was that of a temple, the inner portion, with arched aisles and fluted pillars, and in the centre an altar, with above it the image of a toad. Below it, on the steps outside the customary railing, bowed figures knelt in bare feet, their shoes and stockings at some considerable distance. The representation was comprehensive. Each figure and detail was drawn with great exactness and clearness. The curious polish it possessed was its most striking feature, especially that brilliancy radiating from the toad. Rosalie bent her eyes closer to it, shuddered to find that there was something horribly repulsive in such an animal, and then found herself attracted by the light shining from its head. Its eyes were meaningless and staring, even in the carved picture, but from its head, and this she only discovered after steady looking, the light shone very curiously. Instead of the white light of the rest, this was almost red. Just a faint tinge of red! All the rest, carved as it were from blocks of ice, was utterly lifeless. Yet it was this tinge of colour, so subtly introduced, which made the whole great difference between an uninteresting and an interesting thing. At last she left it and looked down once more into the garden. She saw that several narrow paths led into the shrubberies at the sides. But what struck her attention most was that glorious rising bank of scarlet lilies and harebells and gladioli, that extended right down one side to the wooded avenue beyond, and reached almost to the height of the wall.

She perceived a narrow winding path led up this bank to its summit, and there a garden seat was placed. This was the highest point of vantage in the garden.

"I believe if I could only get up there I should be able to see away over the opposite wall, for it's lower!" she cried excitedly. "Oh, how glorious to be able to see the city and everything! I'll go."

But alas! from the times of Cinderella downwards, clocks have often had a knack of striking at an awkward time. And now there came the sound of chimes, the silver warning, and then the five plain strokes that told the closing hour of fettered liberty.

Rosalie re-entered the house. In the central hall she met Mariana coming from the entrance door in hat and jacket, and carrying a muff.

"Where have you been?" she cried, running across to her.

"Out for a walk."

"Oh, Mariana! What a shame never to tell me, and never to take me!" And she took hold of her hands hungrily, and kissed her on either cheek.

"Why do you kiss me?" the other asked, smiling.

"To try to get some real fresh air into my lips."

"It is not very fresh. There is quite a fog coming on."

"Ah! But it's free air. I feel all the better just for kissing you. But why do you never take me?"

"It is against the rules."

"But why can you go, and not I?"

"I'm sure I don't know. See, I have brought you some sweets," and Mariana held out a very pretty box containing a delicious assortment of chocolates.

Rosalie took it, somehow more touched than she liked to show by this simple little act of graciousness.

"Come and sit with me after tea, and let us eat them together."

"I am afraid I cannot. I am always busy in the evening."

"What are you doing?"

"Making a wedding-dress."

"Are you going to marry, then?"

"Oh, no; I'm not making it for myself. I don't know that it is a wedding-dress either. However, I am making it very beautifully, and so I am ambitious for it."

"Who is going to wear it?"

Here Mariana's brow puckered, and a puzzled, tired look came on to her face.

"I don't know," she answered. "I expect if I finish it, and no one applies for it or wants it, it will shrivel up again. For there is no wardrobe but what is overrun with moths; and the moths here eat away all colours except red and black."

"Then how can you preserve it till it's done?"

"By steeping the silk I sew it with in tears. But when the last stitch is in the effect has gone. The moths cannot perceive the bitterness afterwards. They eat it all away."

Rosalie stared at her, as well she might.

"Won't you let me see it?" she asked at length; but Mariana shook her head.

"It would be no pleasure to you."

"Indeed it would. Let me see it, Mariana, just for one minute. There can be possibly no harm in that."

"The room I sew in is very damp for such as you."

"But I'm stronger than you. I'm accustomed to hard work."

The other looked at her and smiled, with more sadness than mirth in her expression.

"What strange ideas you get about things, Rosalie. The work I do would kill you in a month."

"But you will let me come with you, will you not?"

"Yes, if you wish it very much. After tea at six o'clock I will come for you."

CHAPTER XII

AN ACT OF DISOBEDIENCE

At six o'clock Mariana knocked at the little sitting-room door, and Rosalie opened it, quite ready to accompany her, armed with the box of sweets.

"You must not bring those," said the elder woman.

"But I want you to have some."

"I'm not like you. I'm not fond of sweets, and have no intention of making my fingers sticky."

Then Rosalie put them down, and followed her in silence and obedience.

They went downstairs together, and took the door opening into the central hall to the right, the one through which Rosalie had not yet passed.

But at the threshold Rosalie stood still. It seemed to her as if a great spider's web was barring their further progress. A breath of darkness and dampness was wafted out to meet them, and inclination bade her turn back there and then. Mariana evidently noticed nothing of this hesitation; she passed through the door, and held it open for Rosalie to follow. The gigantic cobweb was nothing but delusion evidently, and melted into nothingness.

"Don't shut the door," Rosalie whispered; but it had closed silently even as she spoke.

And here was darkness and cold dampness. She heard her heart beat wildly in the stillness, and groped for Mariana's arm. It seemed cold and lifeless, having no animation.

"Can't we get a light?" she whispered, with dry lips, and her voice sounded hollow in her own hearing.

"The light is farther down the passage."

That, at least, was reassurance. It was Mariana's voice, no different from what it ever was, just as subdued and gentle.

By degrees her eyes became accustomed to the intense gloom, and when Mariana turned on the one flickering light, she recognised a length of passage similar to that in the other two wings. But here the doors were all quite low, and made of plain black wood. There was no attempt at adornment. The floor was plain wood, the walls, the ceilings, and everything was dreary, damp, and cold.

The doors, too, were numbered all in red, and it was before No. 13 that Mariana stopped. It opened to her touch, and together they entered.

"This is the room I work in," said Mariana, and again turned on one feeble light. It seemed the only one in the chamber.

The black rafters of oak hung low above their heads, and their heaviness perhaps helped to increase the gloomy aspect of the place. A long table of deal ran down the centre, with a chair at either end. This table was covered with a white cloth reaching the ground on either side.

Two chests of oak, shabby and worn, were the only articles of furniture the room possessed. The walls were whitewashed. Here and there the plaster had fallen from them, with a dispiriting effect. There was neither fireplace nor window in the room.

"Can you work in here?" Rosalie asked, looking round with an involuntary shiver.

"Yes. One becomes accustomed to surroundings. I never notice them; I'm too absorbed."

She went to the table and drew away the cloth, folding it, and placing it upon one of the vacant chairs. Below, a shimmer of satin, and gold, and silver, all strikingly in contrast to the bareness and poorness of the room, met the eye.

"How lovely!" said Rosalie, drawing her breath. "Do you know, I thought that big white cloth was the material, and it looked to my eyes more like a shroud."

"This is only the material," said Mariana. "I finished it the day you came, after being engaged on it three years. It is all hand-spun and woven, but now I've put the loom and spinning-wheel away in those big chests. One does not want too many things about."

"But who taught you?"

"Oh! it is knowledge one acquires. It needs a certain kind of brain and a given pattern, that is all."

Then she went over to one of the chests and opened it, and took from it a parcel which she untied. It contained a quantity of most lovely lace, the like of which Rosalie had never seen before.

"Did you make this?" she asked.

"No; it belongs to the Master. I found it in the lumber rooms among the attics, and asked him for it, and so he gave it to me."

"Gave it to you? It looks almost priceless."

"I know—reckoned from some standpoints. But I liked the design. It is lovers' knots, and sprays of lily of the valley. Have you noticed it?"

"Yes."

"It was that that put it in my head about the wedding-dress. When I have finished, it will be a beautiful creation."

"But do not the moths attack the lace?"

"Oh, no; you see it belongs to the Master, otherwise it would have been eaten long ago."

"But why do you not wear it yourself, if he gave it to you?"

Again the tired, puzzled look came over Mariana's face.

"I have no use for it. Besides—I don't know. I think it has something to do with sacrifice or freedom. I can't tell which."

"Will you give it to Lady Flamington, do you think?"

"I shall not give it to anyone, except the one who asks."

"But you will be besieged."

"How can that be when no one knows about it?" And she spread the lace upon the ivory satin, and drew it into graceful folds, just as an understanding artist would. As she did so, even by the meagre light Rosalie perceived its exquisite beauty.

"Who is to be fitted for it?" she asked.

"I don't know. One does not like to trouble people; I think I shall use my own discretion. After all, I scarcely hope that anyone will wear it."

"Could I be of use to you?"

"It is too cold for you to take off your dress."

"Oh, no! Let me do it, just to feel I've done something in the day."

"Thank you," said Mariana. "You are neither too tall nor short. I think it would show to advantage on a figure like yours. I'll fit it for just such a one as you."

She cut a piece from the soft piles of satin, and began to shape it to a bodice lining.

"Are you going to try it on with *satin*?" asked Rosalie, astounded at such extravagance.

"Yes; inside and out must be both alike for a perfect finish. I might use silk, but I prefer the same material."

What a marvellous fitter on she was! and yet how wonderfully patient Rosalie stood, the whole long evening through. It was no light twenty minutes—not even an hour—but dragged out into three.

Mariana forgot herself evidently in her occupation, and had no mercy on the model she was fitting. She treated her as a thing of wood and stone till she had realised the full effect in fit of bodice, skirt, and train, which, when perfected, she removed and folded into tissue papers, all labelled for the purpose near at hand. Then suddenly when all was finished she looked at her, and saw how deathly white her face had grown under the lengthened strain.

"Ah! now you are ill, and I am to blame for it," she said.

But Rosalie shook her head, though she shivered.

"It's the cold; everything is so damp down here."

"Yes. Indeed, it has been kind of you. I never hoped to get a model. We can't ask favours of each other here, and I'm sorry if I tired you; but—but—I don't know whether it may not be against the rule, so it was best to complete it before the Master came, in order to plead ignorance."

Truly this last was the most human thing Mariana had ever said to her, the only deviation from a hard, set rule of living.

"Yes," said Rosalie, smiling despite the faintness and shivering that overcame her. "When you've done a thing no one can say anything, can they? At least, they can't say much."

Mariana helped her on with her customary dress, and just then the clock outside struck nine.

"My work-time is up now," she said. "I will return with you."

Perhaps no one ever greeted fire, and light, and warmth as Rosalie did when back in the small sitting-room in the storey up above. In bed at night she remembered the moths that had flickered round the dim light, and round her also, as if claiming this work as soon as finished, and identifying her with it, so it almost seemed to her. And yet how beautiful the thing had looked, how out of place with its surroundings! Suddenly great tears of bitterness fell on the pillow for this lonely woman, so utterly without the pale of human sympathy, and yet so uncomplaining. How beautiful she was! Once during the fitting on she had thrown a piece of satin on her shoulder, too busy for the second to turn round and put it down. And how its ivory smoothness had matched the smoothness of her neck and cheek. How well it had contrasted with her dark eyes and hair. And then there was about her such a nameless grace and gentle refinement! Yet there she had worked in the cold, damp cell, and been content to work, with apparently no hope for the future, but moths and mildew and decay.

It was in the midst of these reveries on Mariana that Rosalie fell asleep, to wake many times throughout the night, shivering, to think herself alone within that gloomy room below, tried on for shrouds by ghosts with horrid grinning laughter.

It was a night in no wise likely to raise Rosalie's spirits from the curious depths of unreality and pain where they had fallen; yet towards morning she fell into a sleep so deep, that she never awoke from it till Mariana came to call and waken her.

"Mariana," she said, "you promised you would show me Mr. Todbrook's portrait yesterday, and you never did."

"It is in the picture-gallery. You could have found it for yourself."

"I don't know where the picture-gallery is."

"I had forgotten. If you wait for me in the corridor after breakfast I will show it to you."

So after breakfast Rosalie went out into the passage to wait for her.

The gallery was downstairs in that same wing, facing toward the gardens, where the conservatory was.

It was a very large gallery, longer than broad, with polished floor, and seats upholstered in red velvet stood along the walls. The light was admitted from the roof, but very beautiful electric candelabra hung from the ceiling, which was all panelled and carved in black oak.

Mariana led the way to the portrait of the late owner of the Marble House. There he stood in the correct evening dress for a man of his position, with one hand leaning on a table and the other by his side. He was slightly built and scarcely of middle height, with a refined, delicate, and quiet face, and a look of wistful melancholy in his eyes that interested and attracted Rosalie.

"Who painted it?" she asked, after studying it for some time.

"I don't know. There is no name to it. I think myself the Master may have done it. It was painted after death."

"From his corpse?" asked Rosalie, in horror.

"Oh, no! From memory, I should say."

"Does Mr. Barringcourt paint, then?"

"In his spare time, yes. I think he must have done this. I don't know who else could. Even millionaires are bad to remember when once they've passed away."

"Is it like him?"

"I don't know. But Everard says it is almost lifelike."

"Who is Everard?"

"The man who keeps the door."

"I don't like him at the door. Do you?"

Mariana looked up with almost startled eyes. "Don't like him? I like everyone."

"I don't like him," persisted Rosalie. "He's one of those men who always does what he is told. If Mr. Barringcourt told him to wring your neck round, or mine, he'd do it soon—as soon as wink."

"Of course," said Mariana, as if that were the acme of perfection.

"Well, he has neither heart nor head. Now, if Mr. Barringcourt told me to wring your neck, I'd tell him to do it himself, I'd had no practice that way."

Mariana looked at her in utter surprise, and then suddenly she sank back upon the velvet seat, and began to laugh. Unhappily, her merriment did not last, for almost as suddenly she jumped up again, her face white with pain, and her features drawn and contracted.

"Oh, for Heaven's sake don't make me laugh! The pain at my heart is something terrible," and she caught Rosalie's arm in her hand, quite unconscious of the strength of the grip she had taken.

In surprise and alarm, the unconscious offender stood still.

"What is it?" she gasped at length. "Is the pain very bad?"

Mariana looked at her and nodded.

"Talk about one's heart breaking," she said, with a wintry smile. "Every time I laugh I get that feeling."

"Let us go away," said Rosalie, noticing that the great pallor of her face did not decrease.

"Yes. It's time I was back at—at the wedding garment."

"But you're not going to that damp, dark place this morning, are you?"

"Yes."

"Then I shall come with you."

"No. I told Everard, and he does not approve."

"But he is not master here."

"No; but his advice is very good to go upon."

"Did I not tell you how heartless he was?"

"You mistake what is meant for kindness. Let us go."

In the central hall she took leave of Rosalie, and disappeared inside the gloomy eastern wing. And Rosalie made no further attempt to come with her, for her horror of the previous night was still fresh in her mind.

"I don't know how Mariana can do it," she thought, standing still in the great hall. "It's killing her. She looked like death this morning. And to go there right away, to be buried in that damp sepulchre! It's terrible, terrible! I *hate* Mr. Barringcourt! He's bad—right-down bad! The worst man I know!"

But then she knew so very few.

She was awakened from this reverie to find Everard, the doorkeeper, coming toward her.

Her first impulse was to turn away and walk toward the staircase, which she did.

"Miss Paleaf!"

His tone attracted her immediate attention. There was a certain strong gravity in it that appealed to what gravity and steadiness there was in her.

"Yes," she answered, turning round to view this wringer of necks in prospective.

"You have endeavoured to do an incredible amount of harm since coming here. Don't you think it would be advisable to practise a little self-control?"

"Yes. I think if it were practicable it would be advisable to shut myself up in a tin box, or oak, perhaps, and turn round once a week for recreation."

"You rush from one extreme to the other without any attempt at reason."

"And—and you?"

"For Mariana's sake I wish to advise you to be careful."

"Not for my own?"

"No. I know nothing about you, and you seem pretty capable of looking after yourself."

Rosalie looked at him, not knowing whether her dislike was growing or lessening.

"Do you know you're taking a great liberty?" she said, her colour rising despite her efforts to keep cool.

"Yes. And under the circumstances it is pardonable."

"What circumstances?"

"You are doing your best to destroy the happiness and peace of a working woman."

"Happiness! Happiness! Do you call it happiness to be fastened up in there the greater part of the day-time?" And she pointed to the door through which Mariana had passed a short time before.

"When she is contented it is, at least, the nearest approach to happiness. And your ignorant meddling can never have a good result."

Then Rosalie was silent, and with no heart to answer she turned away, and went upstairs to the little sitting-room.

Her own heart ached enough in all conscience. O God! to be free! away from all this coldness and hardness, and gloom and silence.

She buried her face in her hands and cried from utter dejection. When she went to wash her hands and face for dinner, she was dismayed at her own plain looks. She was very far from being ready for a meal, and made little attempt or pretence at eating what was placed before her. At last the young man who waited on her presented a red lozenge to her on a silver plate.

"What is it?" she asked, not being accustomed to this particular dish.

"The nutriment you require to keep you in health. You have eaten nothing, and this is less troublesome if you have no appetite."

She frowned in indecision, and for one minute looked at him and then at it. Then without another word she ate the contents of her plate, and afterwards a plate of plain milk pudding.

But when alone again the same weak desire to cry began to gain upon her, and it was only after a very hard fight she overcame it.

"I don't know how it is," she sighed. "They make you do things here however much you don't want to. I wonder now if the eating of my dinner was a lesson in self-control."

Then she went back to her bedroom and shut the door, and knelt down by the bed to pray, if prayer it could be called. Despite her efforts, everything was most incoherent and jumbled, broken by big sobs, and ending in no prayer at all, but silence. At last the silence must have brought its effect of soothing, for Rosalie rose from her knees with scarcely a vestige of the past emotion upon her face. She combed her hair and smoothed her dress, and then went for her hat.

"I'll go into the garden," she said, "and see if I can see the city."

It was a glorious afternoon, with just sufficient sharpness for autumn in the air. It was considerably after three by the tower clock, and she recognised with regret there was time for little more than an hour there. Her hopes were realised. From the top of the red bank of flowers she could view the city very plainly. She saw right across to the high-standing temple, with every building of note and height rising in between. Behind her she could see nothing, for the wall rose exceptionally high, but from here she could look in the direction of the old home, and to that other magnificent erection that contained all the best prayers and aspirations of her dumb life.

After all, to look on to the sights of freedom is in a measure to the prisoner freedom itself.

From the city beyond, Rosalie's eyes wandered back toward the mansion. There was something wanting in it; its magnificent outline attracted and repelled.

"What a lovely fairy story one could write about it," she sighed. "It seems to me a kind of haunted, sleeping palace; and everything looks so strong, and dark, and silent, and yet beautiful, that I don't know whether the story would have to turn out well or ill."

She sat down on the rustic seat with the arbour of trailing leaves twining above it, and dreamily contemplated the wide expanse of city.

Suddenly she heard the ominous striking of the mansion clock.

One! two! three! four! five!

Rosalie turned her eyes from the sky and looked at it. A faint pink flush from the sun was shining on it, and she clasped her hands.

"I won't go in. They can't do anything to me if I don't. Five o'clock! the very nicest time of all the day—the only time to see the city and the sun look at their best. It isn't wrong of me; I know it isn't. I haven't done anything wrong that I should be a prisoner. I haven't, really. I feel I haven't!"

The sunset deepened.

Suddenly the great gates leading from the garden flew open to admit a dog-cart and one chestnut horse driven by Mr. Barringcourt. Behind him sat a groom, and as they took the sweep of drive leading past her toward the terrace steps, her eyes fell on the horse and man in livery.

She saw that they did not belong to this place. What was there about everyone who lived here that made them different from all else? That groom was just the ordinary groom that one saw every day within the streets and parks.

As Mr. Barringcourt passed below he suddenly looked up, and catching sight of her, took off his hat and smiled. Rosalie's heart gave a leap of excitement.

The flush of evening had dyed her pale cheeks, and given lustre to her eyes. She watched the light vehicle draw up below the central steps, saw Mr. Barringcourt dismount, and the groom lead the horse away by the shorter carriage drive. Rosalie clasped her hands and watched, and made no sign of moving down.

And the sunset deepened.

For one minute Mr. Barringcourt stood on the steps looking at his boots, or maybe on the ground, in apparent thoughtfulness; then he turned round with sudden decision, and crossed the lawn to the path leading towards the bank of flowers where she stood. Yet no step downward did Rosalie take in that direction, and so he came up the narrow, winding path, and very shortly reached her.

And how different from all the others he appeared! How full of life and animation! how strong! how quick at seeing, and therefore understanding!

How weak and lifeless her hand felt in his! And suddenly she felt that intense admiration for strength which all weak things must have. Yet she searched his face narrowly for that tired and weary look that she had seen there twice before.

Her scrutiny was well returned. Out of the purity of a lonely spirit longing for some companionship her clear eyes had looked full into his, the ending of a day of weakness and tears and silent waiting. And under the deep scrutiny of those stronger eyes she had not power to look aside till every little secret not worth hiding had been read. Then having got rid of all the weakness, Rosalie came to the reserve strength.

She drew her hand out of his, and asked suddenly, with an everyday interest:

"Have you any horses of your own, Mr. Barringcourt, or do you hire them all?"

"I have my own; but they're too good for everyday work."

"But when do you exercise them?"

"Occasionally at midnight I give them a run round. They are black, so they don't show. Nor do they advertise their coming by too much noise."

This time she looked at him with puzzled incredulity.

"What do you mean?"

"What I say. Why are you waiting here?"

"To see the sun set."

"It has set."

"I'm waiting for the afterglow."

And as she spoke, the whole sky from east to west flushed to a sudden lowering crimson. It was reflected on his face, on hers, shone from the many windows—red—red—a sea of golden red and copper colour, dyeing all things.

"But you have no business out here after sunset, have you?" he said.

"I don't know. You should be judge of that."

"I'm judge of nothing except the mood I'm in, and today I'm not sorry to find you here; but it's rather a dangerous game to play in a place where strict discipline is observed. Don't you know it?"

"No. I couldn't imagine any punishment worse than being a prisoner."

"Could you not? Oh, there are many worse. You are a prisoner at large, you must remember."

"The reason why I stayed out is because I could think of nothing I had done wrong."

"Are you a good judge of your misdoings?"

"I don't know. A tongue makes things so complicated."

He laughed. "What have you been doing since I went away?"

"Trying to be contented, and help Mariana."

"Help Mariana?"

"Yes. I tried on a dress for her last night, but the room was so gloomy I dare not go again this morning."

"What kind of a dress were you trying on?"

"A wedding-dress that gave me the shivers. Do you know, Mr. Barringcourt, I think Mariana the most splendid woman I ever met."

"Indeed."

"Yes, and I think she's the most shamefully ill-used woman, too."

"No one is ill-used, except dogs and dumb animals in general."

Rosalie gave him one of her sidelong penetrating glances.

"Well," said she, "there are dumb animals and dumb animals; Mariana is dumb."

"Indeed!"

"What I mean is, she never complains."

"Very sensible of her. There is no one to listen."

"There is Everard! She asks his advice upon everything."

"She told you that?"

"Yes. She talks about everything but her own hard life."

"That is why you wish her to speak about it. Did she do so, you would wish her silent. The world is very contrary, Rosalie."

He stepped aside to let her pass before him down the narrow path. There was no alternative but to obey, as the sunset had now completely died away, and the dusk of night and its accompanying chilliness had wandered in, bringing a sense of desolation, of misery.

The Master did not lead the way to the side door, but approached the central one. He let himself in by touching some spring acting in the toad's head, and Rosalie followed with a creepy sense of awe as she passed between these high doors, with their magnificent workmanship all hidden in the dusk.

The darkness of the big conservatory was partly dispelled by tiny electric lights, coloured crimson, that glimmered here and there among the foliage like glow-worms in a forest. As they passed the picture-gallery, Mr. Barringcourt noticed that the door was open.

"Who has been in there?" he asked.

"Mariana and I went this morning to see Mr. Todbrook's portrait. Who painted it?"

"I did—from memory. A man's best friend should represent him most faithfully. Don't you think so?"

"But had you nothing to work from?"

"Oh, no! Nothing but memory. Memory is a very wonderful thing if one only cultivates it."

"If I died, do you think you could paint me?" asked Rosalie, turning her face up to his.

"No," he answered. "I have not known you quite long enough. I could attempt nothing better than a caricature at present."

She laughed, and said: "I must endeavour to live a little longer, then."

CHAPTER XIII

THE FOLLY OF SIMPLICITY

Together they entered the central hall, and saw Mariana standing waiting there. When she saw Rosalie she stepped towards her, but on seeing Mr. Barringcourt beyond her she stood still.

"What are you waiting for?" he asked.

"For Rosalie. It is long past her time for coming in."

"You have wonderful patience to stand here waiting. Anyone else would have gone to look for her."

"If one waits long enough one generally gets what one wants," she answered, rather irrelevantly.

"Well, don't stand there any longer. You're not needed."

"Thank you."

She turned away with grace and easy dignity, and walked toward the staircase; but when there she looked across at Rosalie.

"Tea is ready."

What a dungeon-knell there was in those three words! Tea in that little shabby sitting-room, away from everything of light, or life, or understanding. A piece of bread, a cup of tea and whatever else was going, eaten alone, and the dreariness of a long dull evening beyond. And somehow or other the thought of the evening frightened Rosalie. It was so dark. The long passages above so ghostly, dim, and silent. And below? She shivered and looked towards the door of the eastern wing, that in some unaccountable way seemed to pervade all things with its shadow and odour of graves.

So though Mariana, after she had spoken, stood still and waited a while for the effect of her words, Rosalie delayed to follow her.

The freedom and grandeur of the sunset was still running in her veins; the pleasantness of conversation and companionship had its influence on her also.

"Ought I to go?" she asked suddenly, looking up at Mr. Barringcourt.

"I don't know, I'm sure. If you admire Mariana as much as you profess I think you should go."

"It isn't a case of Mariana. It's me—myself."

"Well, what of you?"

"I'd much rather stay, and have my tea with—with you."

"I don't indulge in tea."

"Then do they insist on your eating a red lozenge instead?"

"Oh, no! They recognise that I am quite able to look after myself."

"Everard told me I was capable of doing that. And yet at dinner-time today I was presented with a red lozenge on a silver salver to take the place of ordinary food."

"And you accepted it?"

"No, I didn't. But if you don't have tea, I'd better leave you."

"I'll waive a point tonight. I have had so pleasant a holiday that it is somewhat distasteful to settle down again. Go and remove your hat, and come down."

But when Rosalie essayed to move towards the staircase she found Mariana gone, and suddenly she stood still.

"Why do you stop?" he asked.

"Oh, I'm frightened! I really am! I dare not go about this place at night by myself. I don't know how it is, but I dare not."

"Nothing will hurt you."

"It's the shadows and the darkness—and the silence."

"Run along. It's your imagination."

"Are you sure there's nothing to be frightened of?"

"Nothing!"

So Rosalie went, and returned like the wind. Her eyes shone with fear, and her breath came in quick pants.

"What did you see?" he asked, laughing.

"Nothing! I did not stay long enough."

So then, in the comfortable cheerfulness of Mr. Barringcourt's study, they had tea.

Rosalie sat in the big arm-chair by the fire; he in his customary one drawn from the table. Very proud she felt to pour out tea, and quite forgave the youth who waited on them for his officious behaviour of the morning. Besides, this was such delicious tea. It was not a bit like that which she had upstairs. The china was superb, with far richer colours than Crown Derby, or anything at all resembling it upon the planet Lucifram.

No wonder that, in the midst of all this luxury and comfort, with a glorious fire and sufficient light, she heaved an unconscious sigh of great contentment.

"Still discontented?" asked Mr. Barringcourt, breaking the heavenly silence.

"Oh, no! Just the opposite. I sighed because I was so happy."

"Have you any book on etiquette?" he continued, casting an eye round his own well-filled book-shelves thoughtfully.

"Etiquette? What is that?"

"Good behaviour, I think, but I'm not sure."

"No, I haven't any book on etiquette; but I remember what my aunt taught me."

"Well, what did she tell you?" he asked, leaning his head against the chair-back, and looking across at her out of half-closed eyes.

"She told me always to be polite to people, and unselfish. You see, there wasn't much else she could tell, because I couldn't talk."

"To be polite and unselfish! Umph! that's good behaviour, is it? I think I've explained etiquette wrongly to you, then." After a silence he continued: "I believe etiquette has to do with correct behaviour. Do you know anything about that?"

"Oh! I expect that is being stiff. No, I don't know anything about that. We weren't at all stiff at home. You see, there was no need to be. We had no servants nor anything, and we always said what we thought. At least, uncle and aunt did, and I listened. But why are you asking about it?"

"I'm very undecided in my mind about you."

"Yes. I get very undecided about myself sometimes. I don't think aunt would approve of me altogether now."

"In what way?"

"My tongue. It is so sharp, you know. You said it was."

"Oh! I'm not thinking about your tongue. I am trying to settle whether we are breaking the laws of etiquette in thus drinking tea together."

"Oh, no! The curates always do it, and they are more correct than anybody. They like you to offer them tea. Aunt used to say so."

"Then we are just as we should be?"

"Yes. Does Lady Flamington never come to have tea with you?"

"No; I generally go there."

"Well, it's just the same."

"Who told you of Lady Flamington?"

"Mariana. Mariana does not give you a very good character, you know?"

"And is your strength of mind great enough to withstand her libels?"

"Well, yes. I like to form my own opinions. Besides, the best fun is, Mariana does not understand she's saying anything against you. She tells me all kinds of things, taking you quite for granted."

"When do you find time for these interesting conversations?"

"At night—and sometimes in the early morning. She never neglects her work to gossip. But when she talks it's always to the point."

"Rosalie, if you wish to possess any fascination, which is another word for beauty, you must learn to keep all your thoughts, opinions, and feelings to yourself. It is not conducive to interest to be told of a person's state too freely. One must be left to find it for oneself."

"Do you find me uninteresting?"

"Very much so. I do not know another man of my acquaintance on Lucifram who would tolerate your company for half an hour."

Her eyes travelled to his with a very real and living pain in them.

"I don't know anything about men except that they're very clever. But I'd be quite content to earn the good graces of the women."

"Why either?"

"Oh, because one must be friendly somewhere. It would be awful to have no friends at all, men or women."

"How many friends would you need for happiness?"

"As many as I could get. You see, when you're poor you can't expect to have many."

"And when you're rich you have less."

"No, indeed. I'm sure you have heaps of friends, Mr. Barringcourt."

He laughed in a harsh, dry sort of way.

"You flatter me. In reality, I have no more friends than you."

"But Lady Flamington?—Why, Mariana says she is in love with you."

Mr. Barringcourt bit his lip; but the smile debarred access there travelled to his eyes.

"Well, what if she is in love with me, as you call it. That makes her one of my worst enemies."

"Oh, no! To love anybody is to be their best and biggest friend."

"I grant if the love be disinterested; but then, how often is it so?"

"What does disinterested mean?"

"I don't know, I'm sure," he answered impatiently; "you must look it out in a dictionary."

"I'm sorry," Rosalie answered meekly, "but I thought disinterested meant unselfish—and I can't understand love being anything else."

"Can't you? Then you have much to learn. Why do you love the Serpent?"

The question came with unexpected rapidity.

"I don't. I—I—I—" Another pause upon the thrice repeated unlucky vowel—and Rosalie shivered from head to foot quite coldly.

"Is this an attempt at fascination?"

The tone was so cold and cruel, and the words carried so sharp a sting, that they cut Rosalie's heart like some whip might have done.

She shook her head.

"I don't understand the Serpent," she said, rubbing her hands against the chair arm. "How, then, can I love it?"

"That implies that you *do* understand the Serpent, and therefore you are not disposed to love him."

"You aspire to understand me better than I understand myself."

"Oh, no! I take you at your own word. I asked you did you love the Serpent, and you said, 'I don't.' Surely there was not much to understand in that."

"Don't let us quarrel," pleaded Rosalie.

"Quarrel? Quarrel? Oh, no, certainly not. I had no intention of quarrelling with you. I remember your telling me the other day you had no particular affection for the god of Lucifram."

"But do *you* love the Serpent?"

"Oh! I—I—I—"

"That is unkind of you, and not polite."

"We ought to have your aunt here to act as chaperon. They say it's scarcely wise to leave a man and woman to themselves, and now I recognise it."

But Rosalie was not far behind in the argument. From cold shivers she began to experience a certain amount of heat.

"I don't know about a chaperon," she said. "I thought a chaperon was a woman who looked after a woman, and I should like to know who looks after the men? Chaperons are silly and stupid, and women, if they were honest, would say they wanted to have nothing to do with them. Besides, it was you who lost your temper then. I didn't a bit. I haven't yet, only you annoyed me by the way you spoke."

"I? lost my temper?"

"Yes, of course. You know you did. You think I've got a secret, and I haven't; so if you don't like, you needn't be nice to me any more."

And Mr. Barringcourt laughed. Under that laugh Rosalie shrivelled up like a white butterfly under the breath of ice.

"But I do like," he answered, still laughing. "You must not quote from Mariana. It is too absurd. And so you have no secret. I can scarcely imagine a woman without one, nor a man."

The merciless mocking eyes were fixed on her, so that she seemed incapable of moving. There rose within her a terrible weakness, a longing to lean on him, to be guided by his advice, to speak of all those doubts that preyed upon her mind, and state the few plain facts that raised them. Again, as before in the garden, she recognised that he was strong, and she was very, very weak. She looked across at him. There was little of sympathy on his face—much of contempt and ridicule—and Rosalie, sensitive to both, shrank from it and him.

A very awkward pause followed—to her, at least.

"I think the tea-party is ended," he said, getting up and pushing his chair back to the table. "It was very enjoyable whilst it lasted, but there is such a thing as folk outstaying their welcome."

But still she sat still, and made no effort to rise.

"What has made you angry?" she asked.

"I don't know, I'm sure. You say I'm angry, so I must be. You should be able to discover the cause when you've noticed the effect."

"I can't. But when I stumble or stammer I notice it always puts you out."

"Then don't do it."

"I'll try not. But if I sometimes said the things I thought, they'd sound so foolish that you'd laugh at them."

"They could not possibly be more foolish than the things you say."

"Are all the women of your acquaintance very sensible and clever?"

"More or less so. Of course, they have the advantage of education and upbringing; but still that does not do away with the fact that they possess many natural gifts."

"It must be very nice to possess natural gifts."

"Yes. Few women are born without them."

"Am I one of the few?"

"So far as I can judge you are. With talent and cleverness, you should be able to escape from prison."

"But I'm staying here on principle. I never thought of trying to get away."

"That shows your inherent stupidity, and a surprising lack of spirit. Cannot you find a door of escape?"

Rosalie shook her head and sighed.

"No," she answered. "I thought of the chimney once, but that was absurd."

"Can you think of no other door?"

"No. It's no good my trying to get out where every door is either locked or guarded."

"You have not wit enough to think of one, you mean?"

"Perhaps so," she answered, and looked at him with eyes full of a great and wistful longing to be told.

"Well, I'll tell you. There is the door of my heart. Any other woman would have thought of it at once."

She shook her head.

"I've had no practice that way. I shouldn't know how to go about to find it."

"No? As women go, you are intensely stupid. You possess all the disadvantages of a school-girl, without any of the attractions of youth."

"I'm not very old," said Rosalie. "I'm only twenty-three."

"There you are again. You can keep nothing to yourself."

"I only told you what my age was."

"Well, I've none of the curiosity of a census paper, and women who tell their ages are a pest."

"But why?"

"Because it is either a boast or a lie. Both are objectionable. Keep your age to yourself. No one wants to know it, and if they do, let them find out or guess."

"Is that what the clever women do?"

"I don't know. If you become a clever woman at second hand, you will become an abomination."

"What must I do then?"

"Remain stupid."

"Then I'll never get away."

"Oh, no; as soon as I pointed the way I blocked it. Had you discovered it yourself, it might have been unguarded."

"I don't believe you would have let me through, even if I had found it out."

"Of course not. One never believes that which touches one's vanity."

Rosalie sighed. What a contrary mood had suddenly seized him! She got up, with little of life or spirit in her movements.

"Then if you find me so very dull I won't come again. Three years seem a long time, but I have no doubt God will help me to live through them."

He laughed.

"God, being dumb, refuses no one, least of all religious women, they force themselves upon Him so persistently. Yes, I shall be glad to be relieved of your company for a while. And so please confine your wanderings to the upper storey where you live. And leave the garden to those who can appreciate its beauty sufficiently to be in by five o'clock."

Rosalie looked at him. Pain and fear was on her face.

"Live upstairs!"

"Yes; live upstairs. And eat red lozenges when your appetite is bad. You can't die, you know."

She turned toward the door.

"Good-night!" he said, drawing an open book toward him on the table, and sitting down.

"Good-night! I see now my fault and punishment in staying out of doors beyond the time."

For only answer he laughed. As he did so the door closed.

CHAPTER XIV

BROKEN SPIRITS

So full of pain and heaviness was Rosalie that all her childish fear had vanished. She passed up the slippery staircase into the corridor, from which her own small sitting-room was.

Never to go downstairs again for three long weary years! Never to be out of the grey, silent, ghostly shadows of those upper rooms—never to have human companionship or friendliness! A part of the meaning floated through her mind, and cast its heavy shroud on all things.

It was still early in the evening, too early for Mariana to return from the work which held her. She sat down in the high-backed chair before the fire, and listlessly looked into it. The flames burnt low. There was none of the brightness of the other day in them—no whispered message of hope.

Rosalie's spirit ached more from the cruel heartlessness of the Master's conduct than even from the thought of coming imprisonment. For this was in the present—that the future. None had ever spoken so to her before—sharply, no doubt but never with this harsh and cruel coldness. Every feeling in her simple nature seemed outraged and lacerated. Once only she moved uneasily in her chair, as one undergoes some great pain, and cried, or rather moaned:

"It's unfair—unfair! I haven't done anything that's wrong, and it was silly and stupid of me to ever think of coming back again."

At last the door opened, and Mariana entered with supper. Rosalie did not turn round till they were alone again, and scarcely even then, till Mariana came and stood beside her, and looking down, said:

"Rosalie, why did you not come in at five o'clock?"

"Don't ask me. I was foolish. There is no other reason."

"Is Mr. Barringcourt's company more agreeable than mine?"

"I thought it was, and have paid the penalty. Don't reproach me. I can't stand it tonight. Perhaps tomorrow."

"I don't wish to reproach you. Once I thought the same, for an hour or two, like you. But I got over it as you have done. You will not care for his company now?"

"No."

"That is well. I suppose you know you are not to go downstairs again?"

"Yes. What am I to do, Mariana, to pass the time away?"

"I don't know of anything. I wish you had come in by five o'clock. There are so many interesting things below."

Rosalie laughed.

"Oh, I didn't come in, so there's an end of it! I'll take supper now and go to bed."

She sipped the glass of warm milk silently, and then together they went to bed. How cold it was in the corridor. How ill lit and melancholy it appeared And Rosalie lay awake, with burning tears, which were never shed, in her eyes.

Three years! And Mr. Barringcourt had said a woman of brains or spirit would have forestalled them and have escaped.

And then it seemed as if across the silence there came that clear, pure voice that spoke to her before, after her aunt was dead: "Neither brains nor spirit, but the path directed."

And silence and sleep and comfort fell—night's gentle curtain and soft pillow for all weary heads.

Sunday, Monday, Tuesday, long or short, according to the circumstance. Each resembled some long and silent eternity of Nothingness. Here was nothing to do. Mariana said there was nothing, and she knew best.

"Bring me a little bit of sewing."

But she shook her head. "I cannot bring it from the workroom."

"Then something from above."

"There is nothing. Each has her work; for you there is none."

"Have you no books?"

"Mr. Barringcourt has the key to the library. I can ask him for one if you like."

But Rosalie shook her head. "No, thank you."

And how difficult she found meal-times, when she must force down food against all wish and inclination. Sunday and Monday it was managed fairly well, but on the Tuesday at dinner-time Rosalie recognised the task was quite beyond her.

"All this tastes of cobwebs and damp soil," she said. "If I must have one, give me one of those little lozenges you offered me the other day."

It was brought. She took it with a glass of water, then rose from her seat. When she got to the door she turned round. Her pretty eyebrows were slightly raised, and she laughed.

"That was essence of cobweb, I believe. Thank you; I feel better already for it."

All was lost upon the youth; he bowed gravely, and returned no answer, and Rosalie went away.

Up and down! Up and down the long dim corridor she walked, with nothing to do but think or mope, or grow melancholy through despair.

After tea Rosalie did not venture out beyond the sitting-room, for the old fear of the darkness had returned; and moreover, tonight a strange weariness oppressed her. At last she fell asleep. Her head rested on the table, and she slept there for nearly an hour.

A little after nine came Mariana and the supper.

"How is the dress progressing?" asked Rosalie.

"It is doing very well."

"How is Everard?"

"He is very well."

"Have you seen Mr. Barringcourt today?"

"No. He is away till tomorrow."

"Have you taken a walk this afternoon?"

"A short one."

"Where did you go?"

"My customary round. But you must not ask so many questions."

"But why?"

"Because," Mariana's voice sank to a whisper, "if we talk much I must leave you, and Sybilla will come. And she never speaks all the week, except on my one night out, and then in a language I never heard before."

Rosalie's pale face grew paler. Suddenly she took Mariana's hand and held it very tight.

"Are—are you making fun of me?" she asked.

The other shook her head, and thus abruptly the conversation ended.

At midnight Rosalie suddenly awoke, to hear the great clock striking—a sound which she had never heard before in that room. The ache and weariness of the evening had entirely vanished. She sat up in bed and looked round the room, lit by one meagre night-light. All was as usual, very still; the corners of the room were all shadowy. In another second Rosalie was standing on the floor looking around her in a puzzled sort of way. Understanding came with the swiftness of lightning to her brain. She stood alert, listening, listening, but there was no sound. Quickly and silently she dressed, holding her breath, fearful of being found thus dressing in the middle of the sleeping night. Then with courage screwed to desperation she went toward the door.

"If I'm found out, God only knows what will happen," she thought and turned the handle.

It had one advantage with all the rest of that big house: it was silent.

Mercifully, a few straggling moonbeams lit up the room, shining from door to door, leaving the rest in obscurity. Without glancing toward the shadowy bed, she crossed to the outer door, opened it, and stood in the corridor. The fears born of reality and action had quite killed those of imagination. She no longer started at shadows, nor trembled at the darkness, but went on quickly till she reached the stairhead. Her shoes she carried in her hand to prevent sound. She feared the slippery staircase, lest she should stumble and waken some light sleeper. But tonight it seemed scarcely so slippery as before. Perhaps it was the descent in her unshod feet. At last she stood safely at the bottom in the large hall, with its Spartan plainness and great richness. Chairs, each worth some small fortune, statues in bronze and marble, and above all the great, oppressive shadow, emanating from that eastern door of glass, polished like diamonds, all met her fearful glance.

"If—if I fail—if I'm caught, that's where I go—"

The thought flashed like lightning through her mind, and she looked round breathlessly to find a doorway.

That leading to the conservatory—it stood wide open. On! On! along the corridor, dark but for one dim electric light, such as was also shining in the hall. Then through the palm-house, and toward the central doors. A red spot gleamed upon the centre—the toad's head—for this door was carved alike inside and out. Instinctively she touched the shining knob. The door flew open. The cold damp air of night wafted toward her as she stood thus upon the threshold of the garden. Then, closing the door behind her, she moved forward to the steps. And here again Rosalie returned thanks to that light upon the ugly head. For whereas within it showed her where to touch the spring, here it shone with a direct brilliancy that lit up the entire straight path across the garden, right across and through the wooded shrubbery at the farther end, that led toward the stables. For though the faint light of night might have been strong enough to guide her to the avenue of trees, nothing could ever penetrate this heavy gloom, save only a light such as this steady red one, that lit up the whole long path, right to the stables, as clear toward the end as at the beginning. So without trouble she came to the doorless building. One gigantic slab of marble, between two pillars, was slid back into the wall, and the red light penetrated in beyond. She followed on the path it lit for her, and stood within a sumptuous building. It was certainly a stable, though at the moment it was empty.

Here she looked round, not from curiosity, but to find some means of exit. She walked round many times, but found nothing but one small door, more like a cupboard than a door, built low in the wall, and quite beyond her power to open.

She wrung her hands in despair, and a terrible sweat broke out all over her. No way of escape! Up to now all things had been so easy, as if aiding and abetting her in this wild dream and dash for freedom.

Suddenly upon the still and ghostly midnight air came a sound: the rhythmic trampling of horses, and then a neigh half-echoed by another, as the sound came nearer.

"God help me!" she said, and leant against the carved partition of two stalls, with that deathlike sweat and fear robbing her limbs of any strength of motion.

"The key! The key!"

What voice was it that rang so clearly on the night?

She fumbled in her pocket, and found the old disused one of her uncle's safe.

With nothing but desperation for a guidance she applied it to the little door, close-built to the ground. It fitted and turned. The door flew open. As it did so, from the garden came the crunching sound of horses' feet on gravel, and of wheels.

The little door closed again. Rosalie was without the precincts of Marble House, and breathed her first long sigh of freedom.

CHAPTER XV

A WAYSIDE HOUSE AND GLOOMY CELL

But what and where was this place that she had come to? Instead of coming out upon a mews or narrower street of that big city on the planet Lucifram, she stood upon the borders of a wood. Foxgloves, cowslips, and pale wood anemones bordered its shaded paths. She passed onward, conscious of a new sweetness in the air, and a certain subdued light which, though faint, was quite devoid of shadows.

And oh! to tread upon a path of velvet—velvet of Nature's making, all soft and soothing to the foot.

And though the beauties of the forest awed, they did not trouble her, for their shade was instinct with the mood that she was in—a mood which had much of quiet thankfulness, but no elation. With little feeling of fatigue she walked along the pleasant path, coming out at last upon a city all deserted. Its buildings were the most majestic she had ever seen. There was no ordinary streets of houses all in a row. The buildings had the strength and beauty of past ages. With courtyards of green, and gates with armorial bearings, the windows of the houses were narrow. During the ages, here and there a cornice or a step had crumbled, giving a certain hoary majesty to the houses, showing they had long withstood the inroads of all-conquering Time. No sound of life enlivened the scene; all was silent as the house which she had left. In the central square two churches stood, one in a state of erection, one in the middle stage of being pulled down. Truly it was very curious. All around betokened signs of recent workmanship. But as in dreams one cannot pause to reason, neither did she.

Through the silent empty streets she passed, and came once more on to a stretch of country which rose in hills not far off. These were steep and high, as Rosalie found on coming nearer to them, but the path bordered with wild flowers led her to and up them, and when at last she stood upon the summit of one that rose amongst the highest, she looked down upon a country of gentle slopes and valleys, and dark stretches of forest. A broad and glorious river rolled its even course picturesquely, curving to right and left, here disappearing in the shade of the woodlands, here glittering in the rising sun. With more heart and renewed vigour she descended from the hill-top into this pleasant country beyond it. The path led along the boundaries of a wood, and suddenly there came in sight a low white house, lying far back within a wide expanse of garden, banked with wild flowers of Nature's growing. On the sunny side it was unshaded by the forest, and deep-coloured peaches were glowing in the light. A low verandah ran along the façade, and many sweet and lovely creepers twined about its slender pillars. The big front door stood open, also the garden gate. Rosalie, with tired feet and thankful heart, went up to it and knocked.

Within was a simply-furnished hall, arranged with simplest taste. Bowls of roses stood upon the tables, and the windows, in the recesses formed by the window seats, were open, admitting straggling stems of flowers that clustered upward from below. Built in the wall was a golden fluted organ, the ivory keyboard open, and all the mystic stops clear to the view.

Rosalie knocked.

A door at the farther end of the house opened, and a youth appeared, coming toward her. He was so handsome, and walked with such grace and youthful brightness, that Rosalie's heart went out toward him on the instant. He did not wait for any word of explanation, but said:

"My father will be very pleased to see you. We have been expecting your arrival for almost a week."

"But where did I come from?" asked Rosalie, as taken with his gentle way of speaking as his appearance.

He laughed.

"I don't know; but from a hot place and a great distance, I should think, or else your wits would never have been sharpened to take so long a journey."

"I wonder how old he is?" thought she. "Fourteen at the most. He should have more respect for me than to speak so—so freely; and yet it's nice to be spoken to quite humanly again."

"Yes," she answered; "I've come a very long distance."

"Come this way. See my father, and then you may rest."

He took her to a room furnished simply, and not unlike that of Mr. Barringcourt's; and there, seated at the table, occupied much as he had been in studying, writing, and arranging papers, was the father of the boy.

His hair was very white, as white as silver, and his face was beautiful and clearly cut. He had an appearance of great age, and his tall figure was thin and muscular. In some indescribable way he reminded Rosalie of Mr. Barringcourt. A vague fear began to spring in her mind—for in his dress and manner there was something strangely reminiscent, even though he looked so very old, with his lined face and silver hair.

But he used what Mr. Barringcourt had never used, and that was a pair of glasses; and his glance was very keen as he looked up at her above them with bent brows. And whereas Mr. Barringcourt's eyes were as black as night, his were of a piercing blue, or some colour very like blue. The quality that struck Rosalie most was their intense brightness.

The youth, having admitted her, withdrew, and closed the door behind him.

"You are punctual, Rosalie, and I'm very pleased to see you."

He rose as he spoke, and drew a chair for her, and on the hearing of his kind, grave voice much peace and reassurance settled on her.

"I couldn't help myself," she answered. "I had to come. But you can't be half as pleased to see me as I am to see you!"

He looked at her. "Are you then so much in need of a friend?"

"Yes; but I think I should make better friends with your son than you."

The vestige of a smile crept into his eyes. "But why?"

"Well, I expect you will be too clever. You would soon learn how stupid I was; and then perhaps we should quarrel."

Rosalie looked up shyly as she spoke those last words. The quarrelling, she felt pretty certain, would be all on his side, as it had been with Mr. Barringcourt, for she would never have presumed so far.

"You give Billy credit for being more forbearing than I?"

"Oh, no; I think he will be less observant. I'm very stupid, you know," she continued, with her large, earnest eyes fixed on his; "and people get very soon tired of me. I thought it might be just as well to tell you now, in case you might form a wrong impression, and then be annoyed after, and blame me for it."

"Well," said he, smiling, "that will do for the present. Sleep tonight, and in the morning we will hold a longer conversation."

"But it's morning now."

"Oh, no! It's evening coming on. The sun has set. No travellers ever come to us with morning. The journey is too long for that."

"But everybody cannot come to you just at the same time."

"Well, pretty much at the same time. We live in the centre of a circle, and the distance from every direction is fairly equal."

"Do you get many travellers?"

"Not compared with many wayside inns. But we have a select few that are always very welcome, for we know that they possess some merit, or they would never reach us."

"Ah! Then I am afraid I am not equal to the rest. I have no merits. Nothing but chance and God's goodness brought me to you."

He smiled. "That is curious coupling," he answered. "Chance and God's goodness."

"Well, it was so extremely strange and unexpected."

"We will speak more about it tomorrow. But now I will come with you to see what light refreshment our house affords."

He rose from his chair and led the way into another room where lamps were lit, though there was still much light outside, and a clear fire burning.

"How stupid of me not to notice the sun was setting. I thought when first I saw it it was rising."

"That is a common mistake, much commoner than you'd think, with those coming from Lucifram. You see, it is the direct turnabout, and it is apt to muddle one at first."

"Yes, indeed. What lovely flowers!"

Rosalie was looking at the pretty supper-table and its exquisite decorations. There was something so pure and delicate and delicious about everything, from the snowy linen and flowers all white and flaxen coloured, to the china and vessels of silver and crystal glass. Moreover, there was no shadow lying here. One might eat in happiness and sweet contentment, and the thankfulness born of these.

And moreover, she did not sit down alone. Her host took his place at the head of the small square table, she to the side of him. Every dish was ready served. But first he offered her a little glass of purest sparkling water. Rosalie drank it. The intense fatigue had vanished almost on the instant. She made no effort to talk much, for he said nothing, but ate her supper in silence. Then at last he rose.

"I will show you to your room," he said. "Billy has gone home; he only stayed to welcome you."

"I thought he was your son?"

"So he is. But this is not my home. It is but a temporary lodging, conveniently situated for business purposes."

"Does no one else live here?"

"No one. You need not be afraid. I am sufficient protection."

She followed him with trust and all simplicity to the bedroom set for strangers. When she was alone, by the light of two soft lights hanging from the ceiling, she compared the pure white hangings with the crimson silks at Marble House. Here, indeed, was light-heartedness and freedom from all depression; and with her head once on the pillow, she slept the first genuine sleep of happiness for many a day.

* * * *

Marble House lay swathed in the mist of early morning. The sun had not yet risen, only that just perceptible twilight that makes known the distant approach of day was at hand. But one by one various lights made their appearance in several of the upper rooms. The occupants were rising at their accustomed hour. It was close on six.

Mariana also awoke, and with the first return of consciousness came the consciousness of loss, vague and alarming. When the light was turned on she noticed the door leading to Rosalie's room wide open, and her own upon the passage standing closed but for the catching of the clasp. Hurriedly she passed into the inner room, to find, almost as she anticipated, the bed unoccupied, its inmate gone. She went to the dressing-room beyond. It also was empty. Then turning back to her own room, she dressed with a curious silent haste. A dull, murky grey sky showed through the window. It caught Mariana's eye and intruded itself upon her memory. Then when her toilette was completed she went out into the corridor. There was no sign of Rosalie either in the little sitting-room or dining-room, and the truth forced itself undeniably upon her. Rosalie had gone—escaped in the night. But where? On second thoughts it seemed impossible. Who ever yet escaped from Marble House in Greensward Avenue upon the planet Lucifram? She smiled forlornly to think of such a thing. And then a sudden fear and trembling for the unhappy girl came over her.

She had tried to escape and had been detected—must have been detected. There were many cells in the east wing, and to attempt to escape and fail in it was of all crimes most criminal.

A feeling, or the memory of a feeling, surged in her heart, so cold, and even, and restricted. Like some quick-gliding spirit she sought the staircase and descended, finding Everard arranging a large batch of papers on the table in the hall. He looked up at her approach, and seeing the slight alteration in her features and expression, said to himself, "It's Wednesday," and went on with his work. But the earnestness of her voice attracted him.

"Everard!" There was more in it than her usual simple, even tone.

He looked up again.

"Everard! Where is Rosalie? Where have you put her?"

"Rosalie? I have not seen. Is she not upstairs?"

She shook her head.

"Is she in there? You have not put her in there?" and pointed to the right-hand door.

He shook his head impatiently.

"She is nowhere of my putting or knowing. She should be upstairs yet. Eight o'clock is her hour for getting up."

"She is not there."

"Not there?" He put the papers he held in his hand down, and looked at her.

"No. And nowhere else upon the corridor."

"Have you searched well?"

"Yes. I did not like to wake the others. Do you think she can possibly have got away?"

"Impossible! The doors are barred—and double locked—and spring-locked."

"I know. But where is she."

"There must be a search instituted."

"Thank God the Master is away."

"He came home last night at midnight."

His voice was grim as his information was short.

"Come home! Come home!" repeated Mariana. "What shall I do?"

"You had best go and tell him."

"Is he up?"

"Yes. An hour ago."

"I can't go. Do this thing for me, Everard. I never asked you anything before."

He looked at her with a face half serious, half cold, then turned in the direction of the west wing.

Mariana sat down on one of the many chairs—a solitary figure in that big empty hall, with clasped hands and shrinking form, fearing vaguely.

Everard knocked at Mr. Barringcourt's door, and obeyed the summons to go in. Before Everard could speak the Master looked up, and said, with a pleasantness not always customary in him:

"Good morning, Everard! When Rosalie Paleaf has had breakfast, I want you to see her. Don't forget to tell Mariana. What is it?"

"She has disappeared in the night!"

"Who?" and the dark brows contracted slightly as he looked across at the speaker.

"Rosalie Paleaf."

"Disappeared in the night? Tell fairy stories to those that believe them."

"She is not in her bedroom, nor the corridor to which she was restricted."

"Who has told you this?" said the Master, getting up.

"Mariana."

"Confound Mariana! Go and search house and gardens, and take the search-light, and bring her back in half an hour."

Everard withdrew.

"Disappeared!" said Mr. Barringcourt, left to himself, and his brows came together blackly. "That is impossible, without the help of Mariana," and then he turned to the letter he was writing and finished it, though it was a long one, before Everard returned.

On his entrance the Master looked up.

"She is nowhere."

"You have searched in every place, likely and unlikely?"

"In every place."

Then a very cruel light leapt into his eyes, in that deep shadow that encircled them, and his lips closed one over the other grimly, as he looked across at the doorkeeper.

"Who is to thank for this?"

"It was a circumstance quite unforeseen."

"I don't doubt it. Where is that heavy-sleeping ass, whose snores swallow up footfalls and opening doors?"

"You mean—"

"I mean your first cousin for dulness of perception. Send me that brainless thing called Mariana."

Everard withdrew. He walked along the corridor as evenly as usual. Whether doubt or misgiving was in his mind, it showed nothing in his face.

There, in the outer hall, scarcely having moved during the whole time, sat Mariana. On the opening of the door she looked up.

"The Master wishes to speak to you."

"Is he very angry?"

"Nothing but what may be appeased. But you had better say no more than you can help."

She got up without a word, and went to the study.

"Where is the girl I entrusted to you?" he said, as soon as the door was closed.

"She has escaped during the night."

"At what time?"

"Between ten and six."

"The time is vague. You're a sound sleeper to be able to count eight hours of unconsciousness."

"I merit it by hard work during the day."

"Oh! you should have explained this a little earlier. If your work was too hard, others could have been set to watch. Your excuse is admirable."

"It is no excuse, it is the truth."

"You never heard a footfall, nor a door creak?"

"No. The doors, as you know, have never creaked."

"I know nothing. You will perhaps enlighten me, and not take too much for granted."

"I can say nothing but in answer to your questions."

"And you know nothing of the hour of escape?"

"I know only that I saw her safely into bed last night, looking utterly tired out. She fell asleep almost before I left the room. This morning I found the door leading from my room into hers standing open, and that leading to the corridor off the latch."

"Has she left anything behind her?"

"I found her hat and cloak in the wardrobe; I do not think she can have taken them."

"Your deduction is beyond argument. A little less sleep would stir that muddled, dreamy brain of yours into some semblance, at least, of action."

"I don't think it's the sleep that makes me stupid. It's the dull greyness of the sky."

"Maybe. What penalty are you inclined to pay for your neglect and lack of vigilance?"

"It was not neglect. I slept heavier than I have ever slept before. I believe God helped her, for she was young and good and innocent."

"You seem to entertain no sorrow for your neglect of duty."

Her puzzled eyes, tired and questioning, met his.

"No, I do not feel sorry. How can I? She could not settle to this prison life as I have done. She was of a softer and more yielding nature. What hardens me would soon have killed her altogether."

"Better be killed than get away alive without permission. And you, being the offender, must bear her punishment beside your own."

A wintry smile crept to her lips.

"Oh! I am strong enough for any punishment. I have a frame of iron buried in what seems like flesh. If I have sinned, then name the punishment. But sin at times, if sin this be, brings near an echo of happier things beyond this life to conjure."

"You are too hard-worked, you say."

"I said I slept the sounder for it."

"Sound sleeping is a thing for swine. You shall not work so hard, for you must sleep less heavily. You are intent upon a wedding-gown, I hear. Leave it unfinished."

"But I have worked at it three years; the dullest work is finished. This is the part I love, that makes some compensation for that other thing I worship."

"And for the double punishment, seeing your working hours have been reduced and cancelled, there will be no further need for that night out—excruciating torment for the all unhappy listeners."

"Rosalie loved my playing." Her dark eyes shone out from a face pale as death.

"No. She was bribing you to stop by flattery. Did she not counsel you to give it up?"

"Ah! that is impossible. I ask nothing but two little hours a week. If that goes, I might as well be dead."

"You might then, for you have done with them."

"It was the stipulation when I came here."

"You have broken the stipulation by your carelessness."

"What am I to do, then?"

"Nothing. Learn to appreciate the luxury of idleness."

"You have not weighed the fairness of such a punishment."

"You have angered me."

"Give me but one hour a week, then. Give me but one."

"No, not one! Get away out of my sight, lest I be tempted to kick you out."

"Where must I go? I have no place amongst the others now."

"There is the workroom. You had best guard what you have made from moths. That is sufficient occupation surely for one who hitherto was too hard-worked."

"It is a return to the life I led before I came here."

"The information does not interest me. You live your life according to your own making. Go; I have no more to say to you."

Mariana's eyes glittered.

"I would I could appeal to some power without against this cruel sentence."

"Oh! there is no power without. The world is too busy with its own affairs. You had best sink into silence gracefully. You have got past the age of screaming and past the age of tears. You have let go the only prisoner I set my mind on keeping, and need expect no mercy for it. Imbecile! Go!"

The words were accompanied by an action so indicative of savage irritation that Mariana, without further reply, turned to the door and left the room.

Daylight, unaccompanied by much warmth, had taken the place of twilight. The lights were out, and morning had begun.

Along the corridor into the central hall, with face all deathly white, she passed. She met Everard there. He had waited for her.

He read her untold story by her face, for she never said a word, and glided past him like a ghost in a painted picture toward the eastern wing.

The door swung open. Here no light had ever penetrated by night or day, save only the artificial glimmer and pale ghastliness.

Then at No. 13 she stopped, and opened the low-built door. She gave one hurried glance back to the big double door that shut her off from life, then passed into the damp, dark cell, and closed the door behind her.

No longer the work that filled with a certain pleasure the long hours of day. To sit there idle, without light, or companionship, or occupation—that was her doom now. And then, to give up that precious pleasure and intoxicating dream that came round once a week! She shuddered at the black thought.

Down she sat upon one wooden chair. And as she sat, the moths descended one by one about her. But when she sighed they flew far off again. The moths in flimsy clouds hovered above, and knew quite all too well their time had not come yet.

So there for the present we must leave her—stiff, rigid, and unmoving. Crushed down by pain and heaviness so great, she had no strength to move or cry.

CHAPTER XVI

THE GOVERNOR

The morning came, and Rosalie awoke, light-hearted and ready to arise. No one came here to call her except the sun and singing birds outside the window. None else were needed. When she had dressed, she passed out on the landing and down the staircase, and seeing the door open to the dining-room where she had supped last night, went there. Its open windows opened on the ground. Breakfast was laid for two, and as none else was visible she passed out into the garden, eagerly drinking in the wondrous freshness of the morning air.

At last she saw the stranger of the night coming toward her from a gate in a high yew edge that separated the garden from whatever lay beyond. He carried a basket in his hand, and as he came nearer Rosalie saw that the basket contained small seeds. Though he wore glasses when writing in the house, he evidently did not need them here. In fact, it did not seem to her that a man with eyes so blue and piercing could ever be short-sighted at all, but still it must be so. He wore no hat. The sun shone on his silver hair, a brilliant lustre. He walked with ease and gracefulness, and again the odd resemblance in appearance to Mr. Barringcourt recurred to her.

"Good morning, Rosalie! I think a spray of flowers would greatly improve that sombre dress of yours. Gather what kind you like, and come to breakfast—it is waiting for us."

He passed on as he spoke, and disappeared within the house.

Following his advice, she gathered a cluster of pale roses, and placed them in her belt. Truly, his words, though simple, had had a very good effect. She no longer felt she wore a uniform of black and red. The flowers had given the happiest relief.

After breakfast he invited her to his study, "for," said he, "I wish to have some conversation with you before eight o'clock. After that I am engaged till twelve, and rarely find much spare time till evening has closed, and tonight I cannot spare you even that."

When they were both seated there, he began the conversation by saying:

"Last night you told me you knew of no merit that could have brought you to me, but I think that, between us, we must endeavour to discover one. Perhaps, if you will repeat your story to me, I may be of use in finding it."

So on that Rosalie recounted the story of her early life, simply and truthfully, up to that last visit to the temple. Nor did she omit her meeting with Mr. Barringcourt there, and the short conversation she had held with him. But on mentioning the last visit, after her aunt's death, she came to a sudden stop, and seemed undecided and unknowing how to proceed.

"You say you went once more inside the sacred curtain. But why?"

"I felt I had given up so much that the Serpent must recognise how much I really loved him. Besides, I felt I wanted to get some real strength to go on living after every hope and aspiration had died away."

"What was it made you wish so badly for a tongue?"

"I don't know. I don't think it was me that wished; I think it was something else."

And then she flushed, for that was the style of speech Mr. Barringcourt would have ridiculed. And she herself recognised that truth at times, to the ignorant or wilfully blind, may appear silly and foolish. But this new acquaintance made no remark immediately, only his keen eyes travelled across her face, as if reading something there.

"And that something?" he asked at length.

"I don't know, I'm sure. But it never gave me any peace, and it wasn't myself, I am sure. Sometimes I used to reason that I couldn't possibly receive the gift of speech, and yet the inner voice repeated, 'Go on, go on!' so that, apart from my own great wish, I was obliged to do as I was told."

"And you received the gift at last?"

"Yes."

"On that last visit to the Serpent?"

"No, I—I—I—for that I went to Mr. Barringcourt."

"The Serpent did not heal you, then?"

"Oh, sir, could it?" Rosalie's voice was almost a remonstrance.

"Is not the Serpent the God of Lucifram?"

"Yes, and that is what has troubled me so heavily ever since; far more than imprisonment and harshness."

"What has troubled you?"

"Perhaps if I tell you, you will think me fanciful."

He smiled.

"Fancies are all put to the test here," he answered, and a certain sternness rang in the kindness of his tone that reassured Rosalie, somehow or other, when she thought it would have frightened her.

"Well, after I had resigned my will, and prayed for strength, I closed my eyes, and it seemed as if a great vision flashed before me in the darkness. The Serpent seemed to have turned round, and to show that from the back it was all hollow, and in its three tails, so black and dingy from the inside, three dwarfed jesters sat, with caps and bells, all grinning and pointing, as if to make a mock of everything. And then a fire of purest light and radiance, with a centre of unearthly brightness, more beautiful than any sight I ever saw, rolled over everything, and burnt the hollow symbol to a cinder with its all-conquering strength."

Rosalie's eyes were shining as they looked across into his.

"And in my mind the same thing must have happened. For somehow no longer I thought upon the Serpent. All was changed. Whatever humble love I had to give, and strength to ask, were given and claimed by some wise reasoning Being far above, whose faintest breath could shrivel into cinders this grinning mockery worshipped of man."

"What of the cinder?"

"Oh! I remember it never burned away. It shone like a little ball of gold within the fire, and I wondered at the time why it had never disappeared."

Then suddenly she got up and crossed the room and knelt down beside him, and clasped her hands upon the arm-chair.

"And I believe it," she said. "I could never think of going back to the Serpent after the higher thing; I loved to see the pure white light within that glorious fire. It was so peaceful, restful, strong and light-giving. I hardly think I could have spent the week that followed, with all its brilliant lights and gloomy blackness, and everything so fresh and new, had I not had that light so pure and still to think upon. It was divinest comfort to me even when the blackness tried to quite obscure it, and set such a terrible gap betwixt me and every living thing."

"And after this you left the temple and went to Mr. Barringcourt?"

"Yes; there was nothing more to stay for. And I think the same thing led me to him that has now led me to you—calling 'On! on! on!' in spite of everything."

"And when you got there?"

"Then he healed me, by a very natural process it seemed, that had little of the miracle about it. But I felt no pain, and I remember he was very much surprised at it."

"And the cure was perfect?"

"Yes, I think it was too perfect. My tongue became most glib and voluble. Words slipped out I often wished unsaid."

"You had had no practice in restraining them?"

"Well, no. But I think myself Mr. Barringcourt really did oil the wheels of my tongue too freely, because I don't think by nature I should ever be given to answering back. But when I was there that seemed the one thing in life I was capable of."

She had risen from her knees and walked towards the fireplace.

"But what reason should he have for doing so?"

Rosalie looked at him sideways. Then suddenly she laughed.

"You've got to learn some day how intensely stupid and simple I am, so perhaps you had better know soon as late. Well, I think the reason why he brought my tongue to such a pitch of volubility was because he is very keen on finding out all secrets, and he thought I should save time and trouble by being made very talkative."

"He is keen on finding out secrets?"

"Yes; it sounds silly, but it's true. He was most peculiar. If other men are like him, I pity the women that have to deal with them, and often think how fortunate my aunt was, for uncle was most quiet and peaceable."

"Your experience of people is not very great."

She sighed.

"No; I could not tell whether he was like other men or not. That's how it was I felt at such a disadvantage all the time. Anyway, he wasn't like any of my relations, the girls and women that I knew, nor even like the doctor that attended us, nor the bread baker, nor the butcher, nor any of those. But then Everard wasn't. None of them were, in fact."

"What led to your discovery of his *penchant* for secrets?"

"Mariana told me; and when she told me, I laughed to myself, it seemed so utterly ridiculous. But afterwards I came to understand it. That is why he quarrelled with me, and left me a prisoner in the upper storey."

"In so short a time?"

"Yes. He found I had no secret worth discovering."

"But had you not?"

"No. Sometimes I felt tempted to tell him the real facts of my last visit to the temple, but something always held me back. And after all, if I had told him I should have become a prisoner all the same."

"Maybe. Then in the end you quarrelled with him?"

"No, he quarrelled with me. We were getting on, as I considered, very nicely, and suddenly I could say nothing that would please him. Afterwards I understood it was because he had grown tired of me, and found me unprofitable, so far as secrets were concerned."

"And so you were consigned to shadows, and a suite of rooms in an upper storey?"

"Yes, and it was terrible. I never wish to go through such a time again. It seemed to me eternity. Even now I don't believe it was a week. It was a year of weeks."

"Did Mr. Barringcourt ever ask you any questions about the Serpent?"

"Yes; he often asked me questions."

"And you never told him what you had seen then?"

"No, I couldn't, much as I wanted to. When I got to that part I only stammered, and that used to make him angry."

"Then how can you say he discovered you had no secret worth discovering when you distinctly had one?"

"He would have simply ridiculed it, and said there was no truth in it. So what was it worth to him?"

"You used some little reason, then, in the controlling of your tongue?"

"Perhaps it was I, but I gave the credit elsewhere."

"Now we have to discover the merit that lit the path for you to here."

"Will you not put on your glasses? It will be hard to find."

"How long did you say you prayed to the Serpent for the gift of speech?"

"Over two years; and the prayer was answered in a different way from what I thought."

"By the way, you spoke a little time ago of Mariana. Who was she?"

"A kind of waiting-maid at Marble House. I do not know what else she could be called, unless a sewing-maid. But she was beautiful, and different altogether from any sewing-maid that I had ever seen. And even in a week I grew to love her, for underneath a cold and smooth exterior she had the sweetest, kindest disposition of anyone I ever knew."

"Did she derive much happiness from living there?"

"None, except two hours every Wednesday night. And then she played upon a violin. I never heard such music, though it was weirdly sad. But Mr. Barringcourt blinded my reason to believe there was no harmony in what she played."

"You do not give him an enviable character."

"That is what I said when Mariana told me of him." And suddenly Rosalie shuddered. "How can I give him an enviable character when he was cruel, hard as marble, and vindictive. He was bad, really bad, and the worst thing is I knew it all the time, yet had he been agreeable to me, really agreeable, I would have shut my eyes to everything."

And from a very real feeling of shame, her colour deepened, for Rosalie was not one of those people who are blind to their own shortcomings and weaknesses.

Then suddenly turning to her host, she said, changing the conversation:

"What must I call you? Everybody has a name, but yours I never heard."

"Well," he answered slowly, "I don't know that for the present I have any name worth going by. Some call me the Traveller's Friend, some the Physician, some the Task Master. You may call me what you will for the present. Hereafter we may find a better name."

"Well, Mr. Barringcourt was called the Master. Suppose I call you the Governor, without any abbreviation to a lesser name."

"Why that?"

"Because Mariana told me I was weak, and weak people want someone very strict with them, and I should like to have a good understanding, you know, because I'm very ignorant."

He looked at her.

"Well, you will find me strict enough. And for the rest, it's bound to follow."

Then he got up, and took down a large volume from a book-shelf, and seated once more in his chair, with the book on the table, adjusted his glasses, and opening the leaves, turned them slowly, as one looking through the pages of a dictionary to discover something.

As last he found the place he needed, and for some time read in silence; then closed the book and instantly removed his glasses as he looked across at her.

"I've been through the list of merits, Rosalie, and have decided yours is the questionable merit of clinging on. None others have had much time to develop yet. They may be there, no doubt, but have not, as it were, yet come of age."

"Clinging on! It's very questionable, isn't it?"

"Yes; but you'll have one or two stiff examinations to pass in it before you've finished."

"But—but the people who cling on are—are so insufferable." And it must be acknowledged a very real tear of disappointment stood in her eye.

"Would you have liked some higher-sounding virtue?"

"Yes; I thought you were going to say meekness and gentleness, or some of the great gifts of the spirit. I never read that 'clinging on' was counted much in the Book of Divine Inspiration. Besides, who have I been clinging on to? I deserted the Serpent just—"

"Just at the right time. There is where the virtue comes. Had you been any earlier you would have shown great fickleness. Besides, after all, I don't think you're very heavy, Rosalie. You would not be such an insufferable load to drag along."

"I don't know, I'm sure. But anyway, I'll trust to you."

"Well now, whilst you stay with me there is much work to be done. But for today, until you become accustomed to your new surroundings, you may take holiday. Tomorrow morning be up as early as today. After breakfast I will show you in what direction your work will lie."

After that she went away, and saw no more of him all day. It was an ideal holiday in the sun and warmth and beauty of the outdoor life. And for the noontide meal, Billy came and sat with her, though he only drank one glass of water whilst she ate.

"Are you not hungry?" she asked.

"Well, yes. I'm getting hungry, but it isn't my meal-time yet. You'd be astonished if you saw the amount I eat compared with you," and he laughed in the gayest, happiest tone. After a while he said: "Have you made friends with the frog yet?"

"With whom?"

"The frog. My father's pet frog. It is in the garden, but is rather shy of strangers, but very talkative when once you get to know it."

"A frog? And it can talk?"

"You bet! It has a better fund of words and style of oratory than many a statesman."

"Well, then, it should be a human being."

Billy looked at her, and his brilliant sparkling eyes were laughing.

"Well, no, hardly that. It is quite contented to remain a frog—a very superior kind of frog."

"Do you come every day for lessons?" asked Rosalie, uncertain what to say.

"Three times a week. And the other days I walk over in my spare time."

"Then you have not far to come?"

"Not far, comparatively speaking. The distance lessens as one grows older, I find."

"Then it would be less to me than you?"

Again he laughed.

"Well, no; I expect I've had more practice than you. Good morning!"

And he was gone, leaving Rosalie to ponder on that odd kind of powerful beauty in his face, and that exuberant merriness that made her sigh to lose him. For that was the worst of Billy. He seemed to come and go more like some brilliant spirit, a kind of Mercury, with winged heels, to bring one ray of sunshine, and then depart.

CHAPTER XVII

A PLANTATION

The next morning after breakfast the Governor led her down the garden to the gate in the edge of yew. He carried in his hand the basket she had seen the day before, containing seeds. But whereas yesterday they had looked green, today they had a silvery-white appearance, toning to a liquid aspect as of water in the centre. Beyond the edge stretched a square plot of uncultivated land bordered by willow trees, and at the further side a little hut of wood, just in the shelter of the forest. But here the sun did not shine so brightly. The garden of Pleasure was left behind. This was the field of *Work*.

The Governor led the way across to the hut. It consisted of two rooms, a living- and a sleeping-room, and moreover a little cellar, where she discovered all kinds of garden implements and spades, and one large fork that looked as if it were for digging heavy soil.

He put the basket down upon the table, and then he said:

"This is your little house. These are the seeds to be sown in the strip of land you see without. You must dig and sow, and then wait for the harvest. The books upon the shelves you may study in your leisure, but you must grasp each subject thoroughly before your time of apprenticeship is over."

So saying, without any word of advice or caution he left the hut and crossed to the gate that led to the garden. Rosalie was left alone.

But though on one side lay a great and unknown forest, she experienced no fear at being left alone, even though when she looked out she noticed how uncompromisingly high the edge appeared, shutting her quite away from sight or sound of the pretty wayside house.

But just then a voice attracted her attention.

"Well! well!" said it, most harshly, "what's the first thing that a farmer does before he sows his seed?"

"I don't know, I'm sure," answered Rosalie; "I've never lived in the country," and looked round to find the speaker.

And there on the doorstep was a frog sitting, looking up at her half contemplatively, half pityingly. Its colours were beautifully striped, green and white. On its head these colours blended brilliantly, taking away some of the staring effect of the wide-open eyes.

"Don't know?" it answered. "Well! well! You'll have to dig. Get a fork and dig. Well! well! best to know nothing than to know too much."

Rosalie went as she was told, and brought the big fork she had noticed. It certainly was very big, and looked aggressive.

"Do you mean this?" she asked.

"What else should I mean? Now then, set to work. The quicker you begin, the quicker you'll finish."

"But—but what must I do with it?"

"Grasp it in both hands. Stick it in the ground, and push it in with your foot. Well! well! the sooner you learn, the sooner you'll know."

"I won't!" said Rosalie. "It's a man's work; why, it's digging. I know I was never intended to do that."

The frog, by way of showing its disgust, gave a contemptuous croak.

"Man's work? It isn't the work most men would thank you for giving them. Even as far back as the days of Divine Inspiration mankind was ashamed of it. It's woman's work! What man won't do always falls to the woman."

"But women never dig in our country," said Rosalie, still bent on the argument.

"What country's yours?"

"The biggest in the whole of Lucifram."

"It would be bigger still if the women applied themselves better," said the frog, and a short silence followed.

"Do you really think I ought to do it?" said Rosalie, at last, not being of that stubborn nature that delights in saying "no" and sticking to it.

"Well, I don't see what else is to be done," said her companion. "If you don't dig you'll never sow, and if you don't sow, you'll never reap, and if you don't reap you'll never—"

"Never what?"

"Prove you're anything but a fool."

"Really?" said Rosalie.

"Really!" said the frog; but the expression in each voice was different.

So she stuck the fork into the ground, and found it took a great deal of strength to make any impression upon the surface. But once having put her shoulder to the plough, as it were, there was nothing for it but to go on, for the old voice kept ringing "Go on! go on!" and consequently on she went.

The frog, for some considerable period, watched her from the side, but finally hopped away into the hut. At noonday it appeared again, and summoned her to dinner, which was already prepared in the little living-room.

"Who prepared my dinner?" asked Rosalie, after she had washed her hands and settled to the meal.

"I did," it replied. "It's a woman's work certainly, but if you waited for a woman to do it for you, you'd come badly off. No; I'm a frog, but when there's no one else by I can do other work besides my own. How do you like digging?"

"It makes me very tired, and the inside of my hands are quite sore."

"Are they? Well, you've got to go on again this afternoon, you know. If you don't get the seeds in before very long they'll wither."

She answered nothing, but after the customary hour of rest returned again to the hard labour.

It was slow work and very hard, and not a soul came near all the day long. In fact, during the afternoon even the frog seemed to have deserted her, and it was not till the first faint tinge of evening crossed the sky that she again heard the familiar voice calling from the wooden doorstep:

"Time's up now; tea's ready."

Rosalie let the fork drop on the ground, and turned round as eagerly as her tired body would allow.

Whilst she ate her tea, this new friend sat upon the hearth.

"I shall be as stiff as a board tomorrow," said Rosalie, laying her tired arms upon the arms of the chair.

"No; my master sent down that little bottle on the mantelpiece for you. You must take it before you go to bed, and you will be all right in the morning—so far as stiffness is concerned, anyway. We don't go in for torture here, but we believe in hard work—very hard work sometimes."

When the meal was finished the frog said:

"Now, if you will take this arm-chair by the fireplace, I will remove the table."

She did so, and was surprised to see that when the frog pulled a small knob in the wall the whole table, which, however, was not large, disappeared through an opening partition, and left the room clear.

"If you want to read or study, you must draw that writing-desk nearer," continued her instructor.

"I don't want to do anything tonight. I'm so tired, I think I'll go to bed early."

"That wouldn't be a bad plan, seeing you have only been at work one day, and find it all so strange. You'll be more accustomed to it tomorrow, and get more done."

"Yes," said Rosalie; "I'm all impatience to be finished. It is such dreary work, and I'm quite inquisitive about the seeds. I wonder whether they'll grow up roses, or lilies, or nasturtiums, or dahlias, or hyacinths, or chrysanthemums, or what?"

"Don't you know much about seeds?"

"Nothing. Uncle was very clever that way; but I never cared about seeds—they looked so very uninteresting; I only cared about the flowers."

"If I were you," said the frog, "I would rub a little of that liquid out of the bottle on my hands. If they are blistered and sore it will heal them very quickly. I've had sore hands myself, so I can sympathise. And here's a pair of gloves," it continued, drawing a pair from behind the coal-scuttle. "I made them this afternoon, instead of coming out to keep you company. I might have made them outside, but I thought it would be a little surprise for you."

"Oh, thank you," said Rosalie. "How very thoughtful of you! Where did you learn everything you know?"

"Well! well!" said the frog, with quite a sorrowful croak, "I learnt it in the school where it is most generally taught."

"Where was that?"

"In the school of experience and adversity, for the most part."

"Don't you think that people can be kind unless they've gone through a great deal of suffering?" asked Rosalie.

"Now and again, just now and again, one finds them. But they're few and far between."

"I think suffering and trouble make people bitter, or else break them up altogether."

"Not if they're made of the right stuff," said the frog. "It's the needle's eye that rich and poor men alike have to pass through. If you can't stand sorrow, you can't stand happiness, though you may think you can."

"But we were made to be happy. The Serpent—God rather, meant us to be so."

"God meant us to be happy eventually," said the frog gently. "But like all things else worth having, it takes a great deal of fighting for. Contentment and peace are the nearest approach to it one generally gets the other side of heaven."

"I don't like the word 'peace.' It reminds me of a fat woman, and a dinner of suet dumplings."

"You're prejudiced, or else you've mistaken it for lethargy."

"Well, is not contentment a state of lethargy?"

"No; when you're most contented, you're least so. The two things naturally go together, and keep up a constant flow of action that does away with torpidness."

"How long do you think it will be before my work is finished here?"

"I don't know. It's rather a foolish question to ask. No one knows. It depends upon what time the seed takes to ripen and the bent of your mind."

"And in the evenings must I study?"

"It is your only time. But what you want is plenty of hard work and plenty of deep thought."

"And that is almost everything," said Rosalie.

"I believe it is," answered the frog; and by the simple process of pulling another knob emptied a shovelful of coal on the fire out of the chimney-side.

It was not long after this when Rosalie prepared for bed. She rubbed the liquid on her hands, and found it very soon relieved them. Then she drank the contents of the bottle and retired to the inner room, first bidding the frog "Good-night."

"I sleep on the doorstep," said it, "so you may sleep doubly secure. Nothing evil can cross me, for my life is charmed."

And, somehow or other, there seemed more life, strength, and independence in this small creature than there had ever been in Mariana. Poor Mariana! Rosalie fell asleep thinking of her, wondering how she had taken the news of her escape, and whether Mr. Barringcourt indulged in anything further than a frown when the truth was told to him.

But these thoughts did not keep her long out of the land of dreams. Perhaps it was that Rosalie had enough to do thinking of her own affairs just then. It never struck her that her escape could make any material difference to Mariana. She imagined her living the same even life, with one real pleasure in the week in compensation for its darkness, and saw within her mind the wedding-dress nearing completion, and trembled in her sleep to think it soon must be finished and fade again to nothing for want of one to wear it.

And in the night she dreamt the seeds were sown, the time of harvest came, and every seed appeared as a huge and barren stone. Then in despair and disappointment she wept upon them, and they disappeared.

CHAPTER XVIII

SEEDS GROWING CONTRARIWISE

After that, life began in earnest for Rosalie. For some weeks her days were given to digging, her nights to mastering the alphabet of some unknown language. It was all dry work, and very hard.

No one came near, except the frog, and she often found herself wishing for more human companionship. But still it was not Rosalie's nature to grumble too much at circumstances. She contented herself with an occasional sigh, and for the rest learnt to love the harsh, croaking voice that had something to say about most things, and was always kind enough to revive her drooping spirits with cheering words.

At last the plot of ground was all prepared, and considering it had been digged by a woman, it was not at all badly done. No one would have known the difference if they hadn't been told, though afterwards they might have discovered the depth was not so great. However that may be, the seeds were sown in it, and began doubtless to do their own little bit of digging, and go down so far that no one could find them where they'd first been put. After the sowing came the time of waiting. There was much weeding, and more watering, for no drop of rain ever descended there, and all had to be carried from a stream near by.

Rosalie watched the ground impatiently to see when the first bright blade would appear, but though she waited one month, two, three, four, nothing at all except an occasional weed altered the surface of the ground. And her whole heart was buried in that little garden. It seemed as if it, too, must have taken root down there, away from the sunshine and the warmth.

And the waiting was far worse than the working, for after three months certainly something ought to have shown. But when it went on to four, five, nay, at last came out into six long months, and nothing yet had come to light, Rosalie went back into the little hut, and laid her head upon her arms upon the table, and cried from sheer disappointment and low spirits. For during this time of waiting and subsequent doubt no one had come to see her, no one at all, except the frog.

In this fit of depression, which was the first of its kind, the outcome of disappointment and hope deferred, the frog spoke.

"What is it, Rosalie? I've never seen you cry before."

"I can't stand it any longer, I know I can't. I've waited for six months, with never a soul to speak to but you, and nothing has come up. It's all a failure. My heart is as heavy as a stone. If it gets much worse it will break right in two. I know it will."

"Where is your heart?"

"It should be in my body, but I believe I must have sown it along with the seeds in the garden, and it's turning to stone while they're rotting."

Then the frog spoke rather shyly, as one who fears to be ridiculed, and is slightly apologetic.

"Perhaps the seeds have turned to—to—to—stone, too," and it looked hard in the fire instead of at Rosalie.

She, however, looked across at it with eyes wide open.

"Well, really! It doesn't seem unlikely, considering the time they are in coming up."

"What will you do?" said the frog.

"I'll begin to dig again," cried Rosalie.

"It's the wisest thing you've said since you came here," the frog answered, and its colours flashed quite brilliantly.

So the next morning (for it was evening when they spoke to one another) Rosalie rose with a much lighter heart than for some time past, went out into the garden with the fork, and began to dig. She dug all day, but found nothing, till just at eventide she noticed something shining in the dull, damp soil. She picked it out with her fingers very eagerly. It was a dull enough looking stone for the most part, with here and there a substance in it that shone like glass—not very brilliantly. Whatever it was, it was enough to brighten Rosalie's spirits for the time being, and as just then she heard the frog's voice calling her to tea, she made as much haste forwards as she could over the clodding soil to show her treasure.

"See what a beautiful thing I have found!" she cried, and held it up triumphantly.

"It isn't very brilliant," said the frog, looking at it critically.

"Don't you think so?"

"No. You do, because you've been looking at black soil all the day, but I've been looking at the sun."

"Well, but then the brightest thing would look dull if you compared it with the sun. How am I to find out really what it is?"

"Take it to my master."

"I can't open the gate."

"The gate will open of itself, if you've anything to take to him."

Rosalie turned about to run off at once, but the other said:

"Wait and have tea first. He is never at liberty till six, and now it's only five."

So after tea, Rosalie, having previously changed her heavy boots and generally tidied herself, set off in the direction of the house.

The gate this time responded easily enough to her hand, and soon she was walking through the garden, holding her stone the tighter, in that she was quite sure, from the fact of the gate opening so readily, it must be worth something very considerable.

The door leading into the garden was open, and after knocking she passed through, and went at once to the study.

The curious thing about the sun here was that it always set at the same time of day, and that between five and half-past, so that now twilight had fallen, and the lamps were lit, though the blinds remained undrawn.

The Governor sat as usual, and must have been expecting her, for he held out his hand as she entered, saying:

"Well, what have you brought?"

She placed it in the hand he held out, and waited whilst he looked at it. This did not take very long, for almost on the instant he looked up, and said:

"I'll send it to an expert in the city of Lucifram, and get his opinion on it."

"You think it is very valuable, then?"

"I'm afraid I don't, except in a way that doesn't count. But we'll send it to someone who is unacquainted with the digging, and watering, and heart-burning it has necessitated, and therefore who will be less prejudiced than I."

"When will you send it?"

"Tonight; and you will hear the decision in something like a fortnight."

So then she went away. The next two weeks were passed in waiting, and in the study of those books which Rosalie found more dry and difficult each succeeding day. For there was no one to explain them, and in some parts there seemed nothing but big full-stops and commas, with wide gaps between.

But at the end of that time the frog came to her one morning and said the Governor wished to see her.

Rosalie went in fear and expectation, and the first thing her eyes lighted on was her stone upon the table. This, she felt, was not quite as it should be.

"The decision is that it is rubbish."

That was all the Governor said.

She felt rather miserable. She thought it must be with hurrying across the garden. However, there was nothing to be said, and Rosalie withdrew. After that some very hard, frosty weather followed, and the ground was so hard that for a long time she was able to do nothing—outside, at any rate.

Then when it thawed a little she went out and digged again, and found just such another stone as the one before, only of a little lighter and brighter substance.

After tea she took it to the Governor, as last time. He promised to send it to the city, and get the opinion of an expert upon it. Rosalie withdrew to wait. At the end of a fortnight she was again sent for to the Governor's house. Her stone was on the table.

"The decision is that it is rubbish," said he.

And she felt disappointed this time, but not miserable. One is never quite so sure of things after the first time—that is, if they've miscarried. She went back again to the plantation and the hut. Again the ground had frozen, and for some time it was impossible to do anything, even had she had the inclination.

After this, every time the thaw came Rosalie set to work again, finding the work a change and relief from study. And though the disappointment always lasted out the frost, it always disappeared with the thaw. And every time she went up to the house, the particular stone she had last found lay on the table, and the words were:

"The decision is that it is rubbish."

This went on for a long while, till at last it seemed to Rosalie all the hope had been crushed out of her, and she went back to the garden and found it quite frosted over. But after a while the frost broke, and the frog, seeing Rosalie made no attempt to go to dig, said to her:

"The frost has broken."

"I know."

"Will you not go out into the garden?"

"No; I'm too impatient. I want the seeds to grow quicker than I can learn. I've been thinking about it all, and I feel that I must wait. Bright stones take longer to grow than flowers, because they fade less quickly."

Thereupon the frog let fall a tear of gratitude, but turned the other way during the odd process, so that Rosalie never noticed it.

Then followed a very long and dreary time, with no companionship; nothing but the even days and dull books, and the sympathetic frog. And this went on so long that many a time Rosalie went out to look at the ground, and sighed, but never thought of touching it, because something had said "Stand still." At last, after a very long time had gone by, she went to bed one night, feeling particularly sad.

Some hours later she awoke to find the moon shining full into the chamber. She got up and dressed, and went through into the outer room. The door was open, and the frog was sitting contemplatively upon the step, looking out on to the beauties of the night. Occasionally it gave a croak of satisfaction.

Rosalie went to the cellar and brought out the big fork, and thought she was so quiet the frog had never seen her. But then, poor thing, its eyes were so large, they stared out from every side of its head, and as she approached the door it hopped down, and moved aside to let her pass.

"Why don't you ask me what I'm going to do?" she said, laughing.

"That's plain to be seen," it answered, and hopped after her in the moonlight.

Suddenly Rosalie began to dig, just on that portion of ground where a shaft of moonlight had fallen. For some time nothing but loose soil came up, but at last the fork hit upon something hard. It did not move till a space had been cleared all round it, and then it appeared nothing but a heavy hard mass of black earth, with an irregular surface.

"Well?" said the frog.

"There are other tools in the cellar beside a fork," said she. "But we've done enough for one night. It can stay now till the morning," and she took it in both hands, and lifted it out of the deep trench dug about it.

So then once more night reigned undisturbed. But with the morning work began again, this time with finer instruments to chip away the thick layers of soil and find what lay beneath. It took a very long time, much longer than Rosalie ever anticipated, though in other ways the hours passed quickly under this keen absorption. In many places the soil seemed more like marble than rock, and required much patience to remove it, for none of the instruments were particularly sharp, nor specially adapted for that purpose. But what of that? Working, working, ever unceasingly, on went Rosalie, and one day she looked up at the frog, and half laughed, and said:

"I believe my heart is inside here, and I'll never be happy till it's free, quite free."

But the frog only turned away and sighed, and Rosalie was so intent that she never heard the sigh.

And at last!

Bit by bit a brilliant jewel unfolded itself, all flashing green-and-moonlight colour, and with one gleam of ruby red, just one bright gleam upon the middle surface.

And she pressed it to her lips and kissed it. This was no dull stone with intermittent flashes of light. No, this was *real*—a lovely thing of sparkling colour.

It was finished just at sunset. She scarcely needed any tea, so eager and impatient was she to get away.

And then she appeared before the Governor with this precious prize.

"I've found something really, at last," said she, with bright eyes and cheeks.

As of old he held his hand out for it, but said nothing.

"Why don't you speak?" she asked.

"It is not for me to speak," he answered; and so she went away.

But Rosalie was scarce content with waiting now. She doubted not that all would see the value of the stone she had so lately found, and most of all an expert. And indeed there seemed to be no time for waiting. The voice said,

"Go on." Truly the harvest was beginning. Who would sit down with but one sheaf tied?

And she was justified in doing so. Another lump of hard black earth (to be chipped away slowly and surely) appeared amongst the looser soil. And after a time the under surface partly appeared, and it, too, as far as she could see, was bright and brilliant.

But as this was in process the message arrived at breakfast, the Governor wished to see her.

She did not allow herself to think, because she dare not, but whatever thought rose in her mind it was success.

She knocked at the study door and entered. There, in the same place that all the others had been in turn, lay the shining jewel, and the cold voice answered:

"The decision is that it is rubbish."

The pain within was so great that Rosalie could have screamed, and then came sickness and faintness, so that she leant against the door and looked at him.

"What does it mean?" she asked.

"It is accounted of no worth."

"Oh, but it is! it is!" she cried, and looked at him so hard that he looked back at her.

"I have told you the decision."

"But what do *you* say?"

"I say nothing."

"But what is wrong with it?"

"I believe the decision was that it was gaudy. It shone too much."

She looked at him dully, and then turned and went away.

There in the plantation was the work she was engaged on. Her eyes were too dull to see the sparkle of light, her heart too black to care. And suddenly she laughed, and picking up the fork lying near, began to dig again. The frog sat by and watched.

In furious haste, without apparent thought, she worked, and at last came upon a much smaller mound, containing one much smaller stone of transparent substance that had no lustre at all. But bitter tears were running fast from her swollen eyes, and two of them flashed on it. When she tried to rub them off upon her sleeve they seemed quite hardened, and they never moved.

"Is this gaudy?" she asked, turning suddenly to her companion.

"I don't think so," it answered meekly. And then she sighed.

"It seems to me it's hardly bright enough, except the tears."

And in the evening she went with it again to the Governor.

After that the time was very short till she was again summoned to the house.

And there the lesser jewel lay, just as she had brought it, and the decision was once more that this was rubbish also.

Then she turned to him, and cried bitterly:

"You gave me the seeds—what is wrong with them? I cannot alter them from what they are."

"Perhaps it would be best if now you left the garden," he answered slowly, "seeing it is so profitless."

But she looked at him with straining eyes, and answered:

"I can't. It's the work I have been put to do, and I must finish it. I told the frog I thought my heart was in that first hard mound, and I believe it is. But there's something else beside my heart, and that's there too, and I'll never be free till it is free. And what can I do? I am mad. I see things beautiful that others only stare at, and then pass by with scarcely one comment. And the old cruel voice keeps crying, 'Go on! go on!' and whither can I go? The path is all so black that, forward or backward, I am lost whichever way I turn."

Then because he did not answer, she said at last:

"Send it, the first I brought to you, that brilliant moonstone, to some other place. The man who called it rubbish can't have any eyes."

"Just as you like," he answered.

Then she went away.

In the plantation there had set so hard a frost that everything was white and stiff and ice-bound. There lay the half-chipped mound containing the other jewel scarce yet visible. But Rosalie had no heart to touch it, even had the frost allowed her.

And no result came from sending the moonstone to another place. One general and unanimous opinion: it had no value—that was all. And still for months the blighting frost lay dead on everything.

In vain, with burning fever under the outward chill that froze her too, did Rosalie take the fork and try with what little strength was in her arms to break the iron earth. Nothing moved. It only made her recognise the more the great impossibility, the strength of life imprisoned by the frozen hands of death.

At last (for now the gate within the edge was never fast) she went again to the Governor.

"What am I to do?" she asked. "I can't get on with anything, nor move either way. I've prayed to God a thousand times to give me peace or break the ice, or let me get the price of freedom from that jewel which I brought to you, and nothing ever answers, except in contradiction. I prayed one night the thaw might come—a hundred times and more I prayed it. In the morning a double frost had settled, petrifying hard as iron. Another night I prayed for peace and rest. I could not stand so terrible a strain. I never dreamt as that night. Ten times I dozed and woke again, covered with sweat, all shivering in the cold, to think myself alive within a coffin, buried within the ground. And most incessantly that other prayer to reap the price of freedom with the stone, and as you know, it lies here in your keeping—a useless thing, and judged devoid of worth."

"You say your heart is in the stone," he answered.

"Yes; I think it sends out shafts of brilliancy to pierce to that dull, empty place, and prick it into fearful pain. What can I do? I've prayed to God— what more can I do?"

"There is one thing more. You'd better give it up."

"Oh! but that is everything—the whole of the little garden. For the frost will never break till the stone is free, and I."

"You can give the garden back to God who gave it."

"But why give me a thing and take it back just when it's fit for using?" and then a great pain and fear came into her eyes. "I would do as you tell me, I would really, but I haven't the strength, and I'm afraid. The frost is too strong for me. It freezes my heart, and leaves my mind quite free, so that the blood courses through my brain in quickest time, and then stops suddenly. It's worse than killing me. I'm going mad, and what use am I to God, or how can I see the light of heaven, if once that heavy cloud descends, and coupled with the frost, freezes upon my eyes and lips, and eats out everything?"

"To trust in God is to be sane—have peace," he answered.

"Ah, peace!" she answered greedily. "What does it mean? I know no peace—nothing but the mocking, cruel voice that says 'Go on!' and shows no way."

"It's the stone, Rosalie, that stands in your light, and blocks the way. Can't you see it?"

"I expect I'm very blind. I'm not clever enough to understand. I haven't spirit enough to find a way out. Mr. Barringcourt told me so, and he knew best. I was handicapped from the beginning to be born without a tongue."

"But that difficulty, and still another, has been surmounted."

"Yes, but I did nothing myself."

"Fiddlesticks!" said the Governor, and he spoke so naturally that Rosalie laughed, even though not particularly brightly.

"Well, I didn't do much myself. I don't see how I could."

"You did as much as was necessary, which is never in any case very much; and now there is one little thing more to be done—give it up."

"I dare not," she said; "it would send me mad. If it would kill me I wouldn't mind." And she looked down to hide the light in her eyes.

"Give it up to God. Do you trust God and think He will forsake you?"

"No; it's myself I am not sure of."

"You should be part of God."

"Not here."

"Where else, then?"

"In heaven."

"It begins on earth for those of sufficient intelligence; and for the others, they do not count."

"I'm one of the last, then. It is so hard, so very, very hard, and I have no strength at all."

Then a very long silence followed—the terrible fight between weakness and trust, between blind ignorance and all-conquering wisdom, the spirit's humble discipline; and at last she turned to him, and said:

"I'll give it up! And if I sacrifice my heart or head, it's all the same, seeing God is the receiver, and He knows best."

And then she turned away, with the knowledge of having done some duty that now seemed extremely simple.

But the Governor rose from his chair, and came towards her, and took her in his arms, and kissed her cheek, and the caressing action reminded her somehow of that time long ago, when Mr. Barringcourt laid his hand upon her shoulder in the temple.

Bur that kiss seemed to revive her strength, and give some of that peace she had so lately craved for.

Yet this reward was so very unexpected. It never occurred to her that the Governor could possibly care whether she walked right or wrong, except, perhaps, as a spectator. But the magnetic sympathy of that kiss, and the great, but gentle, strength in his arms as he drew her to him, awoke her eyes to the fact that here was her friend, the only one she had ever known, maybe would ever meet.

But being too full of feeling for words she slipped quietly towards the door, and crossed the lawn towards the hut.

That was her little home, to be filled with contentment and happiness, in which it would be her task to dig graves for bitterness, repining, and wild craving and longing for that which was not to be. It would be a hard task. Rosalie recognised it as she looked at the frozen mounds of soil, whose digging had occasioned so much eagerness and anticipation.

And in her mind she looked below the frozen surface of the plantation to where other jewels all lay buried, and she had given them up to God, and they must lie there.

But the kiss and the strength of those strong arms had worked a miracle for her. She no longer felt the weak restlessness and alternate blackness of despair and madness. She went into the little hut bravely, with tears trembling on her eyelids, partly the outcome of the struggle she had gone through, and partly of a vague sense of happiness and satisfaction that was beginning to glow within, like some glowing light of summer. Later she said to her companion:

"There was a man who healed my tongue for me, healed it with light, and now I think my heart is being healed, and it is still Light, Light, Light, on the poisonous darkness."

"Then you have given up the moonstone. It was a dangerous stone. I like the little tear-stained one the best."

"And I love it too," said Rosalie. "It gave me work to do at the time I most needed it, and set my mind on the road it has travelled ever since."

Then she took down the lesson-books, and found tonight they were much more understandable, and it was with growing lightness of spirit that she slept that evening.

CHAPTER XIX

A HUMBLE CRUCIFIXION

The next morning sunshine and warmth had come, the frost risen and fled. The birds were singing in the forest, and the melting icicles had none of the dispiriting effect of thaw, but sparkled in the sunshine. The ground was free.

Rosalie went out and took the fork and began the old process—digging. It took a long, long time, days, and weeks, and months, to chip away the soil from the new mound.

And at last the first bright ray—uncheckered—burst through. Rosalie started up with a cry. The frog hopped up to witness. Both of them shed a tear of joy and admiration that glistened like a pearl, though dull beside this other. At last a gem of purest brightness was displayed, that shone with so soft a radiance, yet so pure and bright, that it lit up the garden like the bright sun on an early summer's morning, and seemed a dazzling emblem of light.

And Rosalie said: "This is the light which cures as well as beautifies— the talisman against all ills—the gift of God, the pearl above all price; never pearl shone like to it, or diamond, or ruby, or any stone dug from the mines or caves. I'll take it to the Governor. None can fail but to acknowledge its beauty, if but for the one central spark from the raised inner surface."

And she took it to him, but as she offered it, said nothing, and he showed no surprise, but smiled gravely, as one who might approve in silence, but said no words.

So Rosalie waited, and in a shorter time than she had ever stayed before, less than a week, was sent for by the Governor.

The flashing jewel was on the table by his side. He looked across at her, but her eyes were fixed upon the stone. So soon, and it was back! And the time it had taken to dig! and the long months of blackness before! And at last her eyes travelled slowly from it back to his face.

And he said with curious intonation: "The decision is the same as hitherto."

"But God's decision! Tell me that!" and the pain in her voice was very terrible.

"The decision of God is that it is as He has made it."

"That is sufficient. Thank you," and she moved away; strong only in the friendship of that silent man, who in so few words conveyed so much of meaning.

So once more she made her way to the little hut, where the frog as usual sat waiting; but her lips were set in a smile so stony, that she said never a word, but sat down in her chair by the fire, and forgot to try to form even a syllable.

At last her eyes lighted on the frog sitting there upon the hearth. Its big, wide, mournful mouth drooped at the corners, and its round saucer eyes were brimming with tears, yet there was something very comic in its attitude—so much so that Rosalie laughed. At this it jumped so literally that had it not borne a charmed life it would certainly have settled in the fire, but as it was, it came down inside the fender, and then hopped out.

"Ah! when you laugh in sorrow your heart must needs be broken altogether," it said.

"Oh, no! I feel nothing, nothing at all, one way or the other, only hard and empty, and sorry, not for myself, but for others, that they should be so blind."

"It's well you feel hard. It doesn't do to feel soft at times like this," said the frog, and tried to speak cheerfully, but somehow failed.

Outside a white mist was settling, so silently that they never noticed it. But just then the frog piled more coal on the fire, and soon the room looked very cheerful.

"Come and sit on my knee," said Rosalie presently; and she almost laughed again at the rapidity with which her request was granted.

Although they had lived together so long, this was, as it were, the first time she had seen the frog close.

She took one of its little feet in her fingers, and noticed it was pierced with a hole. Then in turn she looked at each foot separately, and found the same mark in each.

"How did you come by these? They look as if they must have been very painful at one time."

"It was very stupid of me," said the frog shyly. "Generally I put a jewel into each, and everyone remarks about my pretty feet, but today, with thinking about your affairs, I forgot. It was most negligent of me."

"Where did you get the jewels from?"

"My master said I found them by myself, but I think he really gave them to me."

"But tell me about these holes, unless you'd rather not."

"It's a short and very common story," it answered evasively; "I don't think it would interest you."

"Indeed it would; you have been so kind to me all along that I know you won't deny me this."

"Well, there was a time when I used to be a very ordinary little frog, jumping about, and eating all that I could get. And I was very vain of my appearance, for I knew that my coat was brighter than any of my neighbours, and I wished them to know it too. But I wasn't content with being admired by my own kith and kin; I thought I should like to gain the admiration of mankind as well. Instead of confining myself to the shrubs and well in the garden, I contrived to make myself plainly seen by hopping about the paths. There were no children in the house adjoining, so that I felt doubly safe, for the two servant maids used to walk in the garden often at dusk, and talk about their sweethearts, and at these times they always found a kind and flattering word for me. Meeting with such kind treatment from them, I grew doubly proud, and formed the erroneous idea that all mankind was equally kind and simple. I made no doubt that had I been taken before the Queen, my manners, colour, and deportment would have astonished her, and called forth her admiration. As discontentment had first grown toward my own people, so at last it grew towards the maid-servants. I wanted more than two admirers, and almost lost my brilliant colour pining for them. About this time, however, my old mother died, and what with the nursing of her, and seeing to her respectable removal afterwards, I had little time for thinking of myself. But when things had settled themselves again, my old longing revived. I must go out along the paths again and try to gain more admiration.

"Now, there lived in that house a man. He always wore spectacles, and whenever he walked in the garden always carried a book, and from what I could gather from the maids' conversation, was really very clever. Now, being myself very ignorant, I naturally admired clever people, and a great longing grew in my mind to gain his approbation and attention. So whenever he walked out in the garden, I watched my opportunity, and hopped along the path beside him. But for a long time he either never noticed me, or if he did do so, was never attracted by my charms. This upset me so much that my health became visibly enfeebled. I felt that if he could but see it, I might become of value in his eyes, and thus raise myself in his good graces and esteem. Still, I felt I could not give in, for I had a friend of somewhat duller coat always watching me, ready to say upon the first occasion: 'I told you so.' So I continued hopping by his side in these walks, which, of late, had become habitual. But one day, as he came down the path, he closed his book, and his eyes suddenly lighted on me. I know not what the expression in them was, but my vanity took it favourably. I sat there as still as a frog can sit, because I had heard it was a sign of good breeding to sit still, and pretended to be gazing at the sun, because I thought it would appear good taste to admire a thing so generally esteemed. And he stood still too, but I was quite content that *he* should be admiring *me*. It would have disappointed me had he turned his attention likewise to the sun. Suddenly he stooped down, and made a grab in my direction. I had almost waited for this, and being prepared, hopped quickly to one side. I felt it would not enhance my charms to be caught too quickly. He made no further attempt to catch me, but went back into the house, and I heard my friend of the duller coat laughing, as much as to say, 'I told you so.' But I pretended to consider we had made great advances. In a little while, however, he came out again. He carried in his hand a curious string thing, which is called a net, and this he laid with great ingenuity across the path where he and I had previously been walking. This I took as a great compliment; the ground was evidently not good enough for me to walk upon. Over this he spread a few crumbs. They were not, certainly, to my mind, as I liked more tasty things, but I thought he had probably noticed my fragile appearance, and was showing his sympathy with my delicacy. So to show my trust in and appreciation of him, after a little coquettish skipping on the edge, I hopped straight to the centre of the net. He was kneeling by the side, and I must admit my heart beat loudly at my own boldness, but still remembering the kindness of the maids, the only human beings that I knew, I felt no particular or definite fear. In fact, I felt like some great queen before a kneeling courtier. But the next moment I was much upset to find the net swung over me, and both of us caught roughly and inelegantly from the ground, in a manner I had never before experienced. I struggled, but only succeeded in getting one leg through the net. My position was indeed perilous. The last thing I heard in the garden was the laughter of my friend who had the duller coat. So can the frog heart be upon occasion very hard.

"I was thrown down afterwards upon a table that had neither moss nor anything else upon it, still enveloped in the hateful net, so that there was no chance of me getting away, and there I stayed for a long time, choking with fear and partial suffocation."

A tremor ran through its little body.

"I shouldn't like to speak of all that followed. As frogs go, and being cold-blooded, I can stand a fair amount. But that was neither here nor there. I don't know how long I lived there, but it was a long time, and almost every day I was put to some torture or other. Often others used to come in to see how the different inflictions affected me, and once someone remonstrated with him, and said I must suffer; but he said he was always very careful with me, and the other one seemed satisfied.

"'Besides,' he added, 'it is in the cause of science. And what little inconveniences may be suffered by this reptile may be the means of saving many lives.'

"That night as I was lying in my prison, with every limb aching and swollen, and big pains shooting through my body, I thought on his words. It was only the extreme pain that kept me from growing proud, so instead I felt a little thankful.

"But after that the times of torture were growing more frequent, or I less able to bear them, and I longed and prayed to something I couldn't understand to set me free. And one day, as he took me out of my cell, he said to someone who was with him at the time—I think he called him his assistant: 'This thing is on its last legs; I'll just try one more experiment with it, and then it can be thrown to the midden.'

"That was a little comfort to me.

"But just then he ran something through my hand that made me struggle and gasp with pain, and then the other three, and I was lying fast nailed to a board, and could not even struggle. I'll never forget it, though the worst never comes back to me. It was the last time, the last time with a vengeance, and there I died. And I think I must have looked very queer at the last, for the last thing I was conscious of was that someone laughed. But how could one compose one's features nailed to a board, and suffering agony. And when I woke up I was in this pretty garden, and I was as feeble as a baby. But my master tended me with his own hands, and before long I had grown strong and happy again, and less wishful to been seen. And though my coat is brighter now than ever it had been, I think less of it and more of other things. But even now it's sweet to hear a little praise, and never anyone has come to see my master but they have a pleasant word for me."

"Then why do you stay with me? You should be hopping in the garden, not in this dull place."

"Oh, I asked to come. I knew you'd have a deal of sorrow once you came here; it's meant to be a place of sorrow; and I remembered that period of my own life when I was all alone without companions. And I think if someone could have come to me and said, 'Cheer up, Croaker, it'll soon all be over,' I would have felt a trifle stronger for the end."

"Was your name Croaker?" asked Rosalie gently, for the story had much affected her.

"Yes; I used always to be longing to be called 'Bright Coat' or 'Slim Body,' or one of those names when I was young, but my parents had different thoughts from me, and gave me just a family name. The scientists sometimes called me 'Goggle Eyes,' and I believe my eyes did grow unnaturally big whilst I was there."

"It's very kind of you to stay with me when I'm so dull."

"You're not dull," said the frog. "No one is, unless they do nothing but nurse their sorrow, and expect other people to carry both them and it."

Rosalie laughed.

"Yes, one has a great deal to learn," she answered, and took down a book from the shelf.

And hereafter most of her time was given to learning, for the lesson-books had suddenly developed into coherent reading. They were still hard and dull, and many a time she would have given up but for the ever-ringing voice that revived her lagging spirits, and above all the remembrance of that jewel of pure light, the like that she had seen within the temple.

Outside the mist still continued heavy and white, so that it was impossible to find the way about. It hung like a heavy curtain. This continued for a long time, until one day it gradually lightened, and in a week's time the sky was clear again.

"I'm going to dig again," said Rosalie to the frog, laughing. "I feel I am intended to. The ground is soft, and though my eagerness has gone, I still can work when there is opportunity."

And so in the same way she unbedded another stone, and though it was smaller than the last, and not of the same worth by any means, it had its merits, and one pure flash in the centre to show it was related to the larger one. Having given it into the Governor's hands, she returned to her own dwelling, and waited some short time.

But one day as she was going round the plantation, holding a book and reading, with the frog hopping by her side, she was startled to hear someone calling over the gateway, "Good morning, Rosalie!" and looking, she beheld Billy standing there, his arms folded over it, and his face all laughing, as was usual when he came.

"Good morning!" said she, and her eyes brightened at such a change in the day's programme.

"I've brought you bad news."

"Ah! then don't repeat it. I know already what it is," and Rosalie sighed.

"You know, I don't think you're ever going to get out of this little paddock," said he.

"I don't think so myself. Soon I shall be getting past breaking in."

"How do you like digging?"

"Oh, I've taken to it fairly well, thanks to my little friend Croaker here. I regard myself as a worm, and feel lowly contentment. Many a time I have thought myself dead and the sun set."

"You must be very wretched to wish yourself dead."

"Yes, the day is intensely long."

"The worm will develop."

"With a bruised head?"

"It's imagination! A second miracle, and the worm becomes a serpent."

"I would much rather remain as I am. The worm is harmless—the serpent dangerous; the one a little use—the other useless."

"And you from Lucifram!"

"Ah! your mind was fixed on one particular Serpent. Defend me from it."

"You don't look much older, Rosalie, for all your work."

"But you were tall before, and now you're taller. You actually seem older than I, and when first I saw you I reckoned you quite ten years younger."

"Well, you've been burrowing in the ground. I've been advancing. It makes all the difference. What effect has my news had upon you?" he continued.

"Oh! for a change it has made me angry."

"Has the worm turned?"

"I believe it has been so long in a state of constant wriggle that one turn more or less makes little difference."

"Suppose you leave your unprofitable trade, and come away?"

She took two steps forward with a thankful heart, and then a great stubbornness rose within her. She shook her head.

"I won't go yet," she said. "It would be giving up too early. I have pleased God, and by God's grace I'll please man, and if man is not to be pleased by God's grace, what is it that can please him?"

"That is a question for my father. I should not like to say. What do you intend to do here now?"

"Dig again. Begin today. There is no frost, and the ground is soft and loose."

"Is that the message I'm to return?"

"I can think of no other. It was good of you to bring the news to me."

"I thought it very ill. I never delivered an unpleasant message in my life before, and did it just for practice. I had much rather have told you the other thing."

"Your face was very expressive of sorrow when you came to me."

"I'm glad. I imagined my countenance was too smiling."

She laughed.

"Never look sad on my account. I have no wish to forfeit your company for a sad mask. Indeed, I counted it a very great kindness your coming to me at all."

"Truly, Rosalie, you are improving. I think you must be growing older."

"I've forgotten my age. It's a thing women never remember. Years were a form of imaginative punishment invented by the devil. Some folks are sensitive about them."

"When you have finished this, will you bring it to my father?"

"Most certainly; who else could I take it to?"

"He has brought you little luck."

"It's a word I should never use in connection with him."

"Well, I will leave you, and may you be prosperous. I don't know what else I can say, except that you will forgive me for the news I brought."

So saying, he turned about, and went away again.

And the old work began once more.

CHAPTER XX

A SIMPLE CONVERSATION

One day, when Rosalie had about completed the stone she was engaged upon, the Governor sent for her, by the frog.

"And I think," said Brightcoat, for Rosalie had changed its name, not liking Croaker, "that it would not be at all a bad plan for us to look and see if there are any new clothes anywhere about. This old dress you are wearing is most worn and shabby."

"There are none," said she. "I have looked many a time, and have never found anything except the coarse brown apron I wear to protect my dress from the soil."

"Well, there's a time, and not a time, for looking for things. Suppose we look in the little wardrobe together now. If you stay dinner with the Governor, you must be fairly suitably dressed for it."

And what was Rosalie's surprise, on looking in the diminutive dress-closet, to find a pretty dress of softest silk, white and apple green, just ready made to fit her figure, and everything besides to match, even to silken stockings and pretty slippers, and a cluster of red and golden leaves upon the dressing-table, as simple and pretty as the rest.

Rosalie, from feeling old as the hills, suddenly felt young as a blue-bell blowing on an early summer morning.

"Oh, Brightcoat! I never felt so happy in my life. To get rid of this old black and red thing! Why, that in itself is Paradise. But to wear these! It's past belief. Now, if you were me, how would you wear your hair—high or low? Which do you think suits me?"

"I say in that loose bundle at the back you used to wear when you first came to us."

"The way Mariana did it."

"Was it?"

"Yes. Oh, dear, dear! I'm afraid I shan't do it a bit nicely. When you try to do your hair nicely it always looks hideous; have you ever noticed that?"

"No; you see I haven't got any."

"Of course not! My dress is almost the exact colours of your skin. Have you noticed it?"

"Yes. My master said the colours were chosen out of compliment to me."

"How delightful! Frog green! It's quite an innovation in fashions, and a very pretty one."

Brightcoat's eyes sparkled with pleasure at this little bit of innocent flattery, and if it showed vanity, vanity of a sort is a very delightful thing.

So Rosalie dressed with fluttering happiness and eager haste.

"Your hair doesn't look a bit as if you'd taken pains with it," said the frog from the bed, where it was sitting.

"What do you mean?" she asked, with sudden alarm.

"It's very becoming."

"I'd rather your flattery was a little less open. I know you mean well, but it's embarrassing to have one's defects spoken of so charmingly."

By this time the dressing was completed, and in the eyes of her simple companion no one had ever looked more lovely.

"You must come too, Brightcoat. I shouldn't think of leaving you here alone. Besides, you are always welcome at the house, and I am only there on suffrage. If I behave badly I must go. It's a very terrible thing that, when you think about it. Enough to make me tremble and shake all over."

So the frog jumped lightly from the bed on to her shoulder, and made a most delightful ornament.

As they walked across the garden to the house the nightingales were singing in the soft still air of night.

The Governor, who was walking on the terrace, greeted his guests, and they passed into the house, which was all brilliantly lit to receive them.

"This is your last night with us, so I have asked you here to dine with me," said the old man.

"My last night?" Her voice was full of wonder and sadness.

"You surely will not be sorry to leave the soil?"

"Ah! but you and Brightcoat are here. I would much rather stay. Besides, my heart is in the garden yet, and here with the jewels that I brought to you. Oh, you have been my friend; and there is none other. Where else can I go? Let me still live in the little hut, with the freedom I have bought tonight."

But he shook his head and smiled as they sat down to dinner just alone.

"You imagine you have become attached to the hut. But there are other and better places, believe me."

"And does the way back lead as I came?"

"Pretty much so, I believe."

"Into Marble House, with its shadows and cobwebs. I'm sure I daren't go."

"Perhaps it has become less shadowy since you were there. There is spring cleaning, you know, in all well-regulated houses."

"But it is not well regulated. There is one part all moths and mildew, and people live in it, or rather work there. I know, for Mariana does. How I should love to see her once again! And upstairs it is wretchedly lit. In fact,

Mr. Barringcourt's private room was the only human-looking place I ever saw there. But perhaps by now he has a wife. But she'll need great strength of mind to get the necessary repairs done, I'm thinking. He seemed as if he would be very conservative, except where things affected his own comfort."

"I don't think he's got a wife yet," said the Governor.

When they had finished the meal, and the frog had had its full share of the dainties that were to its taste, the Governor led the way to his own room, and placing a chair for Rosalie near the fire, he drew his own to the other side of the fireplace and sat down.

"Do you object to smoke?" he asked.

"Oh, no! Uncle had a pipe that he had smoked for years and years and years. And the night before he died he let it fall, and it broke. I remember how sad he looked at the time—and perhaps there was more in it than just the breaking of the pipe, for he said nothing, but that he could soon get a new one. And if all things had been right I think it would have angered him."

"You were greatly attached to your uncle?"

"Oh, yes! I loved them both. No one could have been kinder to me than they."

"And now, when you go back to Lucifram, you have neither friend nor relation to go to."

"No. Must I indeed go?"

"I see no other way for it. But there are some friends of mine live there, or friends of someone that I know. They will fill, to the best of their ability, the old place."

"How do you know? They might take the utterest distaste to me on first sight, and then what would happen?"

"They are not people of prejudice."

"I wish I were not."

"You fear, then, you may take a dislike to them?"

"Oh, no! I'm always trying to get the better of my feelings, because they are so often wrong."

"Well," said he, "second thoughts are best. I give you the benefit of a second opinion upon most things."

"But there is where I fear to go back to Lucifram. It's a place where one is so terribly misjudged, and it's a place, too, where you have just the knack of saying the things you wished unsaid."

"Well, then, choose. Will you go back, or will you stay?"

But Rosalie, on second thoughts, made answer:

"You know best, and it is for you to choose. Somehow, I could not think to doubt or question what you say; and after all, why should one bother about tomorrow, if one does one's duty today."

"And I have promised you friends in the place of your aunt and uncle."

"Yes; but I thought Mr. Barringcourt might have a word to say about that."

"Well, we're all bound to trust the future to a certain extent. There is no telling; on second acquaintance he might prove kinder."

"When must I go?"

"Tomorrow, in the early morning. The journey takes a day; it will be dark before you reach your journey's end, for autumn is far advanced with them."

Here the frog, who had so far sat quiet on the hearthrug, put in a word.

"It will be very lonely going back to Lucifram alone. My advice and companionship might be of some little help occasionally."

"Oh, yes!" cried Rosalie eagerly. "You have been such a faithful and loving friend to me, that your brightness would dispel half the gloom, I'm sure it would."

Both of them turned their eyes toward the Governor to gain his opinion.

"You bear a charmed life, little frog," said he, "so I don't see what harm or inconvenience can happen to you. In fact, I think the outing would be a pleasant trip for you, and add something to your store of knowledge."

"You don't think," said Rosalie anxiously, for second thoughts were beginning to intrude themselves, "that any harm could come of it. I remember Mr. Barringcourt saying something about vivisection once. It would be terrible if anything happened, and I was powerless to prevent it."

"I don't think anything could happen," replied the Governor. "A frog that has once jumped from Lucifram successfully to heaven could, on a pinch, repeat the process with much less inconvenience."

And soon after this the interview and evening ended.

CHAPTER XXI

A MAN WHO STOOD ON HIS HEAD,
ACCORDING TO LUCIFRAM

The two wanderers were standing once more in the cold, inhospitable streets of Lucifram. But they were not alone. A tall lady descending from her carriage had noticed the forlorn Rosalie, and pitying her tired condition had taken her within her house, promising her one night's shelter at least. It may be simply stated to whom Rosalie in this hour of need had come. In this particular house in Lime Tree Square of the chief city of Lucifram there lived a very great painter and his sister. In his early youth he had had a hard struggle, not so much because he was poor, but because he was original. Now, for a man to have his own ideas in the city of Lucifram was to set all the dogs barking, the mob stone-flinging, and the Riot Act fluttering.

It was very strange, but thousands of years of experience had taught little or nothing.

The painter, as has been said, had his own ideas, and so at first they said he was an upstart, and very justly laughed at him. But laughter never yet cured madness or stamped out the truth, and as the painter seemed to be giving surreptitious invisible spiritual bites all round him, and setting the infection flying, it was recognised at last there must be some truth in his madness, and to a certain extent they let him be.

And so from being badly abused the painter at last sprung into fame. He was a shy and reserved man, and somewhat irritable in his temper. But that was because his temperament and his work were of a kind that wear the nerves unevenly. But still when he liked he could be very charming, even Lucifram admitted that, and for the hidden virtues, they left those with a shrug to God the Serpent.

And so in comparative early middle age he found himself the recipient of a knighthood; that is, he received a title very similar to "Sir"—and for simplicity we will call it such. Some spiteful people said this was on account of his good looks, but as it was a man sovereign who gave him the title, it's hard to see what that could have to do with it. Now, Sir John himself had little belief in titles, but his sister had great belief in *him*, and though herself the simplest of plain women, she had ambitions so far as he was concerned.

"A title's an empty thing," said he, looking at her in his serious, thought-ful way.

"No one knows it better than I," she answered, in her downright one. "And if you hadn't the real thing to outshine it, I'd hate to see it offered to you. But it's a courtesy you owe to the world in return for its courtesy. If you don't accept it, you are churlish. Besides, I always think it's the greatest honour that can befal a sovereign, to confer distinction upon genius, so that, even on a royal consideration, I think you ought to accept."

And so plain John Crokerly became Sir John, and was just the same be-fore and after—neither more or less brilliant or imposing.

From being poor he became rich. He never married, but continued hap-pily in the society of his one unmarried sister. The affection and understand-ing were very mutual, and perfectly to the contentment of both.

On this particular night Miss Crokerly entered her brother's presence with some trepidation. After all, she had a reputation for common sense, though, like him, maybe a little eccentric, and the brightness of the frog and the prettiness of Rosalie's face hardly seemed pretext enough on second thoughts for inviting her into the house.

"John," said she, betraying no misgiving in her voice, as she closed the door, "I've invited a young girl from the country, who is lost, to come in and shelter for the night."

"What's her name?" and he looked up over the top of the paper which he was reading, for daylight was precious just then, and morning meals too hasty to allow of much newspaper indulgence during them.

"I don't know; she is a perfect stranger to me. I came to see if you ap-proved."

"It won't matter to me. I shan't see her," he answered.

"Of course not." Then, after a pause: "You think I'm not running any risks by bringing her in?"

"I don't know. You can't very well turn her out again now you've done it. Small-pox is pretty prevalent, to be sure. Did you make particular inquiries if she'd been successfully vaccinated?"

"You have no objection to what I've done?"

"Not after you've done it," and he relapsed once more behind the paper.

But Miss Crokerly, after turning to the door, looked round again.

"I should like you to see her," she said, for her, very hesitatingly.

"In the morning," he answered.

"In the morning you will have less time and inclination than now."

"But what purpose should I serve in going to look at her? Is she different from the generality of country folk?"

"I don't know," she replied slowly; "but I think she is much prettier. And she has with her a frog with the most brilliant colour I ever saw."

At this he laughed. "My curiosity is not excited in the least," he answered.

"But mine *is*," she said, with a return to her decided manner; "and you really must come, if but to see the frog. It is a marvel."

"Bring it here to me, then."

"Certainly not, unless I bring her too. You are growing terribly lazy, Jack."

"Well, come along," he said impatiently. "Only please don't drag me into any more of your charitable whims, frogs or no frogs."

"Of course not. This is an exception. You might ask her her name and address. I quite forgot to do so."

So together they went into the hall where Rosalie still sat. The frog, with a wisdom born of its dead vanity, had again settled itself conspicuously to attract attention on her shoulder.

Rosalie's pale face and large bright eyes also possessed a peculiar beauty and fascination, although she was tired with the journey and sick from want of food.

Now, Sir John's heart was as kind as that of his sister, and, moreover, he had a great admiration for woman when her beauty was of that delicate yet exquisite type that approaches the ideal, and contains little of the heaviness or substantiality of flesh. As they both came toward her, Rosalie rose, and her movements were so quiet, graceful, and well-bred, that one might have thought the frog's spirit of wishing to do the correct thing for the sake of admiration had settled upon her. All his irritability, which was not of a very lasting or savage kind, vanished.

"You have a delightful little companion there," said he pleasantly, looking at the frog.

"Yes."

"It is rather an uncommon kind of pet," put in Miss Crokerly; "and how brilliant! Is it real, or some highly-polished stone?"

Rosalie laughed softly.

"Oh! it is real enough, and can jump prodigiously." And she put her hand up caressingly to its coat.

"And you," said Sir John—"you look tired. What part of the country have you come from to get lost in the city?"

"I have been walking all day. I came from a little hut and plantation beyond the forest."

At this the painter looked at his sister and she at him. For outside this city of Lucifram there was a tremendous forest full of jungles, and only the pure in spirit and those led by a light of superhuman brightness could pass through it.

"And did you pass through the forest unhurt?" he asked.

"Yes. We were pleasant company to each other. But I lost one of my garden clogs. I think that was very unfortunate, because I never missed it till it was too late to turn back."

She spoke evidently without any knowledge of the terrors of the forest. But whatever reticence she showed about her journey was from now respected by them.

"Then you have no home to return to?" said Miss Crokerly, after a pause, during which she had revolved things in her mind.

"No," said Rosalie simply, and her wistful eyes filled with anxiety and shadow.

"You must spend the night here, then, as I said before, and in the morning we will arrange things. Come with me."

Then Sir John shook hands with her in that grave, kind way of his, and wished her good-night, and then went back to his easy-chair and paper.

He himself knew something of the terrors and blackness of the forest. It had been responsible for some of his best work. But he was a man whose hair was turning grey, and this girl, whose name, by the way, he had forgotten to ask, appeared so very young. He was interested in, and felt sorry for her, and yet could scarcely credit the tale that she had come hither from the forest; on second thoughts it seemed so utterly improbable.

Yet where else anywhere upon Lucifram could that brilliant frog have come from—or Rosalie's expressive, shining eyes?

So when his sister came back later in the evening, he said:

"I think, for the present, at any rate, we must keep her. Providence has sent her to us, and converts a duty into pleasure."

"Yes, indeed. She has had supper and gone to bed. And strange to say," she continued reflectively, "although for the last twenty-five years I have been trying to cure myself of impulsiveness as one of my besetting sins, and was just thinking as I drove home tonight that at last I had quite succeeded, yet now I cannot help loving her at sight, as much," she added softly, "as if she were my own sister."

"That is fortunate for her," replied he. "She appears so destitute."

"And I don't doubt fortunate for me. It is not often one receives a traveller from the forest."

"You have ascertained, then, that she really came from there?"

"Of course! I ascertained it by attending simply to her voice and manner. One needs no other guarantees."

"Well, I can but hope your friendship stands the test of time. For myself, I can only say, as usual, I think you showed true discernment in admitting her to shelter for the night, though at first, to speak truthfully, I must admit your conduct greatly astonished me. What is her name?"

"Rosalie Paleaf."

CHAPTER XXII

A NEW LEASE OF LIFE

When Rosalie awoke next morning, it was in a comfortable modern bedroom, furnished with regard to health, and a conception of beauty thrown in.

For the first time truly in her life and experience she awoke with a light heart, and such unusual brightness of spirits that she seemed at last, for the time at least, to have realised the pleasure and joy of simply being alive. The tired sickness of the night before had entirely vanished.

The sky overhead was blue and bright, the air cold. Nothing could have been more promising for a new entry into an old world.

Brightcoat, who had spent the night on the marble washing-stand, now took recreation in the basin of water Rosalie poured for him, whilst she, being less cold-blooded, as it were, was nothing loath to accept the warm water that was brought for her.

But this part of the day's programme being finished, Rosalie turned disconsolately to her dress.

"It's so shabby and short," said she.

"Well, look amongst your luggage," said Brightcoat, who was engaged in jumping for further recreation over all the articles on the washstand.

"My luggage," said she, looking towards the little hand-bag. "It can't be in there."

"No harm in looking," said the frog, and jumped clean over the water-jug, and then sat as still as if jumping were the last thing it would ever think of doing.

Rosalie laughed, and then opened the bag and looked.

There was packed into that little leather hand-bag everything to make a perfect though not extravagant outfit. A coat and skirt that no fashionable tailor would be ashamed to turn out, a pretty, simple dress for household wear, the evening dress which she had worn the other night, slippers, gloves, and all accessories. Last but not least, there was a little box of jewellery in perfect taste and finish.

"Oh, Brightcoat, look, look!" she cried, as one after the other she drew out those new delights. "Who can have done it? I don't think it could have been the Governor. I'm sure he never bothered much about one's clothes."

And then the frog's voice fell to a reverent whisper, so it almost seemed.

"I once saw the Governor's wife pack a Christmas box for a little boy a long way off at school, and it was quite miraculous."

"Was he her son?"

"Oh, no! At least, not exactly her son. But she was very fond of him. She forgot nothing, and sent it in such little room that no one thought she was sending anything much at all."

"You have seen her, then?"

"Yes, I've seen her; and never anything more absolutely beautiful. It was she who put her tender, gentle hand upon me when first I came all dead and dull and stunned from Lucifram, and by her radiating brightness changed my poor coat to brilliancy. But have you turned out all the contents of your bag?"

"Yes. No. Here are two letters. One for me and one to Sir—John—Crokerly. Who's he, I wonder?"

"The man who lives here," said the frog, who was primitive, and believed in calling men men, and women women, with no thought of discourtesy, but from lack of education in those matters.

"The gentleman," said Rosalie. "He's sure to be a gentleman if he has a title. But how do you know his name?"

"Well, I heard someone speak of the—the lady last night as Miss Crokerly, and they said something about Sir John. And putting two and two together, I've come to the conclusion it is he who lives here."

"How strange!"

"Stranger things have happened. Have you read your letter?"

"No," and she broke open the envelope. At first she read it seriously, then burst out laughing.

"What is it?" asked Brightcoat eagerly, who, having long ago got over the seriousness of vanity, could enjoy a joke.

"Oh, this letter! It's been written in a kind of rhyme, and I'm sure I don't know what it means. It seems utter nonsense."

"If it's not very private, and you read it aloud, I might be able to help you," the frog replied courteously.

"Well, listen. There is no address. It begins:

"The road of Life
Is the path to my wife.
Its struggles and turmoils ended—
Horses so white they dazzle the sun,
A car of dazzling glory spun,
Driver all fearless of peril.
From depth to height the race is run,
The equipage right royal.
The meet a queen come decked as a queen

In shining garments past satin,
With pearl-sewn tears to laughter changed
And heart-blood drops to jewels.
A thousand colours of rainbow light
The trophies of many a hard-won fight,
Before pale faith was lost in sight
And eyes cease weeping on trial.
A driver find,
A purse well lined,
A gate and road all open.
And horses six,
To avoid the Styx,
Yet climb the invisible mountain. '

There now, Brightcoat, what do you think of that? Can you fathom it? I think it's a very charming puzzle."

"Who do you think wrote it?"

"Why, the Governor! And out of compliment to his wife I feel bound somehow or other to—to endeavour to accomplish the task set me."

"Horses so white they dazzle the sun, and six of them," said Brightcoat thoughtfully. "Do you think you'll ever manage it?"

"I don't know. But there's no harm in trying." And she laughed again, and was most becomingly dressed in no time.

Then together, the frog taking its accustomed place upon her shoulder, they descended the staircase.

In the hall Miss Crokerly and her brother stood talking, he in a thick overcoat ready for going out.

Rosalie approached and handed her letter to him, which he received kindly, though with some surprise.

"I found it in my bag," said she, "and had no idea it was there. I think you are Sir John?"

"Yes."

After he had read the letter enclosed, he handed it to his sister. She read it with evident interest, then returned it to him, and holding out her hand to the new-comer, said:

"We're very pleased to receive you, Rosalie. And as long as you care to stay with us you will be welcome, apart from any considerations except those of friendship."

"I'm afraid I'm too poor to accept your hospitality for a longer time than it takes me to find work."

"Poor? The letter to my brother is from the wealthiest banker of our acquaintance, the safest and surest. And his statement proves you anything but poor."

Then Rosalie remembered the jewels she had found, and remained silent. She had prized them very much and loved them, and now she understood their value, in one of those flashes of perception that occasionally comes to all of us.

After that Sir John went away, and Miss Crokerly led the way into the dining-room, where breakfast was laid for Rosalie only, as the others had long since had theirs.

And that day passed away as healthily and normally as Rosalie could wish, and a morning's shopping was quite a pleasant recreation to her, and in fact the first of its kind she had ever indulged in in her life.

For to be dumb is a great drawback, as most of us can understand, and curtails most pleasures, little or big.

And then for tea some very interesting people dropped in, or so Rosalie found them, and altogether the weary, dead, dull, lonely level of life seemed to have vanished.

CHAPTER XXIII

THE SCANDAL OF THE TEMPLE

Now it chanced one night that Miss Crokerly wrote a letter after the bag had gone to post, and Rosalie, seeing that it was dry and frosty, had offered to take it to the pillar-box, which was a few minutes' walk away at the end of the next square. It was so pleasant out of doors that she took the longest way, and having slipped the letter in the box, prepared to take the same road back.

On turning a corner, her attention was attracted by someone coming towards her, scarcely fifty yards away, reading a letter, so it seemed to her, with apparently no more trouble than if it had been daylight. But that fact, though it afterwards occurred to her, was forgotten in the shock of recognising that here was Mr. Barringcourt.

Rosalie stood still under the gas-lamp, unable to move, paralysed with fear. An instinct of safety should have made her move along, but here she stood, courting observation by standing directly in the path, with big wide eyes fixed upon his face. Just then he looked up with bent brows and eyes. They came directly in contact with Rosalie's white and terrified face. In an instant his abstracted air vanished, and a very present alertness took the place of his thoughts. Like a flash of lightning Rosalie turned and sped the near way home, reaching the safety of the doorstep in less than three minutes. She did not stop to breathe till safe within the friendly shelter of the hall, where something told her to regain a little composure, at any rate, before appearing before Miss Crokerly. She went upstairs and removed her hat and the rich evening wrap she had drawn round her, sat down for a little while to recover her breath, and then descended to the drawing-room again.

Miss Crokerly, intent upon some fine needlework, did not look up on her entrance; but Rosalie had one friend whose eyes were sharper and perceptions more acute. The frog, whom she had left sitting upon the timepiece, looked across at her. Rosalie gained assurance from that glance.

She sat down without any remark, and took up the book she had been reading, making some pretence of continuing her occupation as before.

"I've heard a rumour," said Miss Crokerly presently, "that the Great High Priest is resigning."

"Who is he?" asked Rosalie absently.

"The Great High Priest of the Serpent," continued Miss Crokerly. "I can scarcely credit it, though. He is barely seventy-two. And he can have no reason for it either. It's an office never vacated till death. Dotage doesn't count."

"Maybe he is more conscientious than most," said Rosalie, rousing herself from her own line of thought to take an interest in the conversation.

"I don't know, I'm sure. There have been whispers of it for the last three years. I think he has enemies."

"I suppose all men in prominent positions have."

"Yes; but there are enemies and enemies. Now my opinion of the Great High Priest is that he has hidden enemies, or perhaps he chances to be merely unfortunate."

"What do you mean?" asked Rosalie, beginning to be interested in the conversation.

"Well, it began with a scandal. A rumour got about that he had admitted a woman to see the Serpent, and some said such conduct was nothing short of blasphemous. But that was either hushed up or contradicted. Contradicted, I think, and then hushed up."

"Would it be such a terrible thing for a woman to see the Serpent?" Miss Crokerly smiled.

"Well, there's a great deal of superstition and ignorance mixed up with our religion, as all simple and right-minded people can see. But it grows in suitable soil, so it's strong and holds well together."

"And did it not please the people that a woman had seen the Serpent?"

"Naturally not, after thousands of years of prejudice. Some of the best— by that I mean the *narrowest*—women I know withdrew their support (they were extremely wealthy) from the temple for some months during the scandal. They said they felt the brightness of the Serpent had been sullied."

"Absurd!" said Rosalie; and the blood began to course a little quicker through her veins from indignation.

"Well," said Miss Crokerly slowly, "one can't judge quickly. Of course you know the Great High Priest is not allowed to have a wife. She is separated from him the day he takes up office, and if he did admit a woman from idle curiosity to see the Serpent—well, judged from one point, it was very serious."

"Maybe," said Rosalie, whose tongue was itching to say much more. "But do you think there was any truth in it?"

"Well, yes. A woman's handkerchief with a red rose embroidered in the corner was found upon the altar."

"Never!" said Rosalie, with such a visible jump and accents so sharp that Miss Crokerly looked up, and the frog's eyes grew wide with warning.

"It was so, indeed. My brother had it on good authority. One of the Golden Priests went in that evening to offer the prayer at the New Moon. He found it there. And then this hushed-up scandal followed."

Again Rosalie was silent, why, she could scarcely tell. She recognised the handkerchief, which in after events she had never missed. It was her aunt's birthday gift, with a little silk-embroidered rose in the corner instead of a name.

"But why did the Golden Priest remark upon it?" asked Rosalie.

"That is what I say. And it is that which makes me think the Great High Priest has enemies."

"But such a thing as that, once died down, could not make him resign."

"Perhaps not. But I don't think it ever really did die down. And last year at the 'Feast of White Souls,' after the Fast of Black Ones, as he was coming out from between the curtains to sprinkle white confetti down the temple aisles, a most unfortunate thing occurred. The crimson curtain suddenly tore from the rings and fell, and there behind, to the view of a mixed assembly, shone out the Golden Serpent. I was there myself, having gone to hear the music, for on these occasions it is very fine, and was sitting with my brother quite near to the choir stalls."

"And what did you do?"

"Well, it was very strange, but we all instinctively did the same thing. I took one real good look at the Serpent (and I don't know any woman there who didn't, except those who screamed, and some who fainted, for what, it would be hard to tell), and then, from a sense of what was due to the male part of the congregation, we covered our eyes with our handkerchiefs, and all turning our backs upon the God we worshipped, were led solemnly out, with comparatively little confusion. The service could not continue, and that event has made him the most unpopular man on Lucifram."

"Then," said Rosalie, half laughing, half sarcastically, leaning back in her chair, and looking at the fire, "I should say it would not be a bad idea to introduce a 'Feast of Handkerchiefs' to take the place of the unfortunate White Souls. A handkerchief betrayed one woman and saved the rest. It should receive a place of honour in the temple."

"What a pity he did not take it in that way," said Miss Crokerly. "But I've heard since that the occurrence has depressed him terribly. And the last news is that he is resigning."

"And which of the Golden Priests was it who spread the first report?"

"His name is Alphonso. I know him slightly, but do not care for him. I think him ambitious, and unscrupulous, and narrow-minded. I cannot help but think myself he is the greatest enemy the High Priest has, though there are some who uphold him as the strictest and highest principled man within the Church."

"I dislike him already," said Rosalie impulsively.

The other laughed.

"Well, you will have an opportunity of meeting him tomorrow night at the Sebberens'. He is unmarried, so you may be as charming as you like to him, and no one's heart will break. But for all that he's greatly run after by the women. They regard the Golden Priests and the Great High Priest as demi-gods."

The Golden Priests were those whose rank came next to that of the Great High Priest, and when this latter died his place was always filled from this exclusive body of great men, the wealthiest and most powerful in the Church of Lucifram.

"Oh! that will make me dislike him all the more," said Rosalie. "The men who are run after by women, and the women who are run after by men, are both equally detestable. I mean, of course, in excess."

"But that is fascination."

"I prefer the fascination that is clever enough to captivate its own sex."

"Well, men admire him in an intellectual capacity."

"A general favourite? Most insipid!"

"Really, Rosalie!" said Miss Crokerly, and she laughed.

"You cannot expect me to love him. A man should always be loyal to his superior."

"Well, of course, I am only giving you my own opinion. And you must not repeat it on any account; because it is not generally believed or certain that he might be prompted by motives of ambition to make known the incident of the handkerchief."

"I hope that if the High Priest does resign someone less self-seeking takes his place."

"Than Golden Priest Alphonso? But that is scarcely likely. He has Mr. Barringcourt for his great friend, and—What is the matter, Rosalie? Your cheeks are all aflame."

"Oh! I—I—I've had springes of toothache all day, and the sudden pain makes me flush. I'm all right now. What were you saying?"

"Alphonso is sure to succeed to the High Priestship sooner or later. He has much influence on his side—the Prime Minister, and Lord High All Superior for public and official friends, and Mr. Barringcourt, whom I just mentioned, who has great influence in outside circles, and more money apparently than even poor Geoffrey Todbrook had. Now there's a man for you to dislike cordially on the grounds of general favouritism. The women idolise him, and men will hear no wrong of him."

"And what kind of a life does he lead? Is he a good man?" asked Rosalie, leaning forward and looking across at her.

"I don't know. My brother thinks greatly of him, and so do I. But it's hard to tell who's good and who's bad when you come to private life. There are so many things for and against it."

"Of course."

"Still, I think as rich men go, who are young and unfettered by anything, he must be fairly good. I don't remember ever hearing anything against him.

And I know he has carried out all Geoffrey Todbrook's wishes with regard to charities to the letter."

"Is he executor?"

"Yes."

"Then it would be surprising if he fell short of his duties, would it not?"

"Perhaps so. I expect he too will be at the Sebberens' tomorrow night But if you have any conversation with Mr. Barringcourt at all, you cannot choose but like him."

"Is his temper unfailingly pleasant, then?"

"No; it isn't altogether that. I have known him very absent and off-hand. But I suppose people occasionally find that rather pleasant in a world of suavity and insincerity."

"I don't agree with you. I'd rather have people unfailingly suave. It spares a great deal of friction."

"What has upset you, Rosalie? You are most argumentative tonight."

"I expect you are spoiling me, and I've never been accustomed to it. You should treat me with stern severity, and you would find me improve wonderfully."

"And you just preaching unfailing suavity."

"Oh! I preach by the Creed of Contrary."

But Rosalie's argumentative mood sprang really from the irritation that followed on the evening's escapade.

In a cooler moment, and on reflection, she was not over and above proud of the way in which she had fled so precipitately before the enemy. And yet what was there to be done? To have stood still was to have hazarded, so Rosalie thought, far more than she had any intention of hazarding. She registered a mental vow never to go out at night alone again, and wished, oh! wished most intensely, that nothing had tempted her out that night. In her own room the frog broke the silence by saying:

"You seem very upset tonight."

"Yes. I—I met Mr. Barringcourt, and I ran away."

"What made you run?"

"I was frightened of him."

"What harm could he work you?"

"Oh! he might have persuaded me in a moment of weakness I owed him a debt of gratitude."

"And yet you have the kiss of freedom on your brow."

"Yes; but like most abstract things, it sank before the concrete."

"You'll get over it by the morning. Sleep upon it."

"I should have had you with me. You have far less fear than I. The farther off the episodes of Marble House become the more I dread them. They seemed all right, and yet they were all wrong."

"Miss Crokerly said you would probably meet Mr. Barringcourt tomorrow night."

"Yes, I know. And it was only this morning I congratulated myself he was not in her set, and that I should never be likely to meet him."

"If you meet Mr. Barringcourt tomorrow night, you won't run away—will you?"

"No; because it will be light, and there will be people about, and I shall have you. No, I won't run away in any case. But you will come with me?"

"Of course! I should have very much enjoyed the fresh air tonight; but you did not invite me."

"I'm sorry. But I've paid the penalty of my negligence; from henceforth you must never leave me."

"What dress do you intend to wear tomorrow night?"

"The one I have worn all along."

"It's as shabby as if you'd been digging in it. But the morning may bring you another."

"I hope it may not be very heavy, in case I should have to depend on my heels again."

CHAPTER XXIV

AT THE SEBBERENS'

The Sebberens were people who indulged greatly in private theatricals and other sorts of entertainment. With the amateur they included the professional, and in between the acts, songs and recitations were contributed by the latter.

Mr. Sebberen had been engaged in pork, and had made enough money thereby to make the pig respected—as an investment, anyway. He married a waitress in a restaurant, who was neither more nor less charming and handsome than most of her class. She had ambitions, and was young.

But for ten long years they had no children, and never a scrap of the pig was wasted. And those ten years were years of increase. Then to put spirit to an ambition somewhat sordid, a little daughter was born. Both parents were beside themselves with joy. It is not everyone who can manage so much, after breeding nothing but gold or pork, and so they felt. It's a common thing to be a mother after a lapse of one year, but after ten! they grew proud on the strength of it.

And another ten years had trebled the ample fortune, nay, more than trebled it, and Mr. Sebberen, a comparatively young man—scarce forty—found himself with a daughter only ten years old.

Another decade saw her twenty, he in the prime of life, her mother too. "Sebberen's Pork" was of world-wide fame. The king and the chief prince had it on their breakfast tables; the poor still bought the sausages, and doctors still evinced a weakness for onions, milk, and tripe.

No one would have known, to walk into this grand house, that its occupants once lived behind a little pork shop. For Susiebelle was handsome and clever, and had taught her mother a thing or two, and made great friends at school, not from any particular virtue, but from the glamour of outside show. She had a great deal of the outward semblance of that inward spirit that had made her father what he was. She was shallow and brilliant, and a perfect mimic of the world.

When the world wept, she wept. They called her tender-hearted.

When it laughed, she also laughed. They called her gay.

When in a mood for admiration, she, too, had time for adulation, admired arts and music, knotted her pretty brows at science, and bought rich copies of all the works of fashionable poets. And what was all this for?

Susiebelle at twenty made up her mind to marry, and marry as well as could be. Her father had just had a tremendous stroke of luck in business. She set her mind upon a duke, shooting high to reach as far as fortune favoured.

One year had passed away, and Susiebelle's ambition has not yet been granted. A poor baronet, an insipid, weak-eyed lord; not bad for a beginning, certainly.

And this brings us to tonight, the amateur theatricals, and gay company.

Sir John was under commission to paint the lovely Susiebelle, and had undertaken it with a fine courtesy that made her mother glow with pride to think the great were servants of the—the small. And Sir John would do it successfully after all, for she was pretty enough to appeal to the sense of beauty in any artist, and her parents were over and above willing to pay.

And that is why Sir John went to the party—from motives of conscientiousness. And Miss Crokerly went because she wished to give pleasure to Rosalie. She, an ideal chaperon and friend. And Rosalie went because there was no way out of it.

But Rosalie's dress was in itself that night a thing of beauty. Green, as bright and dazzling a green as the frog's coat, that fitted to her graceful figure as perfectly as the shining scales of a serpent's coils, worked with tiny seed jewels and edgings of gold.

"You look just like the mermaid," said the frog, "your hair is so pale, and your eyes so bright, and your skin so fair, and your lips are as red as coral."

And Rosalie looked in the glass just as once before when comparing herself with Mariana, and laughed again just as then, and clasped her hands.

Then, when she was ready, she went to Miss Crokerly's room, who, on seeing her, uttered an exclamation of surprise.

"What is the matter?" asked Rosalie.

"I believe your frog is a beautifier. Take care no one steals it in the crush tonight. Or perhaps I ought to take the credit to myself. I think I shall. You have improved in appearance since coming here, Rosalie, and tonight you look quite radiant."

"Thank you," and with a sudden touch of impulsiveness Rosalie kissed her. "You are so kind to me that the credit is yours."

When they reached the Sebberens' the large party was assembling in the great drawing-room, which had been changed into a theatre for the occasion. Supper was to follow, but light refreshments were being handed round, and proved very useful to take the chill off the commencement, as it were. And music not too obtrusive helped digestion. Rosalie's heart beat quicker as they entered the brilliantly-lit room, advance and retreat covered by Miss Crokerly and her brother, before and behind.

Just inside the wide doors stood Mrs. Sebberen talking to a grey-haired man; Susiebelle was busy behind the curtain, so could not be in attendance upon the guests.

She greeted Miss Crokerly effusively, stared, as is perfectly compatible with good manners, at Rosalie from head to foot, became effusive to her, and then bestowed the same greeting upon Sir John. There was no doubt about it, she was a happy and genial woman. She evidently considered them among her guests of honour or chief friendship, for in person she conducted them to a line of seats near to the front. She was dressed in rich black satin, and looked handsome enough to be imposing.

On the way she talked much to Miss Crokerly, but looked much at Rosalie, her dress, her face, the curious little animal upon her shoulder.

Beyond a certain interest, Rosalie read nothing in her glance. Then when they were seated, she passed away again, and Rosalie found time to look around. Everything and everybody were very brilliant. And she recognised some of her new acquaintances, but none more intimate. At last she whispered to Miss Crokerly—Sir John had left them for the moment:

"Where is the Golden Priest Alphonso?"

Miss Crokerly's sharp eyes travelled round the assembly.

"He is not here yet," said she. "Of course I don't know, but I expect that he will come. There is Lady Flamington and her husband. Is she not beautiful? but very sad-looking."

"Lady Flamington—Lady Flamington! Oh! where is she?" said Rosalie, in an eager voice.

But just then the lady spoken of, who was sitting some distance to the right a row in front, turned round, and seeing Miss Crokerly, rose and came toward her. Her smile was very pleasant.

"I am deserting my husband for better company," said she. "I dragged him here against his will, low be it spoken, and am paying the penalty in sulks. Your brother is easier to manage, Miss Crokerly."

"The privilege of management is not mine. I am only his sister."

The other shook her head.

"You are too modest. There was never a man yet who governed himself; he couldn't manage it. It ends in sudden death or corpulency. Both are dreadful things."

Miss Crokerly laughed.

"You will perhaps have heard what heavy responsibilities I have taken upon myself lately."

"Yes; I hear you have turned chaperon," and Lady Flamington looked across at Rosalie and smiled as pleasantly as before.

Miss Crokerly introduced them.

"Are you fond of private theatricals?" she asked.

"I've never been to any," replied Rosalie candidly.

"She was an only child, and brought up very strictly," said Miss Crokerly, at which Lady Flamington said "Oh!" and looked toward the door.

She remained sitting by them till the play began, talking with both of them. At last she said to Rosalie:

"Do you know, I have the oddest sensation that I have met you before."

"I don't think so," said Rosalie. "I have a very good memory for faces, and I have never seen you anywhere."

"Perhaps I am mistaken. People often resemble each other so curiously."

But now silence was imposed. The play had begun in earnest, and it was quite interesting enough to retain the attention. When the act was over, a song by a very well-known singer was announced; but before this came off a few late arrivals made their entrance.

"There is the Golden Priest," said Miss Crokerly.

He came in with two more gentleman. He was tall and thin, with a narrow face and black hair. His eyes were deeply set and fixed close together. His nose was long, and his lips very thin and straight. He looked clever; beyond that he was scarcely prepossessing, but he was evidently made much of in that assembly. They gave him a seat upon the very first row. And yet he never ceased to preach that the pig was unclean! It was a canon of the Church.

The play had more fine dresses in it than cleverness or substance, but it was received as warmly as the more deserving performances during the interludes.

Everybody was in high good-humour apparently, and the next day the paper said it was the most successful entertainment and supper party Mrs. Sebberen had ever given, which, coming from such good authority, must have been the truth.

When the temporary curtain had fallen for the last time upon general and good-natured applause, a movement was made toward the supper-room.

They put a little round-headed man with weak eyes to look after Rosalie. He blinked upon her critically, and then smiled. Rosalie did not like him.

However, not being dumb now, she needs must talk to him; never had anyone been more tongue-tied. The coldness of the weather, their only conversation, scarcely matched her conduct to him. The supper-room was brilliant; nothing had been spared that money could buy to please the eye or taste. He forgot her in the contemplation of his food, and she was glad; it gave her time to look about.

The table was long, and everyone apparently was seated at it. There was not a plain-looking woman among the number, so it seemed to her; and many of them were really beautiful. But Lady Flamington possessed a certain individual grace, a coldness and sadness under her exterior charm of manner, that raised her much above the ordinary plane. Sir John was sitting by her, and they were talking pleasantly to one another. She gave one the impression that she could be very fascinating.

But as Rosalie's eyes travelled up the table on the opposite side, she recognised Mr. Barringcourt for the first time that evening, and he was sitting next to Susiebelle.

Susiebelle was evidently in good feather, for everyone had been congratulating her upon her acting, and she was simple-minded enough to believe them, which gave her quite a charm. She was talking to him with great spirit and gaiety, and looked quite handsome enough to make any mother proud. Mr. Barringcourt was listening so politely that his attention seemed to lack interest. When she laughed he smiled; when she smiled he listened gravely; when her face was serious, as it rarely was, he took the opportunity to look around.

On one of those occasions his eye travelled across to where Rosalie sat. No sign of recognition was visible in them, but a little later he looked at her again.

Rosalie was annoyed to find that both times she had been looking at him, and for the future looked discreetly the other way, nay, cultivated the acquaintance of her companion, and found him scarcely as uninteresting as at first she had imagined.

But at last the evening was over, and she standing by Miss Crokerly in the hall, waiting for their carriage.

The coldness of the day had changed to snow, and the ground outside was white; a sight which somehow or other always surprises people when first they see it, however much they may have expected it. Thick white flakes were still falling rapidly. People drew their wraps round them and shivered, or pretended to.

Lady Flamington's carriage drove away as Miss Crokerly and Rosalie reached the top step. Mr. Barringcourt had seen them off, and closed the carriage door. Before moving away himself, he looked up at the steps and saw these two descending. He raised his hat, looking at Miss Crokerly.

"Sir John is not returning home with you?"

"No," she answered anxiously. "He said he preferred to walk; but I'm sure he can have no idea of the state of the night. I have not seen him since before supper-time."

"I'll seek him out and bring him to you; it's a beastly night." And he ran lightly up the steps, whilst they got as quickly under cover as possible.

He was not long away, and returned, bringing Sir John along with him.

"You surely are not walking yourself?" said Miss Crokerly, as he proceeded to close the door for them also.

"Yes. It never occurred to me to order a carriage, and I have neither wife nor sister to be concerned about my getting wet."

"Then," said she decidedly, "you must come with us. I noticed as you went up the steps your shoes are not at all suitable to the night."

It seemed almost as if he would decline, then suddenly he said "Thank you," and stepped in beside Sir John, and they were off.

Now, the frog was so bright that the carriage was quite pleasantly lit, for it had crept out from beneath Rosalie's wraps to its accustomed place.

Miss Crokerly then introduced him to Rosalie; but as he showed no signs of recognition, neither did she, but leant back in her corner and listened to the conversation.

"What did you think of the theatricals?" asked Miss Crokerly.

"I did not arrive in time for them. The secretary of Todbrook's Home for Deaf and Dumb came to see me about a Christmas treat for them. For myself, I can imagine no treat that would appeal to incurables. But he has faith in turkey, and I think he said plum-pudding."

"It must be a terrible thing to be afflicted with either defect. What else are you going to do for them?"

"I don't know, I'm sure. I said I'd call to see him in the morning."

"Oh! you should have a Christmas tree, and a cinematograph, and take them all to the Pantomime to see the transformation scenes," said Rosalie.

And she sat up again, and her eyes were very big and bright, because the subject was especially interesting to her. The other three looked at her.

"Are you a philanthropist?" asked Mr. Barringcourt, with a vein of coldness running in his words, in direct opposition to her heat.

She laughed.

"No; but I was told you were," and leant back in her seat, and evidently felt safe enough to betray no outward fear.

"I was speaking last night about your exertions on behalf of the deaf and dumb," said Miss Crokerly, in explanation, recognising, without understanding it, the tone in each of their voices.

"You were naturally prepossessed in my favour then," and he looked at Rosalie again, speaking in a voice not free from sarcasm.

"No. I simply recognised that you were doing your duty."

"Which you must admit is the hardest of all things."

"I take your word for it. From today I honour you as a martyr. I was not prepossessed in your favour at all. Forgive me for my stupidity."

Rosalie's voice was changed from hot to cold. Miss Crokerly heard it with surprise, and a silence must have fallen had not Sir John, whose mind ranged on different topics, put in suddenly:

"I hear that it is quite true the Great High Priest intends to resign office."

"I have heard the same thing," said Mr. Barringcourt. "It is a very unusual occurrence."

"Did you hear the reason of it?" asked Sir John.

"I believe it has something to do with the Feast of White Souls. The episode was rather unfortunate. A great many are in favour of his resignation."

"Might I ask your opinion?" said Sir John.

"Yes. I think the Great High Priest should be above scandal, and he is evidently not."

And he looked at Rosalie, and his eyes were laughing, though his face and voice were as serious as those of a judge.

The old distaste rose in her, as of some dumb thing against a cruel and powerful oppressor. But she said:

"Do you indulge in scandal, Mr. Barringcourt? I thought it was the recreation of idle women."

"Oh, no," he answered, with the coolness of rudeness. "Idle women in these parts are known by the sharpness of their tongues."

"I'm very sorry," she answered, suddenly changing in tone and manner, "but I can't help liking the Great High Priest; and as for Golden Priest Alphonso—I detest him."

"Oh, dear! dear!" said Miss Crokerly, with agitation, laying her hand on Rosalie's knee. "You must not talk like that, Rosalie, indeed, you must not. It is not usual. Remember he is Mr. Barringcourt's friend, and bears an excellent reputation."

But as the carriage drew up, she stopped speaking of necessity.

"You will drive on, will you not?" asked Sir John.

"No, thank you. I'll get out, and borrow whatever Miss Crokerly cares to lend me. I never had a cold in my life. The experience would be new to me."

So he came with them into the house, and seemed in no particular hurry to depart. Rosalie said to him:

"Will you do me a favour, Mr. Barringcourt?"

"To the best of my ability."

"Then give me one good point in the character of your friend."

"Which friend?"

"The Golden Priest."

"He is a man of great integrity."

"What's that?"

"Honour."

"What's that?"

Rosalie's questions were not contemptuous; they were put with a great desire to find out.

He shrugged his shoulders.

"There you have me," he answered. "I'm sure I don't know. The word generally speaks for itself to all but the ignorant."

"Then you cannot defend him on the strength of it?"

"No; he is clever enough to defend himself, I hope. You are wearing a very pretty and uncommon ornament, Miss Paleaf."

"It is not an ornament. It is alive, and one of my dearest friends."

"Such a friend is rather questionable on Lucifram."

"Why?"

"The Serpent has a weakness for frogs. In a natural state they form part of its food."

"My friend has powers of self-defence as well as yours."

"The Serpent has a very big mouth."

"Yes. And is ambitious enough to prefer men to frogs upon occasion."

He laughed, and the conversation changed to general topics.

CHAPTER XXV

THE GOLDEN PRIEST

That night when she and the frog were alone together, Rosalie began the conversation by saying:

"What do you think of Mr. Barringcourt?"

"I like him," said the frog, quite shortly.

"What has prepossessed you?"

"Nothing particularly. But I like him. I'm sorry you were so rude to him." Rosalie flushed. The tone was almost grave enough for a rebuke.

"I? Rude? Oh, Brightcoat, how can you say so? I always try to be polite to him, and it always ends in failure. It is he who is rude to me."

"No," said the frog; "you take no pains to act or to speak sensibly. And to say you detest anyone is absurd, ridiculous, to say nothing of bad manners."

"You've never lived in Marble House, so you can afford to talk. Talk about vivisection! It was Mr. Barringcourt who openly deplored to me there was no such thing in our country. What do you think of that?"

"There are worse things than vivisection," replied the frog. "If it were not for that I should never have been here, or alive now."

"But—" said Rosalie, staring at it.

"Why don't you cultivate a charming manner, Rosalie?"

"I expect I'm not made that way. Are my manners so uncouth?" and her expression was doleful.

"No; but I don't see how you're to get your six horses, chariot, and all the rest, unless you try to be more charming."

"Well, Mr. Barringcourt will never help me that way. You should have seen the look he gave me last night, and then tonight, as if he'd never seen me before. Such folk give me quite a creepy feeling. Besides, talking about horses, his are black. Can't you see he is the exact opposite of what I want? He would do all he could to hinder me. If it were not that once I saw him looking very tired I should detest him too. Oh, how I hate Lucifram! Somehow or other, I never feel at home here," and she sighed.

"And you've got about all it can give you."

"Then I'm like all the rest—ungrateful."

"Rosalie, has it ever struck you you are very pretty?"

"Yes; every now and again it has. But what of that? All the women we saw tonight were pretty. It's the commonest of all things. If I'd a big hook nose now I might appear imposing. But no; even that is common enough today."

After a pause the frog said: "I heard someone say tonight you were the prettiest woman there."

"Please, don't! I'd so much rather you left my personal appearance alone."

But the frog continued:

"It's as well for people to think about these things at times. I know many a lovely woman who has been ruined by thinking too much of her beauty in one way, and too little in another. They know they are beautiful, and that knowledge is all-sufficient to them; their food and recreation, and all in all."

"But I'm not one of those."

"No. I think you might put yours to much more use than you do."

"You speak in puzzles."

"You are not so dull but that with a little consideration you will understand me."

So Rosalie went to bed much sat on by the frog, but maybe profiting, as most of us do, from a little compression and criticism.

Next day everything was sloppy, wet, and dismal. Rain began to fall in the afternoon, and going out, no matter of pleasure on such a day, was not indulged in.

Tea had just been brought in, and Rosalie and Miss Crokerly were preparing to enjoy it alone, when visitors were announced. They were Mr. Barringcourt and the Golden Priest Alphonso.

"I came to return the umbrella, Miss Crokerly, and met the Golden Priest on my way."

"Then you will have tea," said she. "On a wet day you are doubly welcome. No one else has ventured out."

"We are fortunate. Miss Paleaf, allow me to introduce my friend, Golden Priest Alphonso, to you."

And Rosalie, having a severe and cold critic perched upon her shoulder, rose very gracefully and bowed.

"It must have been very important business that brought you out on such a day," said she to him, as they sat down, with charming sympathy.

"Well, I was out begging, and a beggar cannot choose his weather. I was going in search of Mr. Barringcourt for a subscription for a new decorative curtain for the temple."

"In place of the old red one?"

"Exactly. It was old and shabby, despite its richness, and we think it must be rotten. There is every indication that it may give way again, and so we are making all speed with the new one."

"Then you are not superstitious enough to think it gave way before from anything but natural causes?"

He looked at her sharply and narrowly.

"Oh, no," he answered. "One can find a natural cause for everything. Therein lies the greater miracle."

"But how?" said Rosalie, subduing her tongue in deferential attention to the pillar of the Church.

He smiled, as became one of exalted intellect.

"Well, there is nothing like order—cause and effect—to work a lasting miracle. A startling thing has a short life. The rottenness of the curtain was the symbol of something still more rotten. Nothing takes place in a day."

Rosalie's eyes opened innocently, though they were very far from innocent. There is no doubt the frog must have been to blame for it.

"What is still more rotten? But perhaps my questions bore you. I am so inquisitive."

Again he smiled.

"You could never be that. But what is still more rotten is the system that lets old men continue in office after they have proved themselves unfit for it."

Rosalie's eyes betrayed a charming depth of horror at this cold-blooded statement.

"But, sir," said she, "who is to be the judge of their incapacity? And, again, it seems so cruel, and—and—doesn't it make a terrible lot of enemies for you, saying things like that?"

The Golden Priest laughed. The last remark evidently was to some point.

"In the cause of common sense one has no objection to making enemies. And I cannot for the life of me see why the highest position in the land should never be filled by a man till he's nearly in his dotage."

"Oh! it's more restful. Besides, a great and a good man should retain his intellect to his death, however old and feeble he may be."

"Granted! But feebleness is no qualification for an important post. And greatness and goodness should discern its own capacity."

"Is it true, then, that the Great High Priest is resigning?"

"Yes; in a few months."

"He has discernment, then?"

"I think his action is a little too late for that. His plea is ill-health. None of us have heard anything further—not those nearest to him in office."

"And then there will come the general election for his successor?"

(For in Lucifram they chose their highest priests that way. The clergy vote for them.)

"Yes; in a few weeks from now."

"It will be a very distracting time?"

"Scarcely more so than the last year has been."

And so the silent plot of years had worked to a fulfilment, the veil or mask at length being thrown aside. Today was spoken openly what a month ago had been whispered and kept down.

Here the conversation was interrupted by Miss Crokerly.

"Mr. Barringcourt tells me he saw the secretary again this morning, and arranged for all the things you suggested, Rosalie."

"Yes. He has never doubted my judgment before, but I think he must have detected a foreign influence, he looked so dubious."

Rosalie laughed.

"Are they to have force-meat and sausages with the turkey, do you know?" she asked.

"It never occurred to me to ask."

"And you an executor of a will! And never to inquire about the gravy and bread-sauce. It's plain you don't attach enough importance to a Christmas dinner. But if I were you, Mr. Barringcourt, I'd countermand all orders, and give them 3s. 6d. each, and a free day to enjoy themselves anywhere and anyhow, with a night each end, to make a complete sandwich and a delightful holiday."

"You imagine them to be prisoners. On the contrary, those who have friends or relations who care to receive them may have leave from the Home once every month. And for the inmates, you must remember it is no prison that they live in, and they are very happy."

"I suppose so," said Rosalie. "But I always dread those public institutions for defects."

"You are prejudiced," put in the Golden Priest. "They are the greatest blessings in existence. I always regard them as branches of the temple."

"So do I," said Mr. Barringcourt; but the tone was questionable.

"I have the greatest longing to go through Todbrook's Home," said Miss Crokerly. "One hears so much about it. I should like to see the inmates at work."

Rosalie shivered.

"Oh! would you, Miss Crokerly? I can imagine nothing more galling to them than to be watched by strangers."

"But is it such an infliction to them?" asked that lady, turning to Mr. Barringcourt.

"I don't know, I'm sure," said he. "I hardly think so. I think myself it would be better if they had more visitors from the outside world. Lady Flamington is the only lady I have ever taken over the premises."

"I had just left there," said the Golden Priest, "before I met you today. I hear she caught a severe chill last night, and is confined to her room."

"Indeed," said Miss Crokerly; and Mr. Barringcourt and Rosalie looked at each other, from no apparent motive.

When tea was over the two gentlemen rose to go.

"I think," said Mr. Barringcourt, in a lower voice, to Rosalie, as the others were speaking of a special fern which both were rearing—"I think it would not be a bad plan for you to go over the Home with Miss Crokerly. The matron will willingly take you over, and you'll find there are worse things in the world than being deaf and dumb, or even blind."

Then somehow or other they looked at each other, the first time really since the Saturday night. How long ago it seemed now! And each was very curious about the other evidently, for Rosalie's eyes searched his, and his eyes hers, but what conclusion either came to it would be hard to say.

And then she shook hands with the Golden Priest, and the door closed.

"Do you think," said Miss Crokerly, "that Mr. Barringcourt told the Golden Priest your opinion of him, and brought him here today in consequence?"

"No, I don't think so," she replied thoughtfully. "I think Mr. Barringcourt must have recognised the Golden Priest has no sense of humour, and would resent instead of forgiving opinions."

"Your tone proves appearances are deceptive. I thought by your manner you had changed your estimate of him."

Rosalie half shuddered, and stretched her hands to the blaze.

"I was simply carrying out a lesson in obedience. And yet my estimate of him *has* changed. I find him so uninteresting."

"It is the common lot of most of us to be uninteresting."

"Oh, no, indeed. You are interesting; so is Sir John; so was—was—so have been many people I have met—Mr. Barringcourt, for instance. But this man is petrified by ambition. It is eating up his heart and head."

"Well, I am not particularly fond of him myself, as I have told you. Still, I am surprised that with your views you should find Mr. Barringcourt interesting."

Rosalie's brows knitted.

"I don't understand him. I never did understand him. Have you ever met anyone, Miss Crokerly, who at times struck you as being very, very good, and at others almost cruel? And that is how he appears to me."

"But you know so little of him."

"Yes, of course. I forgot. I spoke as if we were almost old acquaintances."

CHAPTER XXVI

CONVERSATION AND A LITTLE PIG-STUFF

After that a short time passed away, during which Rosalie saw much of Mr. Barringcourt and the Golden Priest, though not intimately.

During this time Lady Flamington, young, beautiful, much courted and admired, died. It caused a great sensation at the time, because she had only been ill a week, and the doctor had great hopes of recovery because she was strong. But it was double pneumonia, and whereas many a poor person less well attended to gets well and strong again, she, with all attention, passed away.

Rosalie, though knowing comparatively little of her, was somehow much affected by her death. Sir John went to the funeral, and she was put away in a manner that would have done many a poor person's heart good.

The next morning was bright and frosty, and Rosalie took an early walk in the Park. Walking there, she met Mr. Barringcourt, and as it was daylight, and the frog was with her, she did not beat a retreat. She expected to find him doleful, searched his face for the usual signs, but found nothing. She remembered Mariana's words, and thought there must be truth in them.

"You are out early," he said.

"Yes. I left Miss Crokerly feeding the birds and cleaning the cages. She prefers to do it alone, so I don't offer to help her."

"You are happier with her than you were with me."

"Of course. I was not at all happy with you, Mr. Barringcourt. You knew it."

"I don't think you waited long enough to find out."

"I escaped by the first open door, in case none other should present itself."

"Which door was that?"

"That is my little secret. You must be as charming as charming to me, and I will be sure never to let you know."

He laughed. "Mariana again?"

"Yes, Mariana," said Rosalie, suddenly standing still and looking up at him, for they had walked along together. "How is Mariana? I want to see her again."

"Oh, she is perfectly well, I think," he answered. "But you cannot see her. The guest of Sir John Crokerly cannot fraternise with a housemaid."

"When did you find me a snob?" asked Rosalie. "Of course I can see her. I—I should have written and asked her to call and see me, only things in your house aren't quite on the highest principle."

And Rosalie's nose went one degree higher, and she drew her skirts more severely round her, and moved quite half an inch further away as they walked along.

"What do you mean?"

"Well, the postman would do his part of the work, but I doubt whether Everard would."

"Then, if you don't trust Everard, why not call yourself?"

Rosalie's eyes opened.

"Do you mean to say if I wouldn't trust a letter I should trust myself? How you reason, Mr. Barringcourt."

"You could neither be torn up nor burned."

"No. But it is my firm intention never to enter Marble House again."

"You are the young lady who once said you never had run away, and never intended to."

Her ears began to burn.

"To recall things that are past is mean—and—and abominable."

"I am not recalling things. I merely wish to point out to you people always do the things they say they won't do."

"Do they?" she answered, and turned a pair of mermaid eyes on to his profile, and tried to recall things that he had said.

Under the scrutiny he turned his face to her again, laughing.

"Still the old trick of staring, Rosalie."

"You must be very careful how you speak to me. See, I carry my chaperon in my muff," and she tilted it up and showed the frog sitting there.

"If you had lived two hundred years ago, they'd have called that little animal your familiar spirit, and burnt you as a witch. Where did you get it from?"

"Another secret, Mr. Barringcourt. You must be still more charming, and I'll count twenty every time before I speak. But when may I see Mariana?"

"Mariana has forgotten you."

"Has she married Everard, then?"

"Oh, no! Their friendship is as pleasant as iced milk in summer. If you want to see Mariana, you must come and seek her."

Rosalie bit her lip. "I've told you I won't."

"Why?"

"Because if I came you'd never let me out again."

"You say so, so I should be very ill-mannered if I contradicted you. My road lies this way. Good morning!"

"Mr. Barringcourt."

"Yes," and he turned to find her standing there, with a puzzled and anxious look on her face.

"Would you mind giving me a little advice—telling me what to do, I mean?"

"About what?"

"It's about a handkerchief that was found in the temple, so it seems, some time ago. It belonged to me. I keep wondering ought I to tell, and I don't want to. I would have asked Miss Crokerly, only she knows nothing about it, and might not understand. What would you do if you were me?"

"I'd worry; but being myself, I'd let it pass."

"But it caused a scandal, and did the Great High Priest a great deal of harm."

"Why did you not speak about it at the time?"

"Because I wasn't in Lucifram. I—I—I—You see, I haven't got out of my old habit."

"No," he answered, and raised his hat and turned away again, and spoke with such a short kind of pride, that just the one sharp monosyllable was almost more than Rosalie could stand.

"There now," said she to the frog, as they walked home, she with a burning heart. "Do you like him now? Did I not tell you no one could be nastier?"

"Well," replied Brightcoat, "you ask advice, and only give half the information—not that."

"I see you have conspired against me. If I told him the story of the Governor, and how I met with you, he would only laugh and say I was dreaming."

"You shouldn't stammer when you're speaking. People always misconstrue it, and give it more meaning than it has."

"Because people are so stupid. Well, we've quarrelled again now, and you can blame me if you like; but I blame him. And I would so love to see Mariana again. And to think he called her a housemaid! Housemaid? I've seen no woman to compare to her in beauty or grace since I came here. The only thing she needed was life. And housemaids, as a rule, have too much of that."

It is sad to relate that a few days after this the Great High Priest died, and his death was a general relief. He was little mourned for. The public do not always forgive a man readily, even when he has the grace to die, though it's certainly a great point in his favour. But still there was a certain section still in his favour, or rather, in favour of a certain Golden Priest called Phillipus, who was the oldest of that superior gathering, and likeliest, therefore, to come soonest upon dotage. Now Phillipus, if seniority had anything to do with it, ought to have stepped into the vacant throne, and would have done, if the events of the last two years or so had not undermined public feeling.

He was a man of sixty, so well preserved, and of an intellect so keen, he appeared as one in the very middle youth of life. But when events are against a man, he may be what he will, he doesn't make much headway, from a worldly point of view.

But the death of the High Priest, so unexpected as it was, threw things forward a bit. The election for his successor must come off sooner than was expected. In lieu of this, a famous conclave was called together at a dinner-party—a party at which the dinner was not to be so important as the speeches to follow.

Whilst this was in progress of preparation, cards of invitation were issued for a great ball in Marble House on Christmas Day.

And so it was the day before the big dinner came off, and about a week after the invitations for the ball had been issued, Susiebelle rushed into the drawing-room of her great friend, Miss Groggerton.

Now, before proceeding, it may be as well to introduce this lady cautiously. She lived in Lucifram, not upon Earth. She was so shockingly and vulgarly outspoken that on our modest sphere she would never have been tolerated; but there she was.

And why? Well, the reason is a good one. She had twice been crossed in love. That on Earth makes a woman bitter. Not so on Lucifram.

Crossed once, she does become embittered; crossed twice, she becomes a scourge in the land. And Miss Groggerton had been crossed twice.

She therefore spared no one, man, woman, or child, and in consequence all persons with a spite against anyone went to her. She poured pepper and vinegar upon their wounds; then salt, and healed them.

So it was that Susiebelle rushed into her room, furnished in yellow satin.

"I think it's shameful!"

"What's shameful?" asked Miss Groggerton, laying down her yellow-backed novel.

"The way Camille Barringcourt has behaved!"

"I knew you'd never manage it," said the other.

"Manage what?"

"To get him up to the scratch."

"You've failed often enough; you needn't talk to me.

"I was talking to myself."

"It's scandalous the way that grey-haired old Agnes Crokerly gets into everything. The reason her brother's never got married is because she never lets him out of her sight."

"The reason he's never got married," said Miss Groggerton, "is because he's no morals."

"You know a good bit about people," said Susiebelle, more respectfully.

"I should think I did! People are no better than pigs; they're swine."

"Pa made his money out of pigs."

"They're one degree better than people, then."

"I wish you'd let me say what I came to say."

"Go on. No one's hindering you but yourself."

"Camille Barringcourt's a pig. He's gone and asked old Agnes Crokerly to play hostess at his big do. And I thought now Lady Flamington was gone there'd be a chance for ma and me."

"What d'ye want with *him*?" said the other sneeringly. "He's not a duke. He's plain Mr.! Bless me, you're coming down!"

"Ah! but he's got a mint of money."

"You've got enough money for two and more, if need be. What you want is a title. If you looked back into his people you'd find they kept a chip potato shop, I dare be bound."

"Never!" said Susiebelle, with emphasis, the tears rising in her eyes. "He's so real a gentleman he makes Lord Hysquint look like a twopence-halfpenny waiter in a restaurant I don't want a duke" (her voice was rising), "I won't have a duke! They're common little sniggling things that are too proud for their place. One might think they'd never tasted sausage! I'll marry who I want to, and if I don't marry who I want, I'll make everybody's life a burden to them!"

And her voice rose to a high pitch, for she was hysterical, and had never been much crossed in her life before.

Miss Groggerton was enjoying the oratory so much, she made no attempt at interruption. This would be a delightful tale for repetition. Susiebelle, once having begun to speak, had lost control over her tongue, a state with which many will readily sympathise.

"I went to the temple specially when Lady Flamington died, and thanked the Serpent, because I thought it was my turn next, and—and—and now it's old Agnes Crokerly—old cat!"

"Old Agnes Crokerly!" said Miss Groggerton, with a snort and a sneer. "Old Agnes Crokerly!"

"Well, he's asked her to do the thing for him. And he giving a big affair with Lady Flamington warm in her coffin yet! And never a crape band round his arm or his hat for her."

"Well! Women who make themselves too cheap can't expect to be respected even in their graves."

"She never made herself too cheap. Ma fought tooth and nail to get her to our place, and wouldn't have managed it then if it hadn't been for Mr. Barringcourt, who's more democratic in his views. He brought her to a charity concert when her husband was away in the land of Big Boasts and Loud Voices, and ma improved the occasion."

"And now," said the other contemptuously, "you say John Crokerly's sister has taken her place."

"Yes; it's the way with young men. Mollycoddled by women old enough to be their mothers."

Her tears began to flow again.

"He's not so very young," said Miss Groggerton impressively. "And you bet your bottom dollar it's the other one he's after."

"Which other?" and Susiebelle opened her big brown eyes.

"What's her name? Pa—Pa—Paleaf."

"What!" screamed the other. "The girl with the pug-nose, the green eyes and washed-out hair. Sprung from nowhere! A lot you know about it."

"I know plenty, because I watch. Didn't I see them walking in the Park the other morning? I'll do him the justice, though, to say she kept calling him back when he was all for getting away."

"I don't believe it. She knows how to dress, and there's an end of it."

"She's a right-down pretty woman," said Miss Groggerton spitefully, who would have been just as eager to pronounce her ugly upon another occasion.

"There's no dash, no 'go' about her. She gives one the impression she's been sleeping in a bandbox. I'd rather have Agnes for company than her."

"You would. But then you're not a man. It makes all the difference."

And then Susiebelle, being quite overwrought, put her head on the sofa pillow and cried aloud. Truly Miss Groggerton was cruel. But it was not her nature to remain so long, if justice must be done her. Suddenly she said:

"Are you very gone on Barringcourt?"

"Dead gone. If I don't marry him I'll marry no one. So pa had better look out."

"Well, it's Miss Paleaf he's gone upon now, though it may be only a passing fancy. But why not set yourself to work to do her out?"

"How?" asked Susiebelle, raising her head.

"Well, she never goes anywhere but what she takes a hideous green toad with her. These are days of extreme religion. Let's say she worships it. There would be scandal in no time, and it might end seriously for her."

"Yes; but I'm thinking of him. I don't think he's a very religious man. It might make no difference to him if he's f—f—fond of her."

Miss Groggerton laughed aloud.

"You'll never get married if you're such a greenhorn. D'ye think any man would care for a girl who worshipped a toad when he was there himself to be worshipped? On my word, Susiebelle, you don't know everything."

"Of course not," said the other humbly. "How—how shall we begin?"

"Oh! I have a great friend, a priest called James Peter. I'll speak of it to him as a serious matter and scandal. There's no one like the priests for spreading gossip."

CHAPTER XXVII

AFTER-DINNER SPEECHES

After that Susiebelle went back to her accustomed life, and behaved as a young lady who had been presented to the Emperor *should* behave.

The great night of the dinner had arrived; the following day was to be the great election, and the two most popular and powerful candidates were, to even the inexperienced eye, Golden Priest Alphonso and his brother Phillipus.

Now, since the death of the Great High Priest it was very plain the latter had come into more favour. Why, it would be hard to say. A little whisper here, a little whisper there. "He is ambitious"—deadliest sin in a path of life that fosters ambition. And Golden Priest Alphonso, with his far-reaching, numerous feelers, like the octopus, must have been conscious of it. Yet the poor were his upholders. One night a week, at his own board, they were his guests, and he was seen sitting down with them. *This* man ambitious? The people's friend Alphonso! That means so little and so much, just as in the days of our own French Revolution.

But now the night had come, and everything was a buzz of simmering excitement.

Thanks to tickets sent from Mr. Barringcourt, probably through Golden Priest Alphonso, Sir John, Miss Crokerly, and Rosalie were enabled to go. The Sebberens only got one ticket, as happened in most houses, and that at a side table, still a place of honour, where the wealthiest sat, and were content to sit.

The Golden Priests, robed in their flowing vestments of richest satin and cloth of gold, sat interspersed amongst their guests, at the two principal tables. The great hall was crowded, and so constructed that all speakers, from one end to the other, could be distinctly heard when there was silence.

It was an off-shoot of the great temple, and was called the Golden Hall because its ceiling, walls, and other adornments were overlaid with gold. Men were there in the preponderance, but there were women also from the more influential houses. People were heard lamenting the absence of Lady Flamington. Somehow or other tonight, even in that tumultuous world, her presence was missed.

Rosalie was there. Rosalie, in shimmering grey, like frozen shining *crêpe*, only soft and clinging. She was as one in half mourning among that brilliant throng. On her shoulder was the shining frog, shining in green and white, and for some reason or other her face was very pale, and her eyes big and bright.

On the opposite side, a little farther up the table, Mr. Barringcourt sat. He wore the curious gleaming jewelled pin she had seen before, and the persistent red light it cast was nothing short of wonderful. On the side lower down sat Golden Priest Alphonso. Still farther off sat Phillipus. Tomorrow the race and the fight would be decided.

Now on this great occasion the Golden Priests themselves did not speak. Naturally, a man cannot speak on his own behalf. The only thing he can speak for is a Cause.

But when dinner was over (and it was finished in a remarkably short time, being, as it were, but the trumpet sound calling to greater things), the friends and upholders of each candidate spoke in turn. No names were mentioned—views only were put forward, facts also. Each speaker was allowed fifteen minutes and no more.

The speeches began in earnest, and they revolved round the two chief men of those chosen—for and against.

Now it was plain that the unfortunate episode of the lost handkerchief, or rather *found* one, still rankled deeply in people's minds. A debt of gratitude was still due to the man who discovered and made known this scandalous piece of information. Affairs in the temple had for centuries been kept too close. A Great High Priest was needed whose actions would be as light as day, and character above reproach.

So on the speeches went, all interesting and conclusive, because they all pivoted on one concrete thing, a handkerchief with a rose in the corner. The thing itself was never mentioned, for that would scarce have been diplomacy. Like the Serpent, the handkerchief was hidden out of sight.

And so on one little lie, or piece of misunderstanding, one man was gaining a position which clearly was too good for him. So at least thought Rosalie. She studied the faces of the two candidates, and took a sudden fancy to that of Phillipus. He came from a line of uncrowned kings. The speeches were going against him; he bore it with dignity and polite attention to every speaker.

At last one speaker, bold with champagne, ran full tilt at the red rag, rose, or whatever else it can be called. He spoke of it openly, and the result was—fatal.

For suddenly the frog said to Rosalie, "Speak!" and being obedient, she spoke.

She rose to her feet with one deep spot of colour flaming into either cheek, the rest white as snow. A curious silence fell on the room, which had been silent before.

"I think there has been a little misunderstanding about the handkerchief," she said, in a voice that ceased to tremble. "It belongs to me. I never saw the Great High Priest in my life, but I did go into the most sacred place three years ago, with—with a petition, and by mistake I left it there."

Now there was a certain purity in Rosalie's voice and simplicity in the words that carried conviction.

For half a minute silence followed, then Golden Priest Alphonso broke the silent spell.

"What right had you going there? You! A woman."

"I—I was very much in earnest."

"Then," said he harshly and pitilessly, "you are to blame for all the events of the past three years." Then his voice altered, and he said: "Truth is pleasant. It is a relief to find the late High Priest was better than one thought. But you, what excuse is there for you, to keep silence so long, and let a man go to his grave misunderstood? Fear, I presume, of being found out."

"I knew nothing," said Rosalie, in a kind of self-defence, for the expression in his eyes under the hypocritical sternness was very sinister. And then someone hissed at the far end of the room, and then someone else. Truly the Serpent was alive, and no golden image either.

But hissing was contrary to the dictates of good manners in such an assembly, and the chairman called to order. Rosalie sat down trembling, all colour gone from her face, though she had sufficient strength of will to keep her from giving any further signs of the ordeal she had passed through. Her eyes travelled magnetically from the face of the Golden Priest to that of Mr. Barringcourt.

He was leaning forward, his elbow on the table, looking at her. In his eyes shone the old mocking, laughing light, that said in so many silent words, "Now you've put your foot into it." They showed no sympathy.

Then a man, seizing the opportunity, got up and spoke in favour of Phillipus; another, then another. The tide seemed turning—was turning. Rosalie sat as an icicle. Every now and again she felt the sinister eyes from below, the laughing ones from above, fixed on her.

Who would have thought the popularity of a man hung on such a little thing as a handkerchief?

Then at last Mr. Barringcourt got up. In the midst of passion and eloquence, he was passionless. In spite of his height, in spite of his deep, unfathomable eyes, in spite of his firm mouth and certain lines upon his face, he seemed to be by far the youngest who had spoken, in manner, in voice, in a certain confident easiness. People settled in their places, smiled when he smiled, and became suddenly more good-natured, for at times he had a very bewitching smile.

Rosalie looked at him. She recognised that in Lucifram she had never seen so handsome a man, or one with so much grace. A dull pain and a sharp pain struck at her heart together.

"Ladies and gentlemen," said he, for on these occasions titles were disregarded by the speaker, "the record speech of the evening has been delivered by a lady with a style and simplicity it would be impossible for us to beat." (Popular opinion fluctuated. Was Rosalie so bad as five minutes before they had imagined? The speaker spoke so easily, he made them feel more easy. Wonderful gift of oratory!) "Now I agree with my friend, the Golden Priest Alphonso, the lady should have spoken earlier, when things could have been righted. But her silence no doubt sprang from the best intentions."

"That's all very well," called a voice. "But what about going into the sacred place against orders?"

"When one is in earnest, one goes much farther than one intends. It's an unconscious action. The lady said she was in earnest; she has accounted for what she did."

"She's liable to severe punishment."

"So then are all the women who looked at the Serpent when the curtain fell. I remember hearing a conversation between two sisters who were present at that—that unfortunate service. One fainted, the other retained presence of mind. Since then they have scarcely spoken—one was enabled to see so much more than the other. It is generally acknowledged that all women worthy the name did what was natural."

Whether Mr. Barringcourt were laughing or no, there were few there who took him anything but seriously. They considered this the acme of perfection in simplicity of reasoning, for the time, at any rate.

"But," continued he, "to return to the general subject, the choice of a Great High Priest. It seems to me the greatest fault in the past has been the age of the chosen candidate. What one wants at the head of such a great organisation as the Church is younger men—younger blood—younger principles and ideas."

Dissentient voices.

"You don't agree with me. But lately I was travelling in Lucifram in a country of world-wide respect and renown. It surprised me at first to find all the places of importance filled by comparatively young men—State, Church, professions, even trades. In the centre of their chief city I saw a famous statue in marble of a man, and underneath in letters of gold was carved 'Aged sixty-five.' There was no mistaking it; the smallest child could read and understand it. On seeing this I made inquiries, and was told his history by the High Sheriff, himself a man of about fifty-five.

"His name was Hugo de Bretton, and as a lad he had been an errand boy, and in that capacity acquired an unfailing stock of good manners and alertness, the necessary adjuncts to all successful men who are not boors. From thence he travelled the ordinary roads of success till, in due course, he became a great banker. His own fortune was enormous—his power equalled it. This at fifty. At sixty his wealth was increased. At sixty-five he seemed in the very zenith of his glory—physically and mentally of astounding strength. His name a magic spell in speculations. Then suddenly he resigned from public life." Here a shrewd little smile, almost imperceptible, wrinkled Mr. Barringcourt's face.

"Now, you know," continued he, "that a man who amasses a fortune, a very great fortune, I will not say how great, does the greater part of it by stepping on other people's corns—not intentionally, but he does step all the same. And with increasing gold his feet at times become so heavy they do more than crush corns—they crush life unconsciously.

"This man was no fool. The past had been very profitable years to him; so should the future be. How great a sacrifice his self-resignation was it would be hard to say, but it was done with little ostentation.

"He lived for a period of fifteen years longer, and, I venture to say, in that time he did more practical good than any statesman or soldier of his time. He gave of the accumulated experience of life, generously and widely. He invested large sums for the aid of respected and aged poor, a thing which hitherto had been thought to be the work of the poorhouses. He spent the last years of his life a philosopher and philanthropist, respected and beloved— leaving the outward battle of life for those who had still to win their spurs. So great was the impression left by his conduct that others, lesser men or equal, followed suit. And gradually the law came in that all at sixty-five resigned their office, not as unfit for work, but as having done their full share of labour in the field—ready to give advice when sought, and ready to turn a life's experience into a profitable channel for the good of the community. And with such critics standing by, capable of judging, and unsparingly, it acted as a spur to the generation following.

"And so it is that age is there the most respected. Generation of workers follows generation in perfect order. In State, in Church, in every division of labour there is vigour and freshness. For why is the Church to be excluded? On the plea of sacred exemption? A most sacred fallacy that is so ticklish it won't bear touching, and holds together pretty much as the old crimson curtain in the temple held, till the hand of God, through the agency of moths, tore it down from the rings of gold."

"There's many a man young at sixty-five," one argued.

"Have I not given you a notable example of one who turned his mind from business to philanthropy, and gave his mind and energy and wealth to it."

"There's many a man has died soon after giving up the business of his life, if it's compulsory."

Mr. Barringcourt laughed.

"He's either narrow-minded, with no interest outside his own affairs, or he worships his work above the Serpent. He should be careful."

"Many of our finest clergy are over the age you mention."

"They push out or keep down the younger men who are just as fine. If they wish to remain in office after age, let them work for the love of the thing—for nothing."

Then he sat down. And not long afterwards the guests departed.

"What a curious speech that was of Mr. Barringcourt's," said Miss Crokerly to her brother, as they drove home.

"Yes. He'd argue black was white when in a mood to do so. But I'll call on him tomorrow. According to his verdict, there's only three years good work left in me now."

"He didn't say that," put in Rosalie from her corner, where she had been sitting mutely. "Just think, Sir John! Under certain conditions you might paint the best picture you ever did in your life after sixty-five, and what a great thing it would be if you gave the proceeds to some great scheme of general improvement, that had too much genuine good to have any of the sentimentalism of charity in it. I think it would be a splendid thing, and economise resources."

"Under the new *régime* we'll have to become Spartans," said he, not unkindly. "But tell me, Rosalie, is it true that the lost handkerchief belonged to you?"

"Yes," she answered, breathing quickly and leaning forward. "I went there one day, nay, twice, when I was in terrible distress. I never mentioned it before; I didn't quite know how to. But some day I'll tell you all, but at present I would rather not. Has it made any difference to you? I had to speak tonight. It has weighed so long on my mind. And I couldn't bear to hear them bringing that up as a blot on the late High Priest's life. If it had not been so cruel, it would have been ridiculous."

"We wish to know no more than you care to tell us," he answered kindly. "And it has made no difference. The time was awkward, certainly, but you had not been here long enough to know how things were going,"

"Oh! but it's Mr. Barringcourt," she continued quickly, with a queer ring of pain in her voice. "He knew, and has known all along, and could have spoken and set all things right. It was cruel, cruel! I can't understand that anyone who spoke as he spoke tonight could act as he has done."

"Did he know about the handkerchief?" said Miss Crokerly.

"He must have done. He—he—he was at the temple the same time as I. If only he had spoken sincerely! But it was simply to further the schemes of an ambitious man."

When they got home Miss Crokerly went up with Rosalie to bed. A fire was burning brightly in the bedroom.

"Rosalie, did you ever know Mr. Barringcourt before you met him at the Sebberens'?"

"Yes, indeed. I stayed in his house nearly a week. I met him first in the sacred place of the temple."

"Why were you staying at his house?"

Rosalie looked at her with the look of fear and pain in her eyes that had haunted them half the night.

"If I tell you, you'll never repeat it, even to your brother?"

"No."

"Well, I was born dumb, and I remained dumb till I was twenty-two, and then he cured me completely, just as I am now."

Miss Crokerly would have doubted, but Rosalie's tone carried conviction as before.

"And it took a week for the cure to be completed?"

"No. Afterwards he kept me as a prisoner. I ran away, or something led me away. I don't know which."

"It's a curious tale. Almost unbelievable."

"I know. That's why I never repeat it. I should have gone to be an inmate of Todbrook's Home, but I couldn't bear the thought of it, somehow or other."

Then Miss Crokerly went away. She saw that Rosalie was overwrought and tired, and recommended her to think about nothing till morning, and go to sleep.

When the door was closed, Rosalie flung herself down in a chair before the fire, and the frog hopped on to the mantelpiece.

"Why did you tell me to speak?" she cried. "I did no good. Only incurred cold glances and hisses and hatred."

"Flea bites," said the frog.

"Bred out of serpent's poison, anyway. If I'd followed Mr. Barringcourt's advice I'd have said nothing."

"He always goes by the rule of contrary."

"It's a rule I never learnt."

"It's answerable for a great deal that happens in this world. Why do you take things so much to heart?"

"Oh, I don't know. I'm a lonely, lonely woman."

"I'm a lonely, lonely frog."

She laughed. "You make light of my misfortunes."

"I think you are much more fortunate than you think. I bear a charmed life, and yours is the next best thing. We'll struggle on together, anyhow. Remember, we're in search of six white horses and a capable driver. That's all we've got to mind."

"Of course," said Rosalie. "Life's more like a dream than reality."
Here the frog yawned, and Rosalie, much soothed, was soon asleep.

CHAPTER XXVIII

REVENGE IS SWEET

Next day this particular city of Lucifram was buzzing. The great election was coming off. Yet there was no doubt who was winning. Golden Priest Alphonso had regained his old popularity. When the poll was read at night he headed the list. The people received it with shouts of acclamation. In other circles the news was as well received. He was barely forty. A precedent was established. He was the youngest Great High Priest in the record of time.

But our history is not so much with public events as private persons, and we return once more to Susiebelle and her friend Miss Groggerton.

Neither of them had been at the great dinner, but the one had heard from her father, and the other read from the paper, the trend of general events.

"And," said Susiebelle, with pious horror, "to admit right out she'd been into the most sacred place—a place no woman has ever been in before. Such impudent boldness is enough to make one's hair stand on end. She's a disgrace to our sex. If I met her in the street with the Emperor himself I'd turn my head away."

As this was never likely to be, Susiebelle was very safe.

"Yes; but what I can't understand is Mr. Barringcourt's conduct," said Miss Groggerton. "I hear that he defended her, or the next best thing. Made everyone laugh and then serious at the same time."

Miss Groggerton was green when she said it, but Susiebelle became greener.

"Pa says no right-minded woman would care to hear her conduct made the subject of open criticism, and if she'd had a ha'porth of modesty, she'd have kept her tongue still. But I know the kind she is. Those pug-nosed women are all alike. Pushing themselves to the front if they have to pay body and soul for it. Have you seen brother James Peter yet?"

"Yes. He called the day before yesterday. And I explained to him about her. He was to be at the dinner last night, so he would see her."

Just at this moment, in accordance with the old proverb, brother James Peter made his appearance. He has been previously introduced to the reader at the beginning of this book. Once brother James Peter fell over a footstool, and got lost in the dark, was laughed at by his brother priests, and to this day heard occasional remarks made about his conduct. He remembered very well the source of his misfortunes, and had again scented the innocent cause of them all. He was the first to hiss last night, proving himself to be a true cross-breed of the Serpent. Today he came in as one with news. He had given his vote; for him the day's work was over.

"You look pale, Sir Priest," said Miss Groggerton, who would have called up the devil to prove him another, behind his back.

"The events of last night have distracted me," he cried, sitting down. And Miss Groggerton rang for his favourite collation of whisky and ham sandwiches.

"Tell us, is it true?" they both cried, as the provisions were being prepared without.

"That woman is in the power of the Evil One," said he solemnly. "And the sooner that little squat animal is taken by the hind leg and cast into the fire—the—better."

"Yes, indeed," said Miss Groggerton, in joyful anticipation of slaughter.

"I believe it's that frog that gets her a reputation for beauty. Loathsome little thing!" and Susiebelle shivered, and then laughed.

"Listen to me," said James Peter, raising his fat finger. "Make none of your own little spiteful remarks, but listen to me."

Being a priest, he spoke as one in authority, and the women submitted.

"That woman," said he, "is a dangerous and unprincipled character. Three years ago—listen carefully—she came into our temple and pretended to be drunk—dumb, I mean. She used to come and kneel up close to the crimson curtain, and I believe she contaminated it and made it rot. She used to look up at me with her lovely eyes (she has lovely eyes, Mademoiselle Susiebelle, whatever you may think), and point to her lips, and shake her head, and I—I used to pity her. She gave me to understand she was praying for the gift of speech."

Here the women laughed shrilly, shook with laughing, as he had laughed long since.

"But that," continued he, "was all a ruse. She was waiting her opportunity to slip inside the curtain, eaten up with preternatural and unwomanly curiosity. But one afternoon, as it was getting dusk, I went into the choir stalls to get a psalter that I needed, and thought I heard a curious sound coming from out the sacred place. I could not understand it. I hid myself in the shadow of the carved screen, suspecting theft, and recognising sacrilege. A little later, out came this woman, carrying a light. I know not where she got it from. But seeing me, she ran all down the nave at quickest speed, I following."

"You caught her?"

"The devil helped her. She escaped; and at the door she turned right round and put her tongue right out at me, and said: 'Did you ever know a woman who couldn't talk if she wanted to?' You have the story in a nutshell."

"And you never reported it?"

"Three hours afterwards. I was as one imprisoned in a living grave for three long weary hours."

"But did you not tell?"

"Yes; and the Great High Priest would not believe me. He laughed. That was the beginning of all his troubles. He was too lax, they say. Under the new *régime* there will be greater strictness." And he sighed.

"Why, she's a witch, a witch—an impudent, underbred thing," said Susiebelle excitedly. "Have you told Mr. Barringcourt?"

"I am not personally acquainted with him. But last night, from the way he spoke, one might almost have thought he was excusing her. Of course, there was no putting out of tongues or giving pert answers last night; she spoke as meek and as mildly as you please."

"If it hadn't have come from the mouth of a clergyman I wouldn't have believed it of her," said Miss Groggerton, glad to have such a reliable source of information.

"But—but" continued Susiebelle, "isn't there a severe punishment for going inside the curtain, for a woman?"

"It used to be to have her tongue torn out."

"Who will do it? Who will do it?"

"No one will do it nowadays. The biggest punishment would be a fine. Pawn a few jewels; it's done in no time."

"She doesn't worship the Serpent at all; she worships that little blinking frog," said Miss Groggerton.

"Well, I've got my eye on her. And if there are any heathenish practices going on, you may be sure I will report them before long," said he, and soon afterwards got up to go.

That same night, when all the wear and tear and excitement of the day were over, and all the cabs had rattled home, and all the theatres been closed, the new Great High Priest sat in an arm-chair in Mr. Barringcourt's study, whilst the owner sat in his accustomed one beside the table.

Sacred Priest Alphonso was white and haggard, and the deep lines on his face showed the strain that he had passed through. His arms hung heavily on the arms of the chair, his eyes were fixed on the carpet. Mr. Barringcourt was writing a letter. When he had finished it, he sealed it, and tossed it on the table, then bent his eyes upon his guest as a doctor sometimes does upon an uncertain patient he treats as an experiment. Without saying anything, he got up, and went to a side-table, and poured out two glasses of red wine. One he filled, the other only half, then turned his head round and looked at the Priest. Still he sat in the same weary lethargy. A smile curved Mr. Barringcourt's lips. "Very far gone," he muttered, and filled the glass.

Then he took it across and offered it to him. He took it carelessly and drank all the contents. Mr. Barringcourt drank half his and flung the rest into the fire. It blazed up in a brilliant red light, then died away as suddenly, leaving the fire dark, as if water had been poured on it. But this beverage must have refreshed the High Priest wonderfully; for suddenly rousing himself, he looked up at Mr. Barringcourt, and said, slapping his hand upon the chair arm:

"Today has ended successfully. But the first thing I do on coming into office is to bring that woman to trial."

"Which woman?" said Mr. Barringcourt, sitting down on the opposite side of the fireplace.

"That fool who nearly spoilt everything last night by having too long a tongue."

The wine surely had had a heating effect.

"Miss Paleaf?"

"Yes. The one I took rather a fancy to at the Sebberens', and asked you to introduce me to." And he laughed cynically.

"Oh," said Mr. Barringcourt easily, "you'll let that die down. Set a constant guard of two priests to watch the curtain. Such vigilance will satisfy the people. Besides, Crokerly is doing the work of the panelling, and none can do it like him. You can't afford to quarrel with him over the mischiefmaking propensities of a woman."

"Do you mean to say you would look lightly on her conduct of last night?"

"Of course! She did you no harm. It's herself she's harmed, as she'll find out as time goes on. It's always best to be a bit forbearing with women; they're given to flying off rather unexpectedly at times."

"No excuse. No excuse at all. She did it from malicious intention and love of meddling."

"What do you propose to do, then? Tear her tongue out?"

"Imprison her for life."

"O Lord!" said Mr. Barringcourt, and he laughed. Then he laughed again, and again he said, "O Lord!"

The other frowned, and the light of anger glinted in his eye.

"You seem to rather approve of her conduct," he said. "Certainly I have to thank you for your speech, though, candidly speaking, neither I, nor I believe anyone else, could make head or tail of it" (he spoke in a genuinely puzzled voice), "and for various other things I have to thank you; but in the matter of dealing with this woman, I beg you will not interfere."

"Yes," said Mr. Barringcourt, in a low, clear voice, "I shall interfere. The Serpent is like everything else. It can't afford to get too much talked about, or its reputation's gone. If you prosecute her, you make yourself and it the laughing-stock of Lucifram."

"I uphold its sacredness and sanctity."

"Cant and tomfoolery! You say I made a speech last night you didn't understand—and I didn't take the pains to understand it myself. But if you persist in this, I'll make another before long which will appeal to everyone, and tread on no general corns at all, but that of the individual."

"You are in a quarrelsome mood tonight."

"Yes. I've been in the society of priests all day, and they weary me."

The other laughed.

"That's a hint to me. However, for the present you may have your way, but I tell you candidly, if there's any hubbub made, I bring her to trial."

Then he went away; but walking along the silent streets he said:

"Barringcourt's as spoilt as a child. Cross him in the least thing, and he's inside out in no time. Yet in some whimsical, flimsical kind of way he's been the best friend I've had, and helped on considerably the present affairs. All the same, that girl shall suffer. The thing to do in this world is to teach people to keep their tongues still. It's three parts the battle of life."

And Mr. Barringcourt, left to himself, stood a long time looking into the rekindled fire, which tells so much to those who read it properly. And his face betokened more weariness and contempt than even in the past years, and the lines of his features were finer.

"Revenge first; thanks a very doubtful second," he said at length, and then went off to the stables.

All through the blackness of the night the black steeds galloped, and some mistook their dusky forms for passing clouds, and their wild eyes for distant stars, and the rhythm of their feet for the rumbling wind.

That night, as Rosalie slept, the frog left its customary place on the washing-stand, and came close to her ear. And though all the room beyond was dark, the light round her head and pillow was very white and pure.

All the things the frog whispered it would be unfair to say, for the frog was working for its own ends, as most of us do, and therefore coloured things to its own liking.

Rosalie woke in the morning, and looked at the deceitful frog, now sitting on the washing-stand, and said:

"I've been dreaming that a tiny little angel came and sang to me and laughed. And though I can't remember one word of what it said, I know that everything was very pleasant—so that many a time I found that I was laughing too."

CHAPTER XXIX

A CONFESSION

Time flew on till it was just two days before Christmas, or, at least, the festival which in Lucifram takes the place of Christmas in our world.

On this particular afternoon Rosalie dressed with the greatest possible care, and looked three consecutive times sideways in the glass, to see if her nose was any better disposed to turn downwards; but it wasn't. Still, it detracted nothing from the general effect, and, indeed, might be said to help, if only on the side of morality, to keep her from growing conceited.

The frog, having come to that stage when one evidently regards oneself as quite perfect enough, felt no qualms as to its appearance, took not one doubtful glance into the glass.

Rosalie, when she was ready, put her head through the door to tell Miss Crokerly she was going to pay a call; she did not say where.

Miss Crokerly, busy with festival matters, simply nodded her head. It was just a little after three.

Rosalie left the house, and walked on quickly till she came to Greensward Avenue. Coming here, her steps slackened; but she continued walking till she came in sight of Marble House. Here she came to a dead stand, and looked blindly on the pavement. Her heart was beating so quickly that if the passers-by had not been walking along so heavily they must have stopped to inquire about it.

But from a full stop she ran lightly and hurriedly up the steps and rang the bell. There was no escape now, for within thirty seconds it had opened. There stood Everard, just the same as ever, as silent, as polite, no more surprised.

Rosalie took her courage in both hands. There was that hideous umbrella stand that a dowager-duchess had once exclaimed was the most charming novelty she'd ever seen.

"Is Mr. Barringcourt at home?" said she.

He looked as if he had never seen her before, but after a moment's pause he said:

"Yes. Will you come this way?" And led her through the outer vestibule into the wide and gloomy hall.

There he left her, and went in the direction of the Master's study, but soon returned.

The afternoon had quite faded now, and as he conducted her along the western corridor he turned on the lights.

Mr. Barringcourt received her almost silently. He made some remark about the weather—it was of little importance. He drew a chair for her. Rosalie sat down.

"I came to see you," she began, clasping her hands tightly inside her muff, "because—because—"

"Because," said he, in the most distant of voices, "you wished to see Mariana."

"No. I'm afraid I was too selfish to think of Mariana. I was thinking only of myself."

She did not notice the alteration in his expression, because she had not noticed the previous hardness of his voice. But she got a vague idea he was not particularly pleased to see her, yet was determined to go on.

"It has sometimes struck me," she began hurriedly, "that it was very ill-mannered of me to run away from you. I—I—I escaped by a little door in the stable wall."

A very curious silence followed this remark; then Rosalie continued:

"The country beyond was very beautiful—at least, I thought it was. It—it led me to a white house, with a low verandah and a pretty garden. It took me a whole day to go, and the sun was setting when I got there. In the house I met a youth—at least, I thought he was young; but afterwards he told me he was nearly as old as you. But he seemed to grow very quickly in the time that I was staying there. He took me to his father. At first I thought he was very old, because his hair was white. I had just one day's holiday when I was there, and then I went to live in a little hut all alone, with a plantation in front of it. I sowed a basket of seeds in the ground that the Governor (that is the name I knew him by) had given me. But first I had to dig in the soil, and I didn't like digging at all; I hated it. After that, everything went by the rule of contrary. The seeds never came up; they grew underneath, and looked to me like very beautiful jewels. But they took a great deal of digging out and free-ing from the soil. I took them to the Governor, and he sent them somewhere, I think he said it was to the city, to be tested and valued. But every time they were sent back and marked as rubbish. I've never felt quite the same since. I used to feel young before, but ever since I've felt as old as old. And I do nothing but pretend all day long, in little and big things alike. I pretend least with you of anyone, and that night I ran away from you in the street (you remember it?) I felt quite surprised, and in one way just a little happy. It made me feel just a little more alive. But after a while the Governor said I had better come back again into the world. I didn't want to, because there was nowhere to go to, and I did not want to come back to this house again. I

178 | EDITH ALLON

was tired of prisons. But when he told me to come back into the world I was obedient, because I knew he was much wiser than anyone that I had ever met before. He was kind to me in some ways, although he never threw kindness away. So one morning I started on the return journey, and Brightcoat came along with me for company.

"When we were in the streets, I went along scarcely knowing what I was doing, I was so tired, and at last I sat down on a doorstep. It was Sir John Crokerly's, and when his sister came home she took me in; and I have lived there ever since. There is nothing else to tell you. Now you know all, you need trouble yourself to be agreeable to me no longer. After all, I owed it to you to tell you. You gave me a greater gift than I thought it possible anyone on earth could ever give me. And you no doubt put it down to science, but I put it down to God. And—and about my coming here, when first I did come to you. I came from the sacred place of the temple. I had given up wishing to be cured of being dumb—at least, praying to be cured, because I thought God was not wishful to cure me. And I prayed to the Serpent just to help me to live the right way, because I knew that that was the only thing God really cared about And the Serpent seemed quite to disappear; in its place came the presence of God. Only one little ball of light and gold was left out of all that giant frame and jewelled head. And I don't know quite how it was I came to you, any more than now I have gone to Miss Crokerly."

With these words said, she got up and stood facing him, for he had not sat down during this monologue but stood looking at her, a thing which, after first beginning, she seemed quite unconscious of.

Her words had been simple, her sentences short and abrupt, and at times somewhat disconnected, but Rosalie's voice was so sweet that it seemed to run like a silver bell in and out the mazes of this experience.

Now she held out her hand.

"I have detained you long enough. Perhaps you'll forgive the school-girl style. Though I feel so old, I can find no other."

"Come with me to the stable," said he, "and show me the door. I don't believe there is one."

"You will be able to find it yourself."

"I had much rather you came with me. It is the only way in which I can credit your story."

So together they went through the silent house and silent grounds and silent shrubbery. The red light shone full down the middle pathway to the stable door. But Brightcoat shed a softer brilliancy round about, if not so clearly and direct. But then there was no need for it as guide today.

The stables shone out with a certain curious light of their own—a dusky, shadowy brightness.

At a certain touch the unseen door slipped backward, and revealed the shadowy twilight within.

And as is customary with horses, they turned their graceful heads and looked with wild eyes on the newcomers, and one in the far corner neighed. But they seemed shadowy. All were shadowy. Eyes shone like carbuncles, the only distinctive feature. And there was nothing of warmth there. Everything was cold and chilly as a vault

But Brightcoat's light was useful here. It shone in direct rays on to that little unnoticed door that was built so unobtrusively in the wall.

"There," said Rosalie, and she touched his arm. "I went through there."

"Strange," said he. "I never saw that door before. How did you open it?"

"With the key of my uncle's safe. But that has gone. I don't know what I did with it. I was in such a hurry to get through and close it after me."

"And the path led you to a low white house with a verandah?"

"Yes. Let us return. It is cold here. You'll give your horses rheumatism if you keep them in so damp a place."

"You are not acclimatised. But we will go. Strange I never noticed that door. As for the others, I suppose if they did notice it, they imagined I had done so too."

When they were back again in the house, which seemed cheerful after the intense cold without, Mr. Barringcourt said:

"Will you have tea before you go?"

"No, thank you. Our last tea together had not a very pleasant ending, though it began so charmingly. We're like most people—best friends when parted."

"Then I may not see you again till Festival night."

"Do you still renew the invitation?"

He laughed.

"If I were not very contrary, you would make me angry. You harp so constantly upon an unreasoning subject."

"Ah!" said she suddenly. "Let me see Mariana. Send for her."

"Not tonight"

"Yes, tonight. I will not keep her longer than a minute. Just to see if she is just the same."

"She has not altered. Take my word for it."

"You said if I came here I should see her."

"You must have misunderstood me. I never said so."

"I—I don't believe you ever mean me to see Mariana again," she said.

"Indeed? What makes you think so?" and he laughed again, not at all kindly.

"Because you know quite well that I should do my very best to persuade her to come away with me."

Rosalie bowed, and swept away toward the door, and when she got there she said to Everard, quite loud enough for Mr. Barringcourt to hear, who still stood in the hall:

"When next you see Mariana, please give her my love, and tell her I asked to see her, but was not successful."

He bowed solemnly and let her pass, but took no further notice than if he had been made of stone.

CHAPTER XXX

FESTIVAL

Now came Christmas night. On Lucifram Christmas Day wasn't marred by any subsequent church-going. It was nothing better than a heathen feast; the Serpent had nothing to do with it.

On that day the children went simply wild, and gave themselves incredible airs; demanded their best toys, gorged oranges and apples, made themselves ill with plum-pudding, demanded their full share of turkey, and got it, and looked with expectant eyes on the iced cake when it appeared. Just as if they'd been starving all day! The little wretches!

The grownup world, unless it was going out to an evening party, yawned, and ate its customary Christmas fare, and drank it too. Then the old people played cards, and the young people sang, especially the young men with untrained voices, and the lovers behaved as if they really were in love with one another.

Come and watch Rosalie.

Now that day there had arrived two Christmas presents so beautiful that many an empress might have envied them. The first came early in the morning, before the postman; a curious and unusual thing. There is no doubt Santa Claus was on the war-path, for such a lovely ball and reception dress could only have been made in some magic fairyland. It was like shining silken *crêpe*, all frosted over with tiny sparkling jewels, all in white. It shone like soft pure snow in the sunlight, and fell in folds of simplest grace. It was so very simply, yet so very wonderfully made, that one wondered what it was that gave it such a beautiful effect.

"Is it not too dead white to suit me?" said she to Brightcoat, after going into raptures on its beauty.

"See here, there is a little box below," said it.

And Rosalie opened it, and uttered the most real cry of delight in her life.

"It's my stone, my first stone, that I loved so, all set in gold and ready to wear. Oh, Brightcoat, Brightcoat, look!"

And she sat down on the bed and hid her face in the pillows, and cried from different emotions. At last she wiped away the tears and looked up, her eyes falling on the shining stone again.

"I love them all as if they were my children, and that somehow the most, because it was the first. And I believe it loves me too. Look how beautiful a ray of light it sends towards me! And I never hoped to see it again."

Rosalie took it up, and kissed it, and shed tears upon it, but the light from it was never dimmed; one might have thought it was made tear-proof.

"I need no other colour. This is quite enough. And you, Brightcoat."

"Yes; of course, there's me," said the other thoughtfully.

This was the beginning of the day. But when the postman came, besides bringing letters and cards without end, some of the latter bearing halfpenny stamps after the style of circulars, he brought a parcel, also directed to Rosalie, in handwriting that the frog declared was superior to anything it had ever seen.

It was opened in public, and inside was a pair of slippers as white as snow, and worked in diamonds. And they were such a curious shape they looked as if they must really be antique, because they had little square toes, and gold straps across. They reminded one of the daintiest garden clogs, so light were they, and when Rosalie put them on she wanted to dance right away.

"They're made on the same pattern as the little wooden clog I have upstairs," cried she. "Look, Miss Crokerly, they dance of themselves," and in excess of spirits she pirouetted round the room, and kissed both those elderly people from superabundance of excessively childish glee.

Where they had come from she didn't know. She thought they had come from the same source as the first, although they came by post. So that evening she dressed for the real pleasure of the thing. And when it came to pinning the jewel into the bosom of her dress, her hands trembled just because she loved it so. It shed just the same soft shades on to her dress as the light of the moon might shed on to the snow—a passing green and golden and palest blue that melted into white. And on her shoulder the ever—present frog, and a new light in her eyes, because the ice-tears had rolled out of them.

And underneath the shining jewel her heart beat quickly. She went with Sir John, Miss Crokerly having preceded them in Mr. Barringcourt's carriage some time ago.

"Do you know," said she, "I thought at the last minute you'd change your mind and stay away."

"Oh, no," he replied. "I always go when Barringcourt throws his house open. There are so many things that interest me there."

"Yes. It's quite after the nature of a museum, is it not?"

"Yes. Unlabelled. So that it has an additional charm."

They took their turn in the long line of carriages, and after a considerable time were enabled to alight.

There was an awning from the parapet to the door, and the steps were also covered a deep red.

Rosalie looked for Everard. He was not there. Two powdered footmen instead. They were not inmates of the Marble House. Neither were any of those who personally waited upon the guests that night. There was not a waiting-maid anywhere about to compare with Mariana, and Rosalie could not have imagined her proud and delicate face amongst that throng. But how different did the wide hall look that night! Brilliantly lit, and with huge fires burning at either end. Fires fit for Festival and freezing weather. And no undue crowding of guests to do away with comfort and beauty and enjoyment. The wide doors to the southern wing, leading to the picture-gallery and conservatory, were thrown open. So also were those to the west, containing the reception rooms—no empty, echoing fireless places now, but full of life and laughter and vivacity.

A reception was held first; dancing did not begin till eleven, when a well-known princess was to lead with a gavotte. She was very proud of her instep.

At twelve supper was to be served in the large subterranean hall, a place Rosalie had never been in, nor, indeed, anyone else. And after that dancing began again, and continued till four. Then carriages and home.

On entering, Rosalie was presented with a programme that explained all this. It was book-shaped, with a mother-of-pearl back, and in the centre a perfect little garden clog with a broken string in gold, and underneath "Christmas 0039"—that being the year as reckoned in Lucifram.

"Oh, how charming!" cried one lady, who had just received hers before Rosalie. "An old clog for luck! It is delightful!"

Flowers the most gorgeous and tasteful banked every available corner; truly, the house had been completely altered from darkness into light.

Mr. Barringcourt on these occasions made an excellent host. He had none of the clumsiness of the bachelor host, being for all the world as much at home as if he'd been married and had ten children. Now, it was a dancing night, and thanks to an excellent example, there was not one smoke-absorbed, or card-absorbed, or billiard-absorbed man present. For one night everybody made a delightful martyr of themselves, and secretly enjoyed the process.

Rosalie's programme did not fill so quickly, for there were many there who took her to have religious mania, and doubted they might have something to put up with. Moreover, there were very few persons there that she really knew. At last she was suddenly accosted by Mr. Barringcourt.

"The first and last dance, Rosalie," said he, and they looked at one another. Then looking down at her programme, he said: "What an empty list!"

"It's quite right, thank you. I don't care about dancing. I'd rather watch other people, and listen to the music. Find me some quiet old lady whom I may sit by, and who does not talk too much. It is all I ask of you."

"There are not many present. They are all young and frivolous, or old and giddy. A much easier task would be to find you partners for every dance."

"I should be dead tired before supper-time; I can't talk to strangers, and I don't know every dance. And it takes rather a brave man to accost me; I perceive them mentally screwing themselves up to the pitch as they approach."

"Under those circumstances, it was very kind of you to come. Here comes the Princess. I'll return later."

The Princess smiled so condescendingly all round that everyone was charmed with her. She had a light walk, as one who treads on eggs and fears to break them, and her admirers said she glided as the spirits do.

As soon as she came—and, of course, she came rather late—the proceedings of the evening began. She danced the gavotte, and brought her own dancing-master and fiddler to play, as she was accustomed to be played up to.

When the real dancing began there was one of the best bands in Lucifram in readiness, that all the evening more or less had been playing favourite airs, and another to relieve them when occasion needed.

Mr. Barringcourt sought and found Rosalie.

"Should you not have given the first dance to the Princess?" said she.

"No. My step does not suit her, and she is sufficiently truthful to tell me of it."

"I can scarcely believe *your* step is wrong."

"No? She is easier to deal with than you. She goes greatly on credit. It's a royal failing. Come, let us begin; if this waltz is as it should be, it will be all too short."

And no seventh heaven could have surpassed, if equalled it.

"How lovely," said she suddenly, "if one could die dancing!"

"It would mean company on a lonely road," said he. "And cheat death of some of its tragedy, with well-matched partners."

"Did you—did you send me those slippers that I'm wearing?"

"What makes you think so?"

"The little clog on the back of my programme. It's the exact fac-simile of one I used to wear."

"I had a little story as near as possible to that of Ally Krimjo. For one morning there was found in the middle of my hall a little garden clog without owner or companion. It came there through barred doors and spring-barred doors, and none could make out how it came there. Not even I. I never learnt it till the night when you came to say your lesson. I proved it when you wore these little satin-covered skates tonight."

"You'll give it back to me?"

"Oh, no! I'm keeping it for luck. That is a lovely stone you're wearing."

"It's one I told you of. Dug from the garden with a great big fork and spade, just as a man digs."

"I believe I've seen it before in my father's house."

"No, indeed. Unless your father was the Governor I spoke of."

He laughed.

Then at last the dance was over.

"I've found the lady you asked me for," said he. "Miss Crokerly is my guardian angel tonight. It is she who discovered her. Here is an excellent place where you may sit and see everything, and hear the music to advantage too."

And then he took her to a seat, and introduced her to a lady sitting there. She was so charming a companion. Her silences were never awkward, and now and again she would give Rosalie information about certain people, all of a good-natured if shrewd kind, that was the highest entertainment.

At twelve punctually the company descended to supper.

The staircase down was of black marble, and spiral also, like the one above. It had none of the slippery treachery that characterised its sister staircase, though, and it seemed altogether of a much more reliable make. To a spectator the gay colours of the ladies and their sparkling jewels looked like brilliant multicoloured scales on a gigantic serpent, reared pillar-wise to support the vast chamber below.

The subterranean banquet hall of Marble House was nothing better, nothing worse than a crypt.

It had great and massive pillars of hardened, blackened marble; a fitting support for a fitting house.

Its floors were tiled in marble. Its walls of marble too. But whereas a crypt, if lit at all, is content with lamps of oil, or the feeble glimmer of electricity, this place was deluged with light. The most brilliant candelabra hung from the ceilings, sparkling in the thousand glintings of diamond glass. The tables were covered with finest snow-white cloths, and all the decorations were of silver, purest and brightest and most finely worked. And all the flowers were red.

Here, screened from view, the band was playing gently. A soft and scented air of luxury arose, as if to show that crypts upon occasion have finer possibilities than dining-rooms.

The Princess, led by Mr. Barringcourt, descended first, and half way down stopped to admire.

"Which was the pirate, you or Mr. Todbrook?" said she. "I'm sure you carted off the plan of a cathedral, and the material too."

"That is an open secret," replied he, laughing. "But his was the theft, not mine. I simply inherited what he had left. But he had gloomy taste. Now, were I building, I'd fix upon a little bungalow, a whitewashed place, with a world-wide garden for the summer-time."

The Princess was not of that simple nature that enjoys simplicity, but she delighted in anything odd, as she considered it, because it made her laugh.

"Do you really mean to say you are philosopher enough to grow accustomed to things?" she asked.

"Till I see a way of escape."

"And you see none from here?"

The Princess had not such keen eyes as Rosalie; she was not fond of studying faces, except for what animal beauty they might possess.

"None," said he. "Although 'tis said Todbrook escaped by the back door."

"He died," said she, and looked at him with a vague suspicion of horror in her eyes. She was of a superstitious nature.

But he laughed.

"You talk of death at a dance?" said he. "One might almost think, Princess, you were primitive, and scorned the guarded terms of civilisation."

The conversation had taken a turn not to her fancy. He had thrown a shadow over the brilliantly-lit supper-room. She shivered involuntarily, and looked about her petulantly, and said:

"Are you quite sure this place isn't damp?"

"Not at all! Not a rheumatic dampness, anyway. Spirits do not count; they are above it."

Then their conversation ran into a lighter channel suited to the occasion, and the feast began right royally, when the plumed peacock was carried in, to be admired in death, a lasting tribute to its vanity.

The band played, and the people laughed and feasted and talked. In the whole of Lucifram that night could not have been found a gayer or more brilliant company.

CHAPTER XXXI

MYSTERIES IN MARBLE HOUSE

But there was one person who never came down to supper—at the right time, anyway—and that was Rosalie. She had strolled off alone to the picture-gallery, led to look again on that curious representation of the former master of Marble House.

The silence as the last guest went down below made her heart beat a little faster. She listened to the last echoing laugh, and he seemed listening too. The slightly bending figure indeed betokened an attitude of close attention—almost the hidden smile of one who, listening, understands.

The long line of pictures ran either side of her, each in itself a work of beauty. She remembered that day when Mariana had gone off to the east wing from here.

Tonight the east wing was closed. All this great glare of artificial light never traversed there. A heavy crimson curtain hid the polished door that led to it.

But Rosalie's spirit wandered off in that direction. A great curiosity, with a deeper feeling underneath to give the strength it needed, led her out into the central hall—led her gliding towards that gloomy fatal door.

She drew the curtain back with one white hand, white as snow against this deeper shade, and turned the handle. The door opened. Blackness, damp-ness, and the smell of decay and mildew met her, like a blast of foul despair.

She threw up her head, passed through, and the door slipped to behind her. And for one moment it seemed as if the parting kiss of freedom glowed on her forehead once again. And yet again the darkness was dispersed, for both the frog and jewel, and her own shining dress, that shone apparently without the aid of outer light, gave all the light it needed.

And here, within this gloomy place, at last came life and beauty, and the soft, tender light that lived in its own strength and was unborrowed.

No. 13! How well Rosalie remembered it! Mariana's workroom, a worse place than many a prisoner's cell. Yet it had about it an air of indefinable grandeur, the place of no petty criminal, or one sunk in moral disease. The rusty latch uplifted and disclosed the low-built room beyond, and the dim burner, the oaken chests, the damp, peeled walls, the shadowy corners, the tragedy of silence.

But what of these? They served but as backgrounds to a picture, and fitting backgrounds. For there, beside the long, low table, hid by the sheet, as white today as ever it had been three years ago, sat Mariana. But nothing there equalled the marble whiteness of her face. Her graceful figure bent forward, her hands were clasped on the table, and on her lips was that curious smile of pain, quite frozen there, as, wide open, her eyes stared at this hidden treasure on the table.

Some spider, mistaking the silent figure for a thing inanimate, had weaved a web of finest threads from head to foot, covering her silken hair and rough-spun dress. But respecting the icy chill that hung about those cold-cut features and hands, it had left them free and bare.

All about the cell fluttered the silent moths, settling and rising from the table. Yet they were powerless to canker anything. The bitter iron of living sorrow had too hard a crust.

The light that Rosalie brought with her lit up the room. She stood upon the threshold, gazing spellbound with horror on the central form. Could this be Mariana—this frozen statue, this figure nipped to the spirit with unavailing pain? Oh, never, never! For there this beautiful machine, working so fine a marvel of creation, had come upon a horrid pause, a fearful counterfeit of death, a fearful mockery of life!

Then the spell broke. With outstretched arms she hurried forward. "Mariana!"

No sound or movement came in reply. She placed her hand upon the stiffened shoulder. The cobweb broke; the spider saw, and ran away. She threw her arms around the other's neck, and kissed her stony cheek. No sound or movement in reply.

Burning tears fell from her eyes. They had no power to melt that which had been congealed so long, frozen from ice to marble.

Nothing availed—even when she fell upon her knees, and pressed her warm lips a hundred times upon the death-chilled fingers.

Powerless and weak! O God! for strength, strength, strength of some sort, to give life to the dying or the dead! What blasphemy! what heresy! what presumption!—the ignorant tumult of a still untutored heart. Then she drew back and looked at Mariana, fighting down every emotion to make way for thought. Her eyes fired with indignant protest, and she said:

"I'd rather be a murderer out and out and hanged for it! And to think of this night, when in this very house there is no sound of anything but gaiety and laughter; and people feasting! And here there sits a prisoner and worse, and one man conscious of it. Oh, Brightcoat! How can you think well of such as he! I cannot bear to look at him again." And then she stooped and took the slippers off she wore. "I wore them happily at first, but now they're all so tight they pinch my feet I wonder what sweating or freezing system it was brought them into shape? And I so selfish as never to insist before on seeing whether she were free or no."

The slippers off, she looked at them, then at the silent figure sitting there, and turned away, half-shivering. She placed the slippers upon the table on the sheet.

The moths descending, fluttered round them, yet did not touch; for, taught by instinct, they had learnt what could and what could not return to dust.

Then with one parting call of "Mariana!" one loving kiss, one shivering glance around the dismal place, she went away, closing the door behind her, into the outer passage.

Curiosity bade her try some of those other low and numbered doors; but all were locked. This tragic wing was surely haunted. The air was condensed of sighs—an essence which hung heavy on the heart.

But before opening that crystal door, all rusted iron and cobwebs from this inner side, Rosalie stood still to think. Then she pushed it open, and emerged into the brilliant hall, still silent. From here she passed toward the staircase leading down to the supper-room, where all the guests were now assembled.

But to return to them.

There was no lack of merriment throughout the length of tables. But as the supper progressed, and people became accustomed to their surroundings, general comments were made upon a long and double-folded curtain of heavy material that hung from floor to ceiling at the lower end of the vast chamber beside the staircase.

There was present at that supper a young girl just out that season—as giddy, as merry, and full of happy spirits as one unknown to care or saddened thoughts can ever be.

And to close a spirited discussion with some as young and thoughtless as herself, just as the feast was ending, she left her place amidst a laughing silence, and ran to the farther upper end of the table, where Mr. Barringcourt sat beside the Princess. With the happy assurance of youth never rebuffed, she accosted him.

"I come," said she, still laughing, "to plead on the side of our religion. They say that dismal curtain bears a resemblance, and a very striking one, to the crimson one within the temple. Will you not contradict them?"

He looked across the room toward it "One's black and the other's red," he said, and smiled.

"Yes; but we were discussing what might be beyond," and her face was demure, though her eyes were sparkling with merriment.

"With what result?" said he.

"We all grew curious. Princess, will you be curious, too?"

"Oh, instantly. What is beyond that curtain, Mr. Barringcourt? Tell us, or show us, pray."

The silence of expectation had settled on the guests. Barringcourt leaned forward toward the table, playing with the half-filled glass of wine beside him. And when he spoke his voice was low, yet perfectly distinct.

"You know," said he, "it was a foible of Mr. Todbrook's to collect as many heathen gods and false ones as lay in his power. This house was built on a system—I might say systems—of idolatry; its furniture collected from disused temples sought for all over the face of Lucifram.

"Behind that curtain stands a god, more hideous than any I have ever seen, and I've seen plenty in my time, as maybe most of you have done. The curtain came along with it from the temple where it stood, and in a state of wonderful preservation. Over one thousand years in age."

"What is beyond?" was the general question throughout the chamber.

"A death's-head of unusual size, worshipped and feared of all in the parts from where it came."

"Let us see it." A general murmur of anticipation ran round the room.

"These poor heathens!" said one lady, and her tone was patronising. "How ignorant they must have been."

"And are still in some parts, madam," said he.

"We do our best with the missionaries," she replied.

"Let us see it, please."

This was the voice of the charming youthful pioneer from the back.

"It's a death's-head," said he, and he smiled very kindly as he spoke. "They are not beautiful."

"But I've enjoyed myself so much all evening, Mr. Barringcourt, that I could not bear to be disappointed now. Besides, the Princess has commanded you. Please show us the head."

"It has never to be seen but in complete darkness. It's a clause of the will. It was the condition on which he bought it, I believe, from a few crazy priests, who had no congregation."

But they all wished to see it, light or no light. It was a little novelty to wind up supper and take the place of toasts.

So suddenly the light switched out, and left the place in total darkness. Those who were on terms familiar enough clasped one another's hands. They found the situation not unpleasant.

And then upon the instant the black curtain swung backwards and revealed a space beyond, from which gleamed out, in ashen whiteness and dusky hollows from the blackness, the skeleton head of death. It was the head of some great giant of unusual size, with yellow teeth discoloured, but all present. All looked at it with gloomy interest, and some began to wish, as darkness continued, they'd been less eager to examine it.

But suddenly and swiftly in the silence two gleaming balls of light glared red from the empty sockets, to turn their gaze at every individual round the room, and with a gleam most sinister. This was truly horrible. A room so black and dark that none could see each other. The bleached skull and skeleton of a superhuman head. And above all the terrible gleaming eyes, the only flash of light in the whole room, that had the power of penetrating, and gave each the impression the evil eye was fixed on him alone. A spell of silence had fallen. No woman cried; the laughter of ten minutes since had died; even the very sound of breathing was now quite hushed. This was the deadened, powerless load of nightmare.

Suddenly a light appeared on the spiral staircase. The gleam of snowy whiteness, the soft glow of an undying lamp, and the pure colours of a splendid moonshine. And above all a face and figure of most simple beauty, eyes pure and starlit in contrast to the red gleam. And a crown of mermaid flaxen hair, and expression sweet and thoughtful! It was a wonderful and sweet relief to the ghastly spectacle below.

And on a sudden the full lights flashed on again, and a sigh of relief burst from every heart and many lips. The black curtain had fallen. Rosalie alone remained of the weird scene, descending the spiral staircase. A little thing will often bring about reaction, and from being shunned by many, she from this opportune arrival gained a fair share of popularity.

"Where have you been?" a dozen voices cried, glad to make sound again.

"Trying to find a partner," cried she, and laughed; and others laughed as well, the search had been so long and unsuccessful.

"Supper is finished."

There was no lack of those to offer attention now, and along with this came the general bustle of those leaving the supper-table.

But by the side of Mr. Barringcourt stood the girl who, from a mixture of youthful spirits and curiosity, had asked the first the curtain might be moved.

"I am glad I had finished my supper," said she, with an attempt at laughing still. "I'm sure I could never eat anything in here again."

"It is fortunate refreshments are served upstairs," he answered. "You would not let so small a thing interfere with your evening's pleasure?"

Reassured somewhat by his tone, she said:

"After all, it was only an idol, was it?"

"That's all. They must be very brave folk to worship it, eh?"

"Yes. The Serpent is much less gruesome. Isn't it?"

He laughed. "Well, an empty skull often looks much worse than it is."

"But," said she, "it wasn't empty. I never saw such eyes. Never! Never!"

"You haven't seen the Serpent yet?"

"No; but mother did, and she said nothing about its eyes. She said it was plain to be seen we worshipped the true god, his scales were such a lovely gold. I am going to ask Miss Crokerly to introduce me to her friend. I'm sure if she had not come then I should have fainted right away. And I always laughed at Blanche for fainting. She used to do it so conveniently."

So saying, she slipped away, and to the upper regions, where, so far as she knew, there was nothing gruesome hidden away.

And soon the episode of the death's-head was forgotten, and the evening's enjoyment began again with even greater zest.

Rosalie's programme filled, but she never danced. Who could, when wearing only stockings? But she did not go home, but waited for that final dance, and no one noticed her slipperless feet.

CHAPTER XXXII

DIPLOMACY

"I have not the slightest inclination to dance, Mr. Barringcourt. I've spent one of the most delightfully lazy evenings I ever spent in my life."

"I envy you. I've been going through a species of treadmill. I've danced with every school-girl in the room."

"Myself included. You began the evening badly, you know."

He sat down beside her.

"Where were you all the supper-time?" he asked.

Rosalie looked at him. She detected the old, tired, wearily contemptuous expression on his face. She herself was far from tired. Her eyes were bright. Her cheeks had flushed a pretty pink; she had been under no unwilling exertion to please anyone.

"I stayed upstairs to see how long I'd be forgotten, and when no one remembered me, and I grew hungry, I came down."

"You should have acted the part of the jealous fairy godmother, and blasted us all."

"Well, though I be a school-girl, yet I've none of the attractions of youth, and so I've learnt toleration."

"It's hardly fair to keep repeating what I once said at random."

"Was it at random? I set a whole night apart to weep about it."

"You had nothing better to do, then?"

"The most miserable of all states, you must acknowledge. And through no fault of my own."

"Whose, then?"

"Yours. You have much to be answerable for, Mr. Barringcourt."

He laughed. "I have expiated most of my offences tonight; I have danced the polka."

"With Miss Sebberen. I saw you."

"Let us go into some quieter room. This dancing wearies me. I never was fond of it."

Rosalie's trailing dress hid her feet, and they passed into the picture-gallery. It was deserted.

She sat down under the picture of Geoffrey Todbrook.

"One day Mariana brought me here and showed me this picture. I forget what was said, but somewhere in our conversation she laughed. She said laughing always produced a pain at her heart."

"Mariana laughed? You utterly astonish me."

His face betrayed no signs of conviction of cruelty, certainly.

"Yes," said Rosalie. "It is astonishing, truly. Had I lived here as long as she, laughing would have been utterly beyond me."

"It is a good thing you escaped, then."

"You don't grudge me my freedom?"

"I grudge no man anything if he wins it, or woman either. And far from grudging you your freedom, I'm glad you won it."

"You were glad, then, when I ran away?"

"Well, no—not at the time. I do not know that I ever became thoroughly reconciled to you till you came to see me the other night."

Here a pause followed, broken only by distant strains of music.

"You have another dance on New Year's Eve, Mr. Barringcourt?"

"Yes. You will come? It is the one night in the whole year worth dancing on."

"I would come gladly; but I can find no dress to my liking."

"You have a week before you."

She clasped her hands round her knee, shook her head and looked at him.

"I won't come unless I can wear exactly what I want."

"And what is that?"

"The dress that Mariana was making long ago. But I expect she's finished it, and the moths have eaten it away. But all the same, I won't come unless I have it. It is the one thing on earth I've set my heart upon."

Mr. Barringcourt looked at her. The pretty air of reasonless determination suited her.

"It's impossible," said he.

"The moths have eaten it away, then," and without pretence or acting two big tears rose in her eyes and fell—one for sorrow at his hardness, one for the memory of Mariana in the cell.

But two tears upon occasion can be very fascinating.

"You never did reason, did you, Rosalie?" said he.

"Yes. It's the one thing I've done all my life. But the simpler you are in this world the more you're derided. Let me see Mariana to ask her about the dress?"

"Oh, hang Mariana!"

"Are you speaking broadly?"

"What do you mean?"

"You should never use abusive language towards the individual. I learnt that long ago. If you want to be profane you should generalise."

"Whose lax teaching was that?"

"I learnt it from the Governor; the gentleman whom I met when I ran away from you. But he wasn't lax, I'm sure. Perhaps I misunderstood him."

"I wouldn't put it beyond you. But give me a form of forcible language that would fit in with his exposition."

"Well, the only one that presents itself at all to me is 'Damn it.' You see 'it' means nothing in particular, is quite impersonal, and therefore no one is any the worse for it, yourself included."

"You're an advocate of that particular form?" said he.

"I'd allow it to you upon occasion, but not to myself."

"Indeed! Why?"

"Because if I were a perfect woman I'd never have any inclination to go further than the 'd.'"

"You're striving after the perfect woman?"

"Yes," sighed Rosalie; "but she's very delusive. It's so easy to overstep the bounds and become saintly."

He laughed. "I don't think you'll ever be that."

"But why?"

"The strain would be too great. You'd best remain as you are. I believe the dance is ending."

"And—and never a word settled about my dress."

"Are you so much in earnest about it?"

"Indeed, yes. I went through all the pains and penalties of trying it on, stood three weary hours as model, and it was so beautiful my heart longed for it then, and has done so ever since."

"It's nothing but imagination. You must look for something else."

They rose together, and suddenly she put her hand upon his arm, and said in just such a voice as a mermaid might, half laughing, half plaintively:

"I won't come to dance the New Year in; I've nothing fit to come in. And as for the slippers that you sent to me, you can search for them just where you like. I don't want them, and I won't wear them. I only want the dress." And she showed him her foot in its silk stocking, without slipper or other covering.

"Where are your slippers?" said he.

"I've hidden them, and you may find them."

And suddenly he looked at her quite sternly, and he said: "You've been to see Mariana."

Rosalie returned the glance as meekly as became the situation.

"The doors were all unlocked. Besides, you should have found me a partner for the supper-time. I resented it."

"And what do you think of Mariana?"

"I think that you and I are inexpressibly different in our idea of things."

"Indeed! It is because of you she's placed where she is."

"And because of me you ought to place her where she isn't."

"I am not disposed to laugh. Your constant prying is objectionable."

"I pay dearly for it: hard words and cold glances from everyone, yourself included."

"Not too high a price, it seems."

"Dear me, no! I trust to the luck that saved Red Chin's wife. I'm not in the least bit inclined to cry tonight, Mr. Barringcourt I feel happy enough to dance without slippers on." And she stooped and kissed the precious stone she wore.

He looked at it and then at her. "Give that stone to me," he said suddenly.

Her cheeks paled as quickly. "I love it too well to ever think of parting with it," she answered.

"The price of Mariana's freedom."

"No," and her voice was a mixture of a gasp and weakness.

"And yet you love Mariana! How you do misjudge the word! You don't know what love is."

"Neither do you."

"I make no professions."

"I have no right to give away this stone; it was given to me."

"Keep it, then. I simply asked for it to prove your inherent selfishness."

"You could have proved it by a much simpler test. It is one of the dragon's heads impossible to conquer. Every now and then I give it a sleeping potion, and get some rest. It's very efficacious, I can tell you."

She turned and went away, and they did not see each other again that night, or rather morning.

CHAPTER XXXIII

THE WORTH OF A JEWEL

The next morning, rather earlier than usual, Mr. Barringcourt called to see Miss Crokerly. He saw her alone; but as he was crossing the hall on going away, he was stopped by hearing Rosalie's voice from the staircase, and by seeing her coming toward him.

"I have been waiting for you," said she, raising her finger as if in warning as she came nearer, and speaking very softly. "The dragon is sleeping, completely under the influence of a powerful drug. In the interim I've brought you this. The thing you asked for last night." And she held toward him a tiny jewel-case.

He took it slowly, looking at her, and then at it. Then the contents dawned upon him, and he looked at her again and laughed, though his eyes had a piercing keenness in them that took away the effect of the laughter.

Then her manner changed, and she too laughed. She raised her lips to his ear and whispered:

"I drugged the dragon with *Reason*, think what you will," and still laughing, would have moved away.

Now it just chanced (for those who find no excuse for what followed) that there hung just above them a bunch of misletoe. Miss Crokerly was a great advocate of Christmas parties for children, had had three such since December began, and holly and other Christmas decorations were much in evidence. But neither person concerned was at the moment cognisant of this fact. One was looking down, and one was looking up, but not at the ceiling.

But all the same, in opposition to the laws of etiquette, yet quite in accordance with those of nature, Mr. Barringcourt suddenly stooped and took her hands and kissed her. It wasn't a bit like the ordinary kiss a man would give a woman. It fell as softly on her lips as a breath of snow—nothing of fire—so that she laughed again, and shook her hands free, and saying "Thank you," ran away again.

After that Mr. Barringcourt went away, looking as thoughtful and preoccupied as if he had never been frivolous in his life.

He went home, and passed at once to his own private laboratory and study. He took with him the tiny jewel-case, and going up to one of the big windows facing the front of the house, took out the stone and looked at it. He looked at it so long that a bystander would have grown impatient. Then he went to the other side of the room, and opened what seemed to be a cupboard, but was really a set of shutters opening upon a window looking on the garden at the back. The light from this window showed the jewel differently.

Before it had been softest green and pink; now a constant red ray gleamed from the centre. He noted it, and turned it many ways. The light still remained—no passing brilliancy or change of colour. Then he went into the inner room, and noted the different blendings and the texture by placing it beneath a glass, there to examine it minutely. Finally he poured out from an old flagon, worked and chased in a substance like polished silver, a liquid that flamed up in the crucible like white-flamed fire, intense and beautiful. And into this he threw a stone that matched in some respects the one he carried in his hand. Under this great strength of heat it disappeared; no tiny fragment of lustre or of substance now remained. And quite remorseless to its fate, he next flung in the stone that Rosalie had given him, and bent forward eagerly to notice the effect.

No change! A glimmering blend of colour on the surface of the flame. Then with his fingers, as if the leaping tongues had been but water, he took the jewel out, and dashed the sprays of fire away like drops of water.

A smile, incredulous and all surprised, at first played on his lips and in his eyes as he looked at the jewel. Then after some deep thought, he started as one from a dream, the light of sudden understanding in his eyes. He placed the stone once more within its case, and put it in an inner pocket, then left the room and locked the door again.

Leaving the wing, he went out into the central hall, and passed across it to the eastern side, with its brilliant door and exterior brightness, all so false to the sordid truth behind. But there he paused, and called across the high, empty, echoing space:

"Everard, what is Mariana's number? I forget."

"Thirteen." The answer was simple and distinct.

"That's a lucky number, isn't it?"

"I believe it's a significant one. Unlucky, some say."

"We go by the rule of contrary. I think myself it must be lucky." And he laughed and flung open the great doors and passed inside. They swung to after him.

Then at the door he sought for he stopped, and with the same quick movement threw it open.

Inside, the miserable cell, the scanty furniture, the covered table, the cobwebs, the thick dust, the cloud of hovering moths, the stiff and rigid figure; but to his eyes on entering, not the central figure of attraction. For there upon the table, standing daintily upon the covering cloth, he saw the little satin clogs, with their golden strings and skate-like edges, that turned up daintily, bearing an almost laughable resemblance to someone's pretty nose. For in the same way that many persons' clothes on wearing them become a part of them and look like them, so these, scarce worn, became and looked a part of Rosalie. And in the midst of all this mildew, and decay, and icy lifelessness, they stood a thing of life—an open protest against everything surrounding them.

Without looking toward Mariana, he went and took them in his hand. They were not soiled. They had only danced one short delightful dance, and stood demurely side by side, longing to start again. The moths had never touched them; they were invulnerable. Then placing them once more upon the sheet, he leaned his hand upon the table and looked at Mariana.

Neither pity, distress, cruelty, nor any other emotion played on his face. He stood and looked at her, as deep in thought as if his mind was occupied with pages of a book, a long, long time. Then throwing back the covering from the table, he revealed the thick piles of satin that she had worked at in the three years passed long since. So this was the dress that Rosalie coveted; well, it was worth asking for, or would be when finished.

For the first time on Lucifram, and here in one of its most dismal cells, a smile free from artifice, from cynicism, from pride, from cruelty or contempt, ran on his lips and centred in his eyes.

But the machine? and how to set it working? Only one way. He crossed to Mariana, laid one hand upon her head, the other in her hands, and stooping, kissed her lips.

Then very silently, as some passing from life to death have done, she, with a sigh that trembled gently into every limb, swayed back to life. And on the second breath that stirred her bosom, looked up, and her eyes came to the face of Mr. Barringcourt.

"You've slept long enough," said he. "You can't complain now of being overworked. A long spell of rest, and now comes a short one of work. Are you ready for it?"

"Yes."

She rose from the chair, no stiffness, the old slow, easy motion born of coldness; itself born, who could tell of what.

"Six days to finish this—and alone. Can you accomplish it?"

"For whom?"

"Rosalie."

"Has she asked for it?"

"Yes."

She stretched her arms, then drew them in.

"It's well, because I fitted it for her, having no other model."

"You are to make it especially beautiful."

"It is not necessary to tell me so."

"And jewels? Everard will bring them to you."

Now she raised her eyebrows slightly and looked at him, and a faint smile came to her lips.

"Is Rosalie then so strong to bear so heavy a burden of sorrows as this house affords?"

"Search all you can find from the dust hidden in this room, and he will bring the rest. Did Rosalie appear to you so weak?"

"I loved her on that account I think."

"Part of a cause that changes weakness into strength. You feel yourself strong, Mariana?"

"Oh, no! But cold. The strength of ice, not iron."

"Rosalie has suffered from your complaint, I think. But she's cured."

Her eyes rested on his. There was a thoughtful expression in them, and she said:

"Cured? Then the ice was frozen less deeply."

"Or maybe the fire was stronger. There's something in that, you know."

"Yes," said she; then suddenly: "These moths are a great hindrance. I have no time to spend in sighs if I must work hard and finish in six days."

"Then I'll remove them for six days. After that they'll come back again, but you'll have finished."

"Yes. For Rosalie. And when to wear it?"

"New Year's Eve."

"Thank you. Now you had better leave me. What of these slippers?"

"Sew them with jewels."

"And make her tired feet? Is it some practice of cruelty?"

"No. A whim of mine. To show honour to an escaped prisoner."

"I must wake. Six days to make a dress, and it is rumoured that one of the planets was made in that time! I must hasten."

So then he left her, and she worked alone. And hour by hour some fresh seam in the design became completed, and on the third day Everard came. He carried a large sack, and it was full of jewels of every known description, small and large. Standing there, he said suddenly:

"Can I help you with these? Sorting or stringing?"

"But surely it's against the rules."

"It is advisable to break them in emergency. And I doubt if this be not finished, some great calamity will rise. The Master is away. The work is out of all proportion to the time. For his sake, for yours, and for hers, I wish to help you, for this day, at least."

So Mariana gave way, and one little flame of heat passed over the icy barrier almost unconsciously. The cell, being less lonely now, lost its ghastliness.

Thus the time passed away until completion, the last day of the old year, the eve of the new.

And on that afternoon at four o'clock Mariana heaved a sigh of apparent contentment, for all was now in readiness. And Everard, having done his full share in the arrangement of jewels, and whatever else was needed, returned to the door in order to welcome Mr. Barringcourt, who just then returned.

CHAPTER XXXIV

"A GIFT, A FRIEND, A FOE,
A BEAU, A JOURNEY TO GO."

To return again for a brief interval to that day following Christmas Day. Mr. Barringcourt, when he had left Mariana, went to see the Great High Priest, and afterwards attended with many others the Service of Dedication of the Curtain. Miss Crokerly was there, but not Rosalie. Afterwards Mr. Barringcourt said to the new High Priest when left alone together, and the guests departed:

"Why didn't you invite Miss Paleaf?"

"I have told you why. I am only waiting for a sufficiently good opportunity to bring forward the trial."

Mr. Barringcourt's lips set. "You make a great stir about nothing," said he.

"I don't forget the awkward time at which she spoke."

"And when do you propose to send out the summons?"

"On New Year's Day. A public trial and an ecclesiastical court."

"And you as judge?"

"Oh, no! There is Golden Priest Ferdinand. I take no further steps in the matter publicly."

"And the punishment?"

"Life-time imprisonment."

Mr. Barringcourt looked at him and laughed.

"You laugh? After all, it is worth nothing better. People must be taught a proper respect for established religion."

"In childhood, yes. I doubt when they get older it's too late. And so you contemplate lifetime imprisonment?"

"Could you suggest anything better?"

"Well, there's escape. What do you say to that?"

"Futile. Absolutely futile."

"The Devil has helped her once; he may do so again."

"The Devil! Who or what is that?"

(They were ignorant of such a person on Lucifram.)

"Ah! I had forgotten. He was never fashionable here. The Devil is a libel on virtue; the exact imitator of God."

"And she is on familiar terms with this—this atrocity?"

"I owe a general pardon. I was confounding him with a Superior Being, an error commoner than one thinks of."

"You speak in riddles," said the Great High Priest, and his tone was irritable.

"I mean to say God helped her to escape twice before—nay, three times. You are brave, to say nothing more of it, to put another spoke in the wheel."

"By God do I understand you to mean the Serpent?"

"As you will. To my certain knowledge she has kissed the Serpent. The sensation must have been a new one, almost a dangerous one. After ages spent hearing the dull praise of men coming from lips all stereotyped, one soft kiss would have its—er—its value."

The Great High Priest looked at him sternly, as became his office.

"The Serpent is above such petty considerations," said he. "You speak with too much levity of sacred things."

"A fault of my education. Forgive me for it. And the summons is to be issued on New Year's Day?"

"Or on the eve."

"I understand you. God and his counterfeit will help or hinder you. Good-night!"

Next morning, walking in the Park, he came on Rosalie walking with the frog. Quite unconscious of the impending trial, she stopped on meeting him.

"Good morning!" said she. "You look very thoughtful."

"Yes. I'm thinking of taking a very unusual step."

"What, pray?"

"Paying a visit to my mother," and he looked at her.

"That means your father, too, does it not?"

"No," he answered, still looking at her in the same thoughtful, absent way. "I frequently visit him. At present they are separated."

Now it was her turn to be thoughtful. "That's very sad, isn't it?"

"Sadder than you'd think of; for, but for the irony of Fate, they would be quite inseparable."

"And is it an unusual thing for you to visit her?"

"Yes; I do not care to burden her with my presence, unless there is some reason in it."

"That sounds unnatural. Does she love you?"

"As much as I love her."

"That conveys nothing to my mind. Your powers of love are very enigmatical."

"They're simple enough on a worthy object."

"And she is very worthy?"

He made no answer, but said presently, with sudden decision:

"Mariana has begun upon the dress. It will be finished on New Year's Eve."

"And I to wear it?"

"Yes."

"I went to see her. You guessed at it. But she seemed more dead than living."

"A little extra sleep. She said she needed it."

"What of the jewel that I lent you?"

"It is very safe. I have a request to make to you."

"What is it?"

"I wish to beg the jewel for my mother."

"What is she like?"

He smiled.

"Words cannot describe her; to my eyes, the perfection of beauty and loveliness. As innocent and simple and free from care or evil as the light."

"You don't resemble her, do you?" asked Rosalie, unconscious of the bitterness of her remark.

He laughed, perceiving it.

"You may rest safely assured there. I know no one who resembles her."

"Is she kind?"

"The essence of it."

"Then what of Mariana, and such as she?"

His brow clouded. "You ask questions I'm not disposed to answer."

"Ah! but I'm thinking of my jewel. I love it so. Your mother would not value it a tenth part as much as I. Nay, before today it, and others like it, have been reckoned rubbish. She might think so too."

"Give me leave to take it to her, and await her verdict. If she underrates it, I'll bring it back to you."

"I'm afraid I must give the dragon so strong a dose there'll be no life left in it."

"If it is what you told me, the more honour remains to you in killing it with such a potion."

And Rosalie laughed, but her eyes were wonderfully serious, and she said simply:

"I'll give it to you, Mr. Barringcourt, because it seems to me to love one's mother is the greatest and the simplest thing in the duty towards one's neighbour, if that mother is as she should be. And it is more than pleasant to me to know that somewhere in the wide universe there is someone who has broken through the natural hardness of your heart, and called forth a respect and love of which I never thought you capable."

The remaining days till New Year's Eve passed quickly. The weather was gloriously fine, the sunsets unequalled.

Early in the evening Mariana arrived, and brought with her a large box containing the dress and other things. She came in a carriage drawn by chestnut horses, not occupants of the stables at Marble House.

Rosalie came out into the hall to meet her, and kissed her with affection, which Mariana in her colder way returned.

Together they went upstairs, Rosalie suddenly finding herself very short of words to express her delight at meeting this old friend.

And it was Mariana who dressed her completely, from the arranging of her hair to the tying on of her clog-shaped, satin-jewelled slippers.

And oh! what a dress! With designs of lovers' knots worked in delicately-tinted jewels all over its shining surface, and a train that hung from the shoulders in showers of priceless lace. It was studded with jewels in the bodice, and on her hair was placed a tiara that stood high, and had the same design worked in diamonds. Clasps of gold and jewels were on her arms, and round her neck one fine chain of gold—no other ornament.

"I'm afraid, after all, Mariana," said she at length, "your great ambition has not come to pass."

"What thing was that?"

"You wished it for a wedding-dress."

"I am content to see it as it is, and you so beautiful."

"And when tonight is over you will want it back?"

But Mariana smiled, half dreamily.

"Tonight is not yet over, and you will never wish to part with such a robe. You begged it from the Master, and you'll keep it I know none other who would care to bear so great a load, though in its beauty all forget to think of that."

"I do not find it very heavy."

"It's well."

Suddenly Rosalie laughed.

"I say, Mariana," said she, "suppose—suppose when I come to Marble House it should shine red all round about me. They'd take me for a veritable scarlet woman. I have misgivings. I remember once before."

But Mariana shook her head.

"I heard from the Master you had gained strength from weakness; and I heard from Everard you had jewels of your own that you have worn to counteract the fatal charm of these."

"Not of my own, Mariana; they were of God." "Ah, God! I had forgotten Him. The dream has passed so long ago."

"God is no dream, but a living reality, Mariana."

"I was once bitten by a snake, and here they call the Serpent God. I love not such an image, but live in the never-ending twilight. I think it is the shadowed light the idol throws, placing itself betwixt the world and God."

And suddenly Rosalie took her hands in hers, and drew her to her with a gentle force, and kissed her lips and forehead, saying:

"But soon the idol will vanish out of sight, and the true light come. You needn't live in the twilight, Mariana, any more than I. You only need to trust the Glorious Spirit working behind the leaden cloud, and struggle silently toward the healing light. And some day, even though the waiting time be long, the icy burden will be rolled away, and you all warm and bright again to love and honour God with strength unfettered."

And then Brightcoat said: "I should like to go with Mariana back to Marble House."

"Do you care for such a companion?" asked Rosalie of Mariana.

But the frog jumped across and settled on her shoulder.

"You need me no more now, Rosalie. I have done what work I could for you. But now to Mariana. She may need me as once you did. And though her heart is cold today, the New Year dawns, and with it in the distance I see a fairer prospect and a warmer light breaking upon the horizon of heaven."

And so with this new companion Mariana went away back to the Marble House. Into that gloomy dwelling, though now all brilliantly lit, the frog entered unafraid, and none thought to harm it, for the charm had worked, or perhaps was working.

CHAPTER XXXV

THE SUN RISES ON THE YEAR

A brilliant house again, a brilliant crowd, the eve of the New Year, the death-bed of the Old. Just three hours more to wait.

But as Rosalie drove along, it was as if depression and the highest spirits fought one another for the mastery.

"The effects of wearing fine clothing," said she, and laughed and sighed in a breath. "There is magic in these jewels, I feel certain. Oh! if I could but wear again my own precious moonstone talisman against all heaviness, instead of all this finery, that does its best to cramp my spirits, and half succeeds."

On entering, she was almost immediately joined by Mr. Barringcourt. Never had he looked to Rosalie as tonight, never perhaps she to him. With a scrutiny which had become habitual, they eyed each other, and at last Rosalie said:

"Do you not think I was right in being covetous of such a lovely gown?"

"And the jewels?"

"Oh, they were an extra thrown in. I'd much rather have been without them. You should be kind, not lavish, Mr. Barringcourt. After an hour's wearing they begin to assert their individuality and weight."

"And at first you felt them light?"

"Being alive to their beauty, I was dead to their encumbrance." And then again, this time seriously, she said: "But in truth I must acknowledge, perhaps, their weight cannot be very great, for I have the greatest wish to dance through every dance, and look to you to find me partners. I am not really altered because I stole behind the temple curtain; for one night it might be forgotten."

"The first dance is with me, and the last one."

"Oh, no! I am in a mood of ingratitude tonight. I cannot for the favour of this dress, and all its valuable accessories, even say 'Thank you.' Find me a partner for the dance that's just beginning. No one has come near me since I came."

"The first dance is with me."

"Indeed, no. I'm entering on a life of self-denial. As soon as I want to do a thing I shall cross myself and do the opposite. What chance shall I stand of heaven, do you think, at that rate?"

"You'll never get there. Be guided by me, and be less contrary."

"It goes very much against the grain for me to dance with you. Must I be consistent, or must I be contrary?"

"Become impersonal, and leave the decision with me."

"You are too selfish to be altogether trusted."

"I? Selfish?"

"Yes. I want to dance, and here you keep me talking. I want to study men and form comparisons."

"You can't in a place like this. On these occasions they're all more or less alike."

"And on all others. The similarity of humanity is nerve-destroying."

"A very pleasant state of things. None but a fool would wish it otherwise. But if you wish to dance you shall have partners in sufficiency. I'll say you're quite harmless tonight."

"Say no such thing. Mariana tells me she was once bitten by a snake, and so was I. Since then I've had the greatest inclination to bite everyone who comes near me. She took it badly; I, by God's help, was enabled to take it well."

"What particular snake was it that bit you?"

"I think it must have been the God of Lucifram."

Then he left her and went away, and through the evening Rosalie danced, seemingly happy, on to that hour when the Old Year and the New meet and part again.

Then she sought Mr. Barringcourt, and found him, not amongst his guests, but in that now deserted drawing-room where once Mariana had played for her. He was looking out on to the gas-lit streets, and the window being open, the cold night air blew into the room. The lights in it were shining fully, yet the city without was plainly visible.

"You have left the crowd?" said she.

"Yes," he answered. "They can amuse themselves. You look tired."

She laughed, an apology for deeper feeling, and looked at him with eyes whose tiredness was lost in a certain appeal and pathetic beauty, that characterised them long since in the days of silence.

"I think I overrated my powers of—of endurance. I—I should be very pleased to give the last dance to you. I left it empty."

But he shook his head.

"I have not danced all evening; I do not wish to make myself conspicuous now."

"We could sit it out."

"We might; but I am contrary."

Then Rosalie went up to him and put her hand very gently in his arm, and almost whispered:

"I have a feeling of insecurity that grows with almost every hour. It may be childish, but I never professed to be much different from a child. When I stay with you it leaves me more or less, and always has done from the very first I met you. And now Brightcoat has left me, and I feel quite alone, a thing hardly enviable in any sphere. And I've gone through the evening as best I could, and tried to get the better of my weakness." And then she laughed and drew her hand away, and said: "If such confessions are unusual, you only have this dress to thank for it. The jewels have magnetic power, and draw me to the owner."

At this he turned round from the window and looked at her, and a very curious smile curved on his lips.

"That's your solution, is it?" he said, and scratched his head thoughtfully with one finger. Then he added: "My mother said I was to thank you for the stone you sent her."

"Was she well?"

"Yes. At the first stroke after midnight I go again to her. These guests will then have all departed."

"I, too."

"You say that sadly."

"The magnetism of the stone I sent her draws me to your mother."

Just then Everard entered the room, carrying in his hand a large sealed envelope addressed to Rosalie. At the back it was sealed with the image of the Serpent.

"You, Everard?" said Mr. Barringcourt, with some surprise.

"I heard the door bell ring, and knew it was no ordinary guest of the evening."

She took and opened it. A summons to appear before the High Priest's court, and on the morrow morning, this first day of the New Year.

She read it through, half mystified, the truth with some difficulty dawning upon her. Then on a sudden she handed it to Mr. Barringcourt, her face as white as the background of her dress, and he in his turn read it. Then he turned to Everard and said:

"Who brought this?"

"A priest who, with his companion, waits outside. I did not let them in."

Master and man looked at one another, the same grim smile half visible upon each face. Then Mr. Barringcourt took out his watch and looked at it.

"It wants still twenty minutes till the dance is ended. It is barely twenty minutes after twelve. Are they impatient of delay?"

"I did not ask them."

"We'll go upon the supposition that they're patient." Then turning to Rosalie, he continued: "There was a time you told me that you scorned to run away, and never had done. Afterwards, upon much less occasion, you trusted to the fleetness of your feet. And now? Are you prepared to meet the enemy?"

"Indeed, no. Or perhaps I cannot tell. If you stood for council on my behalf I think I might enjoy it. For myself, I could never get much farther than the truth."

"A marvellous short journey, with a sudden ending, but little reckoned upon Lucifram. What think you of lifetime imprisonment, Rosalie?"

"Ah! It is that that frightens me. I never liked the thought of prison. Must I really go?"

"What plan of escape is there?"

Her brow knitted thoughtfully; then suddenly clearing, she said:

"Take me away with you. Take me to your mother?"

And she looked so very beautiful, with something so imperious in her manner, yet so sweet, that little wonder if the Master consented.

"It's a long journey, and a very final one, and, moreover, my horses are black."

"I'll trust to the rule of contrary where you're concerned, and trust you too. Take me where you will. I have sufficient power given me of my own to guard against a vital evil."

"You trust me to a certain point. No farther."

She laughed.

"I trust you altogether, but wish to show it is not quite from weakness I wish to come with you."

"Then we'll go. My mother is hospitable, and so are others round about her. Some are better known to you, no doubt, than she. A stranger is a rarity among them. You will be welcomed."

"Alas! But who can travel in a dress like this—at midnight, in the depth of winter? It is so conspicuous."

"No dress could be so suitable. Safe-guarded against wind or snow, and simple in comparison of those where we are going. Heat or cold, darkness or light cannot touch it. It was sewn in the inner darkness, and shines in the inner light. Come, Rosalie, the time is up. We must away to see the sun rise on the New Year."

Then he led her through those great empty rooms into the fuller ones, where general hilarity preceded the closing of the dance. But here they never waited. Across the palm-house to the doors of glass with the image of the toad and temple so finely and so clearly worked in them.

At one touch they both flew open, and there, flooded in a tide of light—red—red—and an accompanying silence. It travelled swiftly, yet without sound or violence into the rooms of feasting and of mirth, carrying silence and a vague alarm. And noting where it came from, the guests instinctively crowded out towards that curious garden, on which faced the real front of Marble House.

And there, below the terrace steps, upon the wide carriage drive, stood a chariot of gold, with seats of crimson velvet, and harnessed to it the six black steeds, with tossing heads and eyes of fire, strong, and sleek, and slim.

One youth alone stood at the foremost bridle. And in the midst of all this ruddy glamour shone the pure whiteness of Rosalie's robe, with all its flimsy showers of lace and jewels. And there beside the carriage step stood Mariana, the frog upon her shoulder, and with her Everard, who had preceded them.

Then Rosalie stepped in lightly and gracefully, and sat down. Mariana bent forward, and with the grace peculiar to her arranged the spreading train about her feet. Then looking up, with mutual feeling each drew an arm round the other's neck and kissed. Rosalie whispered:

"You will follow, Mariana, and we'll meet again, in no land of shadows, red or black, but in the sunlight. And you'll bring Everard. A little company along the road is most desirable. But for the present, good-bye!"

And then the Master, gathering the long reins in his hand as he sat down beside her, wrung Everard's hand, and seeing Mariana held her hand toward him too, bent over it and kissed it, by that one act undoing all the past in which she suffered through him.

The Master shook the reins. A thousand tingling stars shook from them upon and round about the coal-black steeds. One wild bound forward all in unison, not on a straight road, but up some climbing steep.

Rosalie turned round. And laughing, half in fear and half in happiness, kissed her hand to Brightcoat.

"Good-bye—till—till we meet again!"

Then the Master turned round also, a face very unlike to hers.

His face was dark and shadowy as it ever had been. The same contemptuous curl lay on his firm lips; a mocking laughter was in his eyes. His glance fell upon Marble House, and the guests all drawn towards the terraces.

With his free hand he felt in the pocket of the long coat he wore.

"I forgot to leave my New Year's presents, Rosalie," said he, and brought out a large handful of precious stones, flinging them down to Lucifram. Then drawing out another, he handed these to Rosalie, and bade her throw them too.

They fell among the crowd, who gathered them and praised their beauty.

But the six black steeds with little apparent effort climbed up the steep mountain-side, or so it seemed to be. And gradually the red light disappeared, and Lucifram along with it, and darkness followed.

And now there was nothing but the wind and icy snow and loneliness— nothing but the path. Nothing was to be seen on either side.

The spirited steeds, wild as ocean foam, flew up and on the mountain track, the winds moaned after them with a song as wild, as full of sad complaint, as if they were embodied spirits of the sighs and tears of broken hearts.

But no feeling of cold came near Rosalie. The jewelled robes encased her, proof against everything. And gradually it seemed as if the darkness gave way to a glimmering of light. At first it was feeble, but grew in distinctness, steady, and still steadier.

Suddenly a ray of brilliant light—light that could never blind the eyes—shot straight across the path. Then came another, another, following thick and fast from every direction.

Swiftly the coal-black horses changed in the flooding light to purest white, visions of inexpressible and perfect beauty. Rosalie's heart beat faster with sudden, unexpected joy. She looked up at the Master, her own face transfigured by the light, as so was his. For all the weariness, all the contempt, all the dark shadows, had vanished from his features, and left nothing but what was full of life, of vigour, and of kindliness. His eyes, still dark and deep, looked into hers, the first time on the long and perilous journey, and he said, laughing, as sometimes of old:

"Do you prefer looking at me to the magnificence of all this scenery?"

But she clasped his arm in both her hands, and leaned her forehead against his shoulder.

And suddenly he brought the horses to a check, and drawing her still closer, bent his head and kissed her cheek. Then she looked up with eyes all wet with tears, and bright with happiness, and drawing back a little, said:

"I never thought that things would come out this way. I—I never imagined that black horses could come out white—nor you become so altered."

He laughed.

"It all depends upon the journey that I take. Sometimes I cross upon another rainbow, that leads us all down hill from Lucifram at almost break-neck speed. Then neither I nor these, my horses, alter much. But look, Rosalie, round about you. This is a scene worth seeing and remembering."

He stood up, and giving her his hand, helped her to her feet.

And then she saw that streams of light and rainbow garlands were flung from a thousand spheres to meet this central road, itself a giant rainbow crossing from Lucifram (a tiny speck of gleaming red in the far, far distance) towards a country quite unsurpassed for loveliness. And all around, from the different worlds of light, came scenes of fairyland.

And now she saw a towered city folded in night, the change from day; and here the bright sunshine of mid-day glinting upon a noble river, with sloping, tree-clad hills, and meadows smooth and green.

Again the sun was setting behind a sea of golden glory, on whose restless surface danced three round boats inlaid with pearl. And in the boats sat three maidens of exquisite beauty, attended by the gentle wind, their servant, who wafted them towards the distant shore. And as they went they sang a song that trembled sweetly on the air and reached in the soft silence to that golden car, ringing tones of happiness and joy.

So on around: a thousand scenes, and all delightful, delicate yet clear, country and city all in perfection spread out everywhere. And each sphere was linked to each with garlands of lights, so that the nimble spirit crossed on them, a perfect path of beauty.

Rosalie looked and breathed a sigh of admiration. Then her eyes travelled to the path which they were crossing. The steep part had been passed. There now remained only a lesser portion, and that sloped gently down. This remaining part was free from danger. Pillars of light garlanded with flowers guarded the sides.

The horses, unwearied with the night's long race, moved slowly towards this nearing country, over whose waking sky the bright dawn was spreading wings of glory, with silver flutings right east to west. The descent led to a regal city, where nothing mean or sordid, no toil and tribulation, no anxious care or killing sorrow, no oppression, no dark deeds, no foul disease, no hardened priests or creeds had ever come. But all was God, the essence of immortal greatness.

And to this city came Rosalie, led by him whom some had called on Lucifram the Master. And being all tired with the journey, Rosalie fell asleep just as they were entering the gates.

For no traveller from a darker sphere can enter there unweary. The soft air, too strong for them, wafts the frail form to tender sleep, that it undergo the great and immortal change.

The sound of laughter and welcome, Heaven's truest music of joy, and then for us a silence.

So ends a little chapter in the life of Lucifram.
A chapter that bore indirectly upon the Serpent, and
helped gradually to its undoing. But that's another tale.